IS *MURDER*
YOUR KI

M000206898

"This story belongs to the hard-boiled school of detective fiction. The characters, particularly the detectives, consume large quantities of hard liquor and indulge in conversation not fit for polite ears, and their morals are, to put it mildly, not above reproach. If you like that sort of stuff as garnishing . . . then this is the book for you."

—Isaac Anderson
The New York Times Book Review
May 5, 1935

JONATHAN LATIMER
available in IPL editions:

THE LADY IN THE MORGUE
MURDER IN THE MADHOUSE
SOLOMON'S VINEYARD

Writing as Peter Coffin

THE SEARCH FOR MY GREAT UNCLE'S HEAD

JONATHAN LATIMER

MURDER
IN THE
MADHOUSE

INTERNATIONAL POLYGONICS, LTD.
NEW YORK CITY

MURDER IN THE MADHOUSE

Copyright © 1935 by Jonathan Latimer. Renewed.
Reprinted with permission of the author's estate and
Curtis Brown Ltd.

Cover: Copyright © 1989 by International Polygonics, Ltd.
Library of Congress Card Catalog No. 89-85727
ISBN 1-55882-023-X

Printed and manufactured in the United States
of America.
First IPL printing November 1989.
10 9 8 7 6 5 4 3 2 1

Chapter 1

IT WAS NEARLY EVENING. Outside there was already that stealthy darkening of late afternoon in a region of hills, but the air was still dry and hot. Tar in the cracks of the concrete pavement oozed out blackly, leaves hung limply from bedraggled trees, and in the parched fields the animals lay and watched the road with detached curiosity. In the ambulance, too, it was dry and hot. William Crane sat on the narrow leather-covered ledge and watched particles of dirt, enlivened by the vibration, dance around the floor. He wondered how far they had to go.

They were traveling very fast, and behind him, through the dirty window, the road unwound like an angry snake. The ambulance swung insanely from side to side, and waves of burning air swept back from the engine. A bug flew in the partially opened front panel and struck William Crane's face. He tried to strike it away, but his handcuffs bruised his head. He cursed. The man beside the driver scowled back at him. "What's the matter, mister?"

"Bugs," said William Crane.

The driver laughed. "Bugs to the bugs," he said.

Both the men laughed. The man beside the driver fumbled in his pocket, pulled out a bottle, and took a drink between gasps. Then he held it between the lips of the driver. The ambulance reeled to the left, struck something with a sharp crash, and swerved back to the right. A car roared by, and there was a receding sound of angry shouting.

"Jees, that's real stuff," the driver said. He turned to peer back down the road, exposing a roll of sooty flesh where his collar touched his neck.

The man beside the driver tenderly pocketed the bottle. He appeared shaken. "That was so close," he stated, "you could've untied that guy's necktie with your teeth."

"Don't let it bother you," said the driver consolingly. "As soon as it's dark I'll turn on the red lights and the siren and show you a little fancy work with a gas pedal."

"How far are we going?" asked Crane.

"We're going to the Astor estate for the week-end," said the man beside the driver. He was a dark man with two gold teeth and a cap. His name was Joe.

"Yeah," said the driver. "A party with those big bugs."

This sent Joe into a hysteria again. "Big bugs," he gasped. "Christ, that's funny!" He was impelled to take another swig from the bottle. The driver took one, too.

Through the back window, William Crane could see the buff banks of the Hudson every time the ambulance rounded a curve to the left. It was nearly fall, and some of the trees were beginning to turn brown. The dusk and the speed made the landscape mottled, as though it were being unwound too quickly on a stage set built to represent scenery passing a train window. The car roared through a town, and there was a burst of screaming. He caught sight of three young girls through the back window.

"Let's pick them up," said the driver.

"Nix," said Joe. "Not with this loony in here."

The driver said: "Hell, he's all right." He gazed back at William Crane affectionately, narrowly missing a passing sedan. "Ain't you ever picked up babes in an ambulance?" he asked Joe.

Joe admitted he had never picked up babes in an ambulance.

"It's the berries," asserted the driver earnestly. "You don't have to find no woods or pay for a hotel room or anything like that."

When the road dipped down into a valley between the hills, Crane noticed a pocket of cool air. It felt good to be cool again, even for only a minute.

"The best part of it all," the driver was saying, "is

that they can scream their damn heads off and nobody will pay any attention. An' even if they do, you can tell them the broad is a patient. It's a snap."

The driver inserted the neck of the bottle in his face a second time. It was nearly empty when he handed it back to Joe.

"We better get some more of this when we stop to get gas," he said.

"Do you know a spot?" asked Joe. He drained the bottle of its cinnamon liquid.

"Sure," the driver asserted. He waved a grimy hand. "You can get applejack at pretty near any of the filling stations. It's good stuff."

"So is this," said Joe. "I got it from Dutch's mob. It ain't been cut."

"I thought they cut everything."

"I work for Dutch."

The driver was impressed. He made a sucking noise with his tongue and gums. "Whew! How'd you happen to quit him?"

"I didn't. I'll go back when this doctor gets through needing me up here."

The driver considered this information for nearly a mile. "What'd you do?" he asked finally.

Joe patted himself lightly under his left arm.

It soon became dark. Trees huddled somberly by the roadside. Lights gleamed in clearings, and the Hudson looked like a black leather belt with an electrically lighted bridge for a diamond buckle. Presently the ambulance decreased speed, came to a crawl, and swung to the right onto a gravel driveway. It halted in front of a pump marked:

"Blue Gas—11¢."

The driver shut off the ignition, and the door of the gray frame shanty opened, reluctantly emitting a cadaverous man with a dead-white face. He spoke with difficulty around a plug of chewing tobacco.

"How many?"

"Better put in ten," said the driver. "Check the oil and water."

Joe got out of the ambulance and walked stiffly over to the shanty. He glanced inside and then came back and spoke to the attendant.

"There's ten acres of woods back there," said the attendant in an aggrieved tone of voice. "What's the matter with them?"

Joe's small eyes wavered as he paused, undecided, for an instant behind the oblivious back of the attendant. Finally he turned and disappeared into the ten acres of woods. The driver climbed out to watch the attendant measure the oil, and William Crane raised his handcuffed hands high above his head. The leather-covered iron chafed his wrists, but the stretching relieved muscles cramped from perching on the narrow seat and resisting the swaying motion of the vehicle. He slid up toward the front panel and looked out.

The attendant held up the gage. "Take a couple," he stated dispassionately.

"Put 'em in," said the driver.

"These here sure take a lot of fuel." The attendant poured in the oil from a slimy can. "Another one, somethin' like this here, comes by every week. They take ten and five most every time." He balanced the can on the engine and straightened his back.

"Check the water," said the driver.

Joe stepped out of the irregular underbrush and strolled toward the station. "I'll watch while you go," he said to the driver. The driver nodded and walked toward the woods. He did not walk in a straight line.

The attendant had finished pouring the water and was screwing on the radiator cap when he noticed ·William Crane through the front panel. His eyes widened as he saw the handcuffs. "I didn't know they was three of you," he said.

Joe was lighting a cigarette. "Three of who? Oh, he don't count. He's daffy."

The attendant studied William Crane's face. "You'd never think it, would you? So young looking. Can't be over thirty. Kin he hear us?"

Joe said he didn't know. He said he didn't care.

"Well, I don't suppose it makes much difference.

They say nobody can tell them they're crazy. They say they don't know it themselves." The attendant was still looking at William Crane.

Joe glanced up and down the road. He leaned closer to the attendant. "You look like a right guy. D'you know where a fellow could get some good stuff around here?"

The attendant looked at him speculatively, without surprise.

"I sorta think I got some in my shack."

"How much a quart?"

The attendant reflected. "Two dollars," he said tentatively.

"O. K."

While the attendant was in the shack, the driver came back. Joe told him about the applejack.

"He makes it himself," said the driver.

Joe said, "I don't care who makes it so long as it's good."

It smelled good, anyway, so Joe paid for it, and the driver paid for the gas. While they were getting in the front seat, the attendant went around to the back and looked at William Crane through the window. The gas station's electric light made his face whiter and his teeth yellower, and Crane decided he looked like an unpleasant horse. He waited for a second, and then he leaned toward the window.

"Boo!" he said. "Boo!"

The attendant's face disappeared from the window.

Once more the ambulance was racing along the highway. Trees, automobiles, houses, towns whisked by with violence, and every now and then the headlights would illuminate the white face of some pedestrian along the way, like a flashlight in a charnel house. With the heat and the weird effect of the colored lights and the speed and the cry of the siren, William Crane felt as though he were being driven down the road to hell.

They tried another drink of the applejack, and Crane saw that it was already more than half gone.

"That ain't bad stuff," the driver said. He smacked his lips. "It's got authority."

"You said it," said Joe. "Is all the stuff around here like this?"

"It varies a lot, but we got some better'n this at the home."

"Where do you live?" asked Joe.

"In Hoboken."

Joe looked at the driver with suspicion. "What good is that going to do us up here, if you got it at home?"

"Got what at home?"

"The liquor."

The driver was puzzled. "I didn't say I got liquor

at home, I said at the home. Besides, the little woman don't allow it around."

"What do you mean—at the home?"

"That's what we call it up here. I wouldn't have none home, the little woman wouldn't allow it."

"Where does the booze come from?"

"They bring it in bottles like this." The driver held up the bottle and then drank from it. "Boy, I'm glad I ain't going home tonight. The little woman's sorta hasty. She don't like me to drink. She said——"

"Say, who's askin' you about the little woman?"

"Why, you did." The driver's feelings were injured. "You were asking me about liquor at home. I told you the little woman wouldn't have it around the place. She said if I ever come in blotto I could just figure on alimony. She said——"

"Nuts," said Joe. "Have another drink."

The driver did.

Presently the highway curved, and they turned down a side road in a wide even skid and started to climb a long hill, the tires crunching against pieces of crushed stone and every once in a while throwing one against the fender with a sharp report. It was cooler as they climbed, and it did not seem as noisy as it had on the main road. Now there were no lights at either side.

"Only four miles," said the driver.

Joe asked, "What sort of a place is it?"

"Not bad. They got good eats and a good place for us to sleep. You don't have to work hard except when some patient gets to making trouble. The nurses is pretty hotsy-totsy, though."

"What d'ya mean, hotsy-totsy?"

"They're swell lookers, but they go for the doctors. You won't get to first base with them."

"I won't, eh?" Joe evidently thought otherwise. "I ain't had no trouble with dames yet." Gold teeth flashed in a proud smile. "I got hair on my chest."

"Don't let Doc Eastman catch you foolin' around."

"Who's he?" asked Joe. "Doc Livermore's the big boss, ain't he?"

"Doc Livermore's the head of the place, but Doc Eastman looks after things. He don't let anybody forget it, either." The driver licked his lips. His face was streaked in the light from the dashboard. "He's engaged to Miss Evans, the head nurse, and is she a honey!—blond and *built*. They say she went to college." He shook his head. "I wouldn't know about that."

Joe did not appear impressed. "How many others?"

"There is one more doctor and a couple of other nurses. They're pretty nice, but they got dark hair. I go for blondes." He thought for a minute. "Still, I'm gettin' sorta chummy with one of the others. I may take a try at her."

"Those docs must have an eye," said Joe. "How many patients they got?"

"About a dozen. You wouldn't think that would be enough to make a place like that pay, but I hear the minimum is five grand a year. They are all worth plenty of rocks."

William Crane looked out the front panel. It was not quite so dark outside. There was a nearly full moon in the sky, and the stone road was chalky. The trees were black, and he could see they were pines. The road was still upward, and the ambulance had settled down to a comfortable thirty miles an hour.

"Most of 'em aren't so nutty," the driver said. "They act all right for a while and then they go cuckoo for a spell. They have to be locked up in the detention building then."

"What do they do with them when they are on good behavior?"

"It's just like one of them classy resort hotels they have in Florida or at Atlantic City. They got a tennis court and a croquet field and a putting green, and they can do just what they please except for meals and treatment. They just got to be in bed before eleven."

"Jees," said Joe. "I thought they kept nuts in padded cells and fed 'em through the bars like lions or somethin'."

The driver snorted. "Some of these people have got

such good sense that it takes the doc a couple of weeks to find out what's wrong. And even then he ain't sure until they have a bad spell."

Joe took another drink. So did the driver. "What are they like when they have a spell?" Joe demanded.

"They are all different. Some get crying fits, and some get tough and try to strangle me or one of the other fellows about the place. One guy, he used to be a banker, gets down and makes out like he was a dog, and one old lady throws off her clothes when she gets one."

"It's too bad the swell blond nurse ain't like that old lady." Joe took another drink. "Do we got to live right with them all the time?"

"It depends upon what you're going to do."

"I don't know," said Joe. "Dutch said I was to come up here and do whatever Doc Livermore said."

"Well, if they put you in the servants' quarters," said the driver, "you'll be able to sleep away from them. But you'll be in the same part of the estate if you get a room in the hospital."

"Hell, I ain't scared of them," said Joe. "It's just that if I'm around them all the time I may get nervous and bust one of them or somethin'."

The road finally stopped climbing and circled through a cut between two hills. There was a deep valley ahead. The driver stopped the ambulance.

"There it is." He pointed down. "I guess we better finish this liquor before we get there."

Joe agreed, passed the bottle. "I got somethin' else I want to do," he said. He climbed down from his seat and walked to the side of the road.

William Crane looked through the panel at the valley. Not far below was a scene as artificial as the setting in a Cecil B. DeMille society drama. Through the tessellated branches of trees seen from above, a pool of water gleamed in a patterned background of paths and flower beds on the estate. Their figuration was nicely bounded by a stone wall, like a frame on a picture, and artistically unbalanced by a cluster of white buildings at one side. Under the light of the moon the estate was at once peaceful and glamorous and illegitimate.

William Crane's contemplation of Dr. Livermore's sanitarium was broken by the return of Joe, who swung back into his seat. "Where is this joint?" he asked. The driver pointed the bottle downward. There was a pause.

"Say, pretty classy," said Joe. "Is all the liquor gone?"

"One drink left," said the driver. "You take it. I feel lousy."

Joe drank as the driver started the ambulance down the hill. Finished, he tossed the bottle out the window. There was a brittle noise of breaking glass.

Chapter II

IRON GATES CLOSED with dull finality. The old man moved after them, crabwise, his face thin with suspicion and curiosity. The driver swung the ambulance up to the porch of the large stucco building and skidded it to a flourishing stop, like a coachman arriving with royalty. Naked of furniture, bare of rugs, the porch gleamed under moonlight which made pearls of pebbles in the driveway.

The driver stepped out to the earth, staggered, clutched the open door for support, and sat down heavily on the running board. He made an attempt to rise but got no more than halfway to a standing position.

"Get dizzy drivin'," he said to no one in particular. "It's fumes."

He made another attempt to stand up; failing, he muttered the word "fumes" and sat down. Joe watched him with apprehension, leaning far out of the seat.

"Buddy," he said, "get yourself together."

The driver sat with his face pressed against blunt fingers. He made a hiccoughing sound.

"Remember," Joe said, "that we gotta take this guy somewhere."

There was a harsh cackle. "He comes in this way every time," said the old man. His voice was high and frail and oriental. "But I'll help you." He was standing back out of the area lit by the headlights.

"Who the hell are you?" asked Joe. He peered pugnaciously at the circle of shadows.

"I'm Andrew," said the old man.

"Sure you are," said Joe, "but what of it?"

"I'm Andrew," repeated the old man. "I watch at night."

"Well, let's see you watch this guy," said Joe.

"He will be well in a little time."

"All right, all right," said Joe; "but what about the patient?" The word had a proud sound on his tongue.

"He is expected. The doctor is waiting for him." The old man moved closer to the ambulance. He blinked his eyes excitedly. "What kind is he?"

"What d'ya mean, what kind is he?" Joe snarled at the old man.

The old man licked his lips. His eyes were like oysters in the moonlight. "Is he violent?"

"Naw," said Joe. "No more 'n yer old lady."

The old man was disappointed. He slid slowly over to where the driver sat on the running board and reached over his head for the leather package of keys dangling from the ignition switch. He carried these gingerly to the back of the ambulance and inserted one of the keys in the lock. "All right," he said. "We will take him."

Joe swung down from his seat. "Open 'er up," he ordered.

With a protesting groan, the doors opened. Crane looked out at the yard. There was an undertone of cricket noise and a heavy exotic odor of flowers. It was as though his sense of hearing and of smell had suddenly returned.

"All right, Doc," said Joe.

"I am not a doctor," said William Crane.

"You're telling me?" said Joe. He climbed into the back. "Come on."

Crane tried to stand. His muscles refused to hold him, and he sank back on the leather bench. Joe seized his collar and swung him out the door, almost upon the pale face of the old man. Rolling, Crane hit the gravel on his back and finally came to a halt with his hands thrust under him, crusted with pebbles. He managed to gain his feet.

Joe jumped after him, fastening onto his handcuffed arms. "Which way?" he asked the old man.

"This way." The old man's voice trembled with excitement. He had retreated to a safe distance.

"Wait!" It was the driver. He stood, one arm hooked

to the ambulance, watching the three. "We gotta remove handcuffs."

"O. K.," Joe said. "But let's get going."

The driver unlocked the handcuffs. His breath was sour in Crane's face. The old man started up the steps, Crane and Joe followed, and the driver staggeringly brought up the rear.

The screen door was unlatched, and they entered the long hall. Red carpet covered the floor, and on wall brackets shaped like candles two yellow bulbs gleamed, casting hungry shadows along calcimined walls. At the first door the old man knocked timidly.

A thick man stood in the doorway. Bunchy muscles pulled his black eyebrows into a scowl. He had on pants and an undershirt.

"What do you want?" he asked.

The old man said, "A patient." His voice cringed.

William Crane pulled against Joe, trying to see into the room. The man put a palm against his face, raised his right shoulder, and shoved. Crane's head hit the other wall of the hall hollowly: he put out his hands to keep from falling. On the calcimine, his fingers, torn from the gravel, left bright red stains.

"Lord Almighty!" The old man ran a tongue across violet lips. "They look like nail marks. . . ." His voice faded. He stared at the blood and then at Crane.

"Dr. Livermore's in his office," said the thick man. He closed his door.

The last door in the hall was also closed. The old man knocked a second time. There was the sound of an inner door being closed. After a long time the hall door was opened by a hand with a diamond ring on the third finger. The diamond was the largest Crane had ever seen.

Dr. Livermore wore a black beard like Gen. Italo Balbo and Sir Hubert Wilkins. His brown eyes were cunning and indirect. There was powder on his coat. He smiled a welcome.

"Do come in," he said. He nodded dismissal to the old man.

"Thish the gent'man from Bellevue," announced the driver. He leaned against the door jamb. His face was ash gray.

Darkly stained wood ran under oriental rugs, and there were lamps with Chinese bases and brocaded shades about the room. A large walnut desk was beside a closed door at the opposite end. Dr. Livermore sat down behind the desk. He pushed a button.

"You are Mr. Kassuccio?" Dr. Livermore looked at Joe.

"Yeah," said Joe. He still had hold of Crane.

"Mr. Campbell will see that you are given dinner. After that, I would like to have you come back to my office."

Mr. Campbell appeared to be the driver. He thrust himself from the wall. "C'm'on," he said. He ushered Joe out, slamming the door behind him.

"This is an outrage," said William Crane loudly. "I demand an immediate explanation." He glared at the doctor.

Dr. Livermore spread both hands, palms downward, on the polished surface of the desk. He leaned forward confidentially.

"Mr. Crane." The doctor's voice was muted like a trumpet. "Mr. Slater has been so anxious about you."

Crane evinced surprise. "Mr. Slater? My uncle?"

"Yes." Dr. Livermore brought his hands together so that fingers and thumbs were touching but not palms. "Mr. Slater was worried about your health. He determined to have you brought out to this quiet spot for a nice rest." Dr. Livermore clasped his fingers. "He was afraid you might refuse to come, so he took this unusual method of sending you to us."

"You're damn right it's unusual to kidnap a man." Crane was furious. "Particularly one doing the important work I am."

The door to the hall opened, and the thick man came in. He was wearing a white jacket.

"What is it?" he asked sullenly.

Crane scowled at him. He returned the scowl.

"Is this another of them?" Crane demanded.

"Another what?" asked Dr. Livermore.

"Another of those thugs of yours."

"Why, Mr. Crane!" Dr. Livermore was very hurt. "This is my colleague, Dr. Eastman. He is here to help you regain your health."

"He looks like a thug," Crane said.

There was a knock at the door. Dr. Livermore said, "Come in," and a pretty girl entered. A nurse's cap perched on her black hair. She took a seat beside the desk. Dr. Livermore handed her a large printed form.

Dr. Eastman pulled an overstuffed chair close to the built-in couch by the three long windows at the side of the room. Crane noticed two of the black cushions were flat on the couch, while the third sat at an angle. The two flat cushions were wrinkled and on one a blond hair caught the light.

"Now, my dear sir, you must know that health comes first of all," said Dr. Livermore.

"My work means everything," said William Crane. "I am a very important man."

"But to have your work go on, your health must be preserved," said Dr. Livermore. "That is why your uncle asked us to care for you."

"But this is an asylum. I am as sane as anybody."

"Certainly," said Dr. Livermore quickly—too quickly. "But those here are merely suffering from a temporary—let us say—attack of nerves."

"You mean nobody here is insane?"

"Exactly. There is no such thing as insanity. Some people are merely suffering from brief periods when their rationality is in abeyance. It is like a nightmare, only it occurs during waking hours. With proper care anyone can be made rational again."

"But I am perfectly rational."

"Of course," said Dr. Livermore, bringing his fingers together again. "Of course. But your uncle felt that a nervous breakdown might be imminent if you kept up your work."

Crane appeared to come to a decision. "As long as I am here," he said, "I might as well make the best of it."

"That's the attitude we like to see." Dr. Livermore put his hands behind his head and swung back in his chair. "Now, we must ask you some questions. Miss Clayton will make a few notes."

Crane noticed that Dr. Eastman seemed to be asleep. Heavy lids shrouded his eyes; his face was as expressionless as a death mask. On either side of him were vases filled with ferns. The windows behind him, Crane saw, were backed with a very fine cheesecloth next to the screens.

"First we shall have to inquire into your past life," said Dr. Livermore cheerfully. "Are you married?"

Crane thought for some time. "No," he said.

"Have you ever had any serious illnesses?"

"Scarlet fever, whooping cough, and boils."

Dr. Livermore said: "Please do not joke, Mr. Crane."

"Have you ever had boils?" asked William Crane.

Miss Clayton uttered a giggle which, when Dr. Livermore turned to her, suddenly became a sneeze.

"Do you have nocturnal headaches?"

"No," said Crane. "Most of my headaches come in the morning."

"Ah," said Dr. Livermore. "You drink, then?"

"Sure, don't you?"

Dr. Livermore glanced at his colleague. One of Dr. Eastman's eyelids moved upward in an acknowledging blink.

"How old are you?" asked Dr. Livermore.

"Thirty-two."

"What church do you belong to?"

"None."

"Can you say Methodist Episcopal?"

"Methodist Episcopal."

Dr. Livermore exchanged another glance with Dr. Eastman. Miss Clayton wrote something on a slip of paper.

"How do you sleep?"

"Alone."

Miss Clayton seemed to think this was funny.

Dr. Livermore was very patient. "I mean, how well do you sleep?"

"Fine."

"When is your birthday?"

"October 3."

"Can you remember where you were on your thirtieth birthday?"

"Sure."

"Where were you?"

"I wouldn't care to say," William Crane said.

"We can't help you if you won't help us." Dr. Livermore's beard quivered indignantly.

"Then you better ask me about some other birthday." Crane winked at Miss Clayton, who pretended to be interested in the point of a pencil.

"Never mind." Dr. Livermore swung his body against the desk. "What did you have for your last meal?

"It's been so long," said Crane, "that I hardly remember."

"Come, now," said the doctor firmly. "Your last meal."

"That must have been breakfast," said Crane. "You know, I think it's nice of you to ask me what I had for breakfast. I like to tell people about my breakfasts. I had a glass of orange juice to start out with; then some soft-boiled eggs, buttered toast, coffee, and some swell marmalade. Of course, on some mornings I have——"

There was a strange noise in the garden outside the windows. The three medical persons in the room froze with attention, like listening statues. There was a tense silence, undertoned with hushed breathing and the susurrant tones of crickets.

Then the sound came again. It was like the sniffing whine of a hound dog hot on the scent of some animal, excited and impatient and immediate. But it was not the sound of a dog. It was not the sound of any animal.

The black pupils of Dr. Livermore's eyes widened. "Quick," he shouted. "Get Charles." Dr. Eastman was already on his way out the door. "Miss Clayton, you stay here." Dr. Livermore pulled a pistol and another object from his desk. Crane saw that it was a baseball catcher's mask. A heavy chain was attached to it, and this Dr. Livermore swung around his arm as he hurried out.

"What the hell!" said Crane. Miss Clayton held a finger to her lips. She was pale, but he could not tell whether it was because of the sound or because she was left alone with him. He walked over to the window.

Outside, the moonlight poured silently on the garden. Hedges precisely circled a fountain in the distance and, in orderly beds, flowers peacefully slept. A great moth, attracted by the reflection of the moon in the pool, fluttered above a nimbus of spray around the fountain. The garden was serene, laved in quiet and light, until, suddenly, the weird whining resumed. It was louder this time, and in its direction Crane saw a dark object moving behind a hedge. It was heading for the pool.

A second later it was out in the open, and Crane saw that it was a man running on his hands and feet. His gait was a wolf-like trot, the more abnormal because of its seeming naturalness. At the pool's edge he raised his head in a swift backward glance and then began to drink. The noise of his lapping reached the window in liquid rhythm. While William Crane watched in surprise, the man finished drinking and again made that swift, furtive scrutiny of the garden. Suddenly he stiffened, crouched flat on the ground. Then, with a smooth outthrust of legs, he leaped in the air and deftly caught the cream-colored moth with a metallic snap of his teeth.

"He's eating it!" Miss Clayton was standing beside Crane. Her face was bleached with horror. "Why don't they stop him?"

Crane was first to see them. He pointed out the creeping shadows to Miss Clayton. Two men were crawling up to the pool from the direction of the window, and two others, much closer, were emerging from behind a clump of small plants. As these two were about to close in, the man saw them and snarled defiance with bared teeth. One attempted to seize his neck; there was a click, and that one drew back with a cry of pain. At the same time the wolf-man wheeled and came loping on hands and feet toward the window and the men hidden just below it. At the edge of the zone of light cast by the windows, the two men leaped upon him.

Uncanny snarling and yelping awoke a hubbub of frightful echoes in the garden, which, duplicated, seemed to be the voices of an entire wolf pack. Once during the struggle the creature nearly got free and, in so doing, his head came within a few inches of the window. It was a head of so inhuman an aspect, with animal cries coming from foam-flecked lips, and mad eyes showing more white than pupils, and sweat and blood and dirt on naked cheeks, that Crane leaped back into the room, seized a chair, and prepared to defend his life.

But in a moment the fantastic noise failed, and in its place came a howling, sad and lonely and tragic. Presently it moved into remoteness and vanished with the closing of a distant door.

Crane looked at the chair in his hand and then at Miss Clayton. "I hope I never run into that alone." He grinned foolishly. He put the chair back on the floor.

Miss Clayton's nice brown eyes widened with interest. "I don't believe you're crazy," she said.

"Sure I am," said William Crane. "Mad as a temper ance worker."

He walked over to Dr. Livermore's desk. A drawer was open, and in it Crane could see the handle of another automatic pistol.

"These are interesting buttons," he said. "What are they for?"

"They call the servants," said Miss Clayton. She was powdering her nose.

"What'll they do with that fellow they just caught?"

"They'll put him in detention."

"Anybody else in detention?"

"Only Miss Van Kamp."

"What's she done?" William Crane looked curiously at the nurse.

"She thinks she's had something stolen. She keeps breaking into places looking for it. They've just got her in there for a day or two."

" How do you get in detention?"

"Just get rough and see."

"Oh!"

Dr. Livermore and Dr. Eastman came into the room from the hall door. There were scratches on Dr. Eastman's face. Dr. Livermore's eyes went to the closed door beside the desk. They were at first anxious and then relieved. He took his seat.

"I think, perhaps, in view of tonight's events," he

said, "we might defer this examination to a more seasonable time." He looked inquiringly at the other doctor. Dr. Eastman's face was impassive.

"There are just a few other questions we should ask now," Dr. Livermore continued. "What is your occupation?"

William Crane leaned toward the desk. "My outward or my secret occupation?"

"Why, both."

"To the world I am a simple bond salesman," Crane announced. "But actually I am a great detective."

"But your uncle's note says nothing about detective work," objected Dr. Livermore.

"He does not know of it," Crane whispered. "No one knows save a few criminals."

Dr. Livermore looked at Dr. Eastman, who seemed interested for the first time. Miss Clayton was taking rapid notes.

"You don't believe me?" William Crane spoke with indignation. "You don't believe I am a detective?"

"Now, Mr. Crane, it's quite all right." Dr. Livermore spread out his fingers. "We are naturally surprised."

"Surprised, hell!" said Crane. "You don't believe me. But I'll show you. What do you do for your hay fever, Dr. Livermore?"

Dr. Livermore's eyes expressed genuine surprise.

"It's too bad to love gardens and not be able to walk through them except at night when the pollen is settled," said Crane. "And now you don't even dare walk outside alone at night for fear someone will attack you. That's bad, too."

Dr. Livermore arose from his chair, but Crane held up his hand melodramatically. "Stop! Who was it you had in here a half an hour ago while I was imprisoned in that ambulance?"

Dr. Livermore did not answer, and Crane turned to Dr. Eastman. "You are engaged, I believe, to one of the nurses?"

Dr. Eastman stared at him.

"It might interest you to know that your Miss Evans is the one who was in this room."

Dr. Livermore looked away from Dr. Eastman.

"But that isn't all." Crane was talking to Dr. Eastman. "It was not upon professional business that she was here."

"Be silent, you madman," shouted Dr. Livermore, pressing the buttons on his desk.

"Let him talk," Dr. Eastman said. He moved closer to Crane. "Go ahead."

"They did a little necking," said Crane. "Right on that couch over there." Dr. Eastman was no longer looking at Crane. "You son of a bitch," he said to Dr. Livermore.

"Be careful of your language," said Crane. "There are two ladies present." He walked to the desk and pulled open the door beside it. Miss Evans was standing there. She had on a wine-colored velvet dress, and her blond hair was mussed. "You should have a back door to your bedroom," said Crane to Dr. Livermore.

Miss Evans slouched into the room. She was like Sadie Thompson, vivid and hot but not quite so defiant. Her skin was very white, and her lips were very red. She said, "What's the fuss about?"

"It's my fault," said Crane. "I was giving a demonstration in elementary deduction."

"Deduction?" asked Miss Evans.

"You see, from the fact that the windows have cloth filters on the screens and there are ferns instead of roses in the vases, I concluded that Dr. Livermore suffered from pollen fever, more commonly known as hay fever." Miss Evans watched him without expression. "Then I observed that Dr. Livermore had a pistol which he carried in his pocket and still another in his desk. No man keeps two weapons near him unless he is afraid of attack."

Crane spoke with a nasty smugness habitual to schoolmasters.

"That you had been in the room, Miss Evans, was evidenced by a blond hair on one of the pillows on the window couch. And you were good enough to leave a bit of your face powder on Dr. Livermore's coat. Hence the vulgar allusion to necking." Dr. Eastman was having trouble breathing. "As for your presence in the other room, Miss Evans, that was revealed by the anxious glance Dr. Livermore threw at the door when he returned from his struggle in the yard. As for being engaged to Dr. Eastman, it is not hard to distinguish that arrow on his white jacket as a sorority pin. You are the only college girl here so it must be yours."

Crane laughed briefly and without humor. "Now, Dr. Livermore, I insist that you release me."

"No," said Dr. Livermore shortly. "These men are going to take you to your room."

The driver and another man in a white jacket stepped beside Crane. Both had blood on their faces, and the driver's ear was bandaged. Crane hit him on his bandaged ear. He tossed a Chinese lamp at Dr. Livermore. Then, as his arms were seized, he kicked Dr. Eastman on the jaw. Then he kicked him in the stomach.

Dr. Livermore shouted, "Take him away. Put him in detention." Dr. Eastman writhed on the floor. No one paid any attention to him. At the door William Crane halted his captors by bracing his feet against the wall.

"You can't lock me up," he asserted earnestly. "I am C. Auguste Dupin."

Chapter III

SUNLIGHT ROLLED into the window and slid across the floor like butter on a hot frying pan. On slender limbs outside a lazy breeze stirred absinthe-shaded leaves and carried into the room the perfume of heavy flowers and the brisk sound of bees in the half silence of morning. Against the upper windowpane a fly hopefully attempted to break through the glass. A spider web, shimmering in the air, reflected rays of light in flashes about the room.

Waking from heavy sleep, William Crane looked at the room with reluctant eyes. It was a plain room. There was a steel table in the corner by the window, a chair of metal against the wall, and a wash rug was flattened whitely on the brown wood floor. On the gray wall hung a colored sampler whose green-and-red thread printed:

JESUS DIED TO SAVE YOU AND ME

Crane turned over so that his face was toward the wall. He closed his eyes. There was a rattle at the door,

32

and he rolled over in bed. It was Miss Clayton. She was dressed in a professionally starched nurses' costume, and her face was starched with professional dignity. She carried a small tray. On it were a thermometer, a bottle of castor oil, a glass of orange juice, and a small bottle of aspirin tablets. She laid the tray on the table and began to tiptoe out of the room.

"Hello," said William Crane.

Miss Clayton let a trace of surprise flutter the calm of her pretty face. "Why good-morning," she said. "How do you feel?"

"Lousy," he said. "What time is it?"

"Nine o'clock," said Miss Clayton. "That's very late for the country."

She went out of the room, closing the door lightly behind her. Crane got out of bed and put on the linen bathrobe that was neatly folded on the seat of the chair. He felt better after he had brushed his teeth. He was glad to find they were all there. There was a cut under his right eye, his ears were red, a rib hurt, his hands were raw, but he decided he had come out of last night's fight pretty well.

He crossed to the window and looked out. Along the building there was a row of stout young trees, continuing in an orderly line to the left until they reached a small enclosed garden. Around this garden and its steel picket fence was a much larger garden, and in it he could see the fountain where the wolf-man had caught the moth. Directly across from him was a large two-story stucco house with green shutters on the windows. It was anchored at one end to the ground by a screened porch, also painted green.

Under the beams from the sun, the garden was a Joseph's coat, bright and vivid and variegated. Aquamarine grass curled around livid beds of earth and sheeted in a backdrop for a confused chorus of flowers. In unsymmetrical isolations about the garden, trees hugged liquid pools of shade, like green umbrellas on a hotel roof. Under one of these, in the small enclosed garden, sat an old lady, in a red-and-green canvas deck chair. There was no wind for a moment and there was a timelessness about the old lady and the garden and the lack of movement, as though she had always been there sitting with her hands folded in her lap in that flowering garden, and as though she would always be there, motionless and grim and implacable. Then she began to knit, her needles twinkling in the light.

"A couple of million dollars," said William Crane, "and no place to go."

He turned from the window and got back in bed. He wondered if he was going to have to take the castor oil. He lifted the bottle and emptied it in the toilet. He was in bed again when heavy footsteps echoed in the hall. They belonged to Dr. Eastman. Behind him was

Miss Clayton. Dr. Eastman's dark face was impersonal. "How do you feel this morning?" he asked.

"I've already been asked that," said Crane. "Lousy."

"Does your head ache?"

"Wouldn't yours if somebody socked you on it?"

"Take his temperature, Miss Clayton." Dr. Eastman walked to the window and waited there until Miss Clayton withdrew the thermometer.

"It's just a fraction below normal," she announced.

"He can have a bath and a light breakfast," said Dr. Eastman.

"How about some clothes?" asked Crane.

"You will find some in your closet," said Dr. Eastman. "Miss Clayton will bring you your breakfast in fifteen minutes."

William Crane felt still better after the bath. He had put on a pair of gray flannel trousers, a white shirt, and was selecting a tie when Miss Clayton returned. She was carrying another tray on which there were a glass of orange juice, a dry cereal, three slices of toast, and a glass of milk.

"What's the extra orange juice for?" he asked.

"You're supposed to take that with the castor oil." Miss Clayton's soft brown eyes widened. "What happened to that oil?"

"I drank it."

"All of it?"

"Every bit," said William Crane firmly. "It has practically no effect on me."

"I hope you're right." Miss Clayton put the tray beside the other on the steel table. "You'd better have something to eat, anyway."

Crane paused halfway through the second glass of orange juice. "What was the matter with that man they fought with last night?"

"That's Mr. L'Adam. He's the worst one we have. He suffers from spells like that every time the moon is about full. I don't know how he got out last night."

"There is an old lady in the yard. Who's she?"

"That's old Miss Van Kamp. I told you she was in detention last night."

"What's she doing in the garden?"

"That's just a part of the garden. It's shut off from the rest and is used by those who are in detention. The main part of the garden is where you saw the fountain, over by the guest house."

"Is that the place right across the way?"

"Yes, but I don't know why I should tell you these things."

"Well, at least tell me this," he said. "Do you think a dark blue or a purple tie would go best with my black eye?"

Miss Clayton had nice teeth. "Anything will do," she said. "We are not at all dressy."

William Crane put on the dark blue tie. It hurt his neck. He took it off and opened his collar and looked in the mirror. He thought he looked like Ernest Hemingway, only smarter.

"You are to have the morning free," said Miss Clayton. "Dr. Livermore is busy."

"Free for what?"

"You can sleep, or you can read in the garden."

"I'll read," said William Crane. "I like to read."

It was very nice in the garden. Coolness hung under the trees and clung to the walls of the house, intensified by the glare of the sun on the flowers. William Crane found a deck chair under a tree almost across from where the old lady sat. She appeared oblivious of him. He sank back in the chair and picked up the book the nurse had given him and began to read. The book was lousy.

It was pleasant in the garden, however, and Crane got up from his chair and walked to where the iron picket fence met the wall that ran around the entire place. The wall was of dove-colored stone, and there were pieces of glass embedded in the top. He thought it would be a hell of a place to get out of. He walked back to the other end, by the detention building, and stopped in front of the iron gate.

The old man of the night before stepped in front of

Crane. He had a hooked nose and white hair, and he wore a white coat. "Where are you going?" he demanded.

"I don't know," said Crane. "Where're you going?"

"That's out," said the man, pointing at the gate.

"Out what?"

"Outside," said the old man triumphantly. His hooked nose became more prominent. Blue veins twisted on his temples.

"What's outside?" asked William Crane.

"Meadows and fields and hills," said the old man. "All basking under the light of His Grace."

"Aren't there any towns near here?"

"No towns fit for Christians," said the old man darkly. "I reckon the nearest is Toryville: that den of iniquity; that abomination in the eyes of the Lord."

"What's the matter with Toryville?"

The old man's wrinkled hands clenched with indignation and his nose quivered in righteous wrath. "Matter with it?" He drew a gasping breath. "It is a veritable Sodom and Gomorrah, a sink of evil, a foul stench in the nostrils of the Lord. But He will cut down the men wallowing in the filth of their drunkenness and reveling in the darkness of their lies, and He will crush in His hands the harlots and the jades and the adulteresses with their soft white bodies, naked under their flimsy dresses no longer than their knees."

"How do you know they haven't anything under their dresses?" asked Crane.

"I know," said the old man. "I bin watchin' them when they didn't know me and the Lord was lookin'."

"What have you been watching them for?"

"I got to watch them and everybody." The old man poked his head through the bars of the gate. "Some are crazy; some are sane. I been appointed by Him to tell them that is from them that ain't."

"Which of us is crazy?" asked William Crane.

The old man said, "You are. I'm a guard."

Crane went back into the garden. Fluid melody came from a bird somewhere in a tree. Outside the gate, behind the guard, he could see the other garden and some people in it. He felt restless in the enclosed plot. The old man went back to the detention house. The guard named Charles took his place beside the gate. He paced in a careful square; three steps one way, one step across, and then three steps back. Crane watched him for a moment and then walked to where Miss Van Kamp sat with the tense immobility of an old lady waiting in a railway sitting room.

"It's warm, isn't it?" said William Crane.

Black, beady eyes came alive for a second. Miss Van Kamp glanced at him and then returned to her original impassivity, neither seeing nor not seeing.

Crane looked around the garden. There was nobody in sight.

"My name is William Crane," he said. "I've been sent here to help you."

"A trick," said Miss Van Kamp. She blinked her eyes like an incredible parrot. "A trick."

"No, your brother sent me," he said. "He received your message."

Miss Van Kamp's button eyes were bright with suspicion. "I sent no message," she said.

Crane leaned over confidentially. He said, "I am a detective."

Miss Van Kamp betrayed no surprise.

"Your brother said I was to help you in any way I could. You are afraid of something in here."

A shadow, like an oil film, softened the hard brilliance of Miss Van Kamp's eyes for a moment. Then her face stiffened with decision. She said, "Go away!"

"They will murder you if I do," Crane said.

The eyes looked at him again. There was anger in them, and terror. "How do I know you are from my brother?"

"He told me to ask you if you remembered Adrian."

"He would," said Miss Van Kamp. She relaxed as though someone had loosened her corset. "Is it safe to talk now?"

"Sure," said Crane. "No time like the present."

"Someone has got my strong box," Miss Van Kamp said. "I must have it back."

"Who's got it?"

"Do you think I'd have sent for you if I knew?"

"What was in it?"

"About four hundred thousand dollars' worth of bonds."

Crane blew his breath between his teeth.

Miss Van Kamp regarded him placidly. "That isn't all. There was one of the two keys necessary to open my safe-deposit vault in New York."

"How much is in New York?"

"Just cash, jewelry, bonds."

"How much?"

"About eight hundred thousand dollars' worth."

"My God!" said Crane. He decided the old lady had got herself in a damn nice mess. "Where did you lose the box?"

"Someone stole it from my trunk. It was in the bottom shelf, covered with a nightgown."

"Who do you think took it?" asked Crane. He looked around the garden.

"I don't know."

"Did you tell anybody about the box?"

"Only Dr. Livermore."

"He's probably the one that took it."

"No," said Miss Van Kamp. "If he did, I'd have

been dead long ago. I think he is searching for it, too."

"You don't believe Dr. Livermore would—er—have you disposed of?"

Miss Van Kamp's eyes expressed superlative scorn. "Don't be stupid."

"How long before it was stolen did you tell him?"

"About a week."

"How long ago was the box stolen?"

"About two weeks."

The garden was murmurous with the minor sounds of insects and the solo notes of birds. In the warm air the odor of flowers was heavy and tropical. The sun was high overhead.

"Did he tell anyone else?"

"I suppose he told the others." Miss Van Kamp impatiently brushed a wisp of thin hair from her eyes. "He probably would."

"Then one of the docs is probably richer by four hundred thousand dollars than he was a couple of weeks ago."

"Yes, and he can get the other eight hundred thousand dollars from my vault in New York by killing me and getting hold of the second key."

William Crane looked at the old lady speculatively. He wondered if she were completely batty. A million, two hundred thousand dollars was a lot of money. Still, her brother had said she had large holdings in

New York real estate. He noticed Miss Van Kamp was frowning at him. "Need a nap?" she asked.

"Wouldn't some of the others around here want the box?" he asked.

"No." Miss Van Kamp was emphatic. "They're all insane in here but me."

"You and me," said Crane.

The old lady's eyes were expressive. She said, "Maybe."

"How did you lose the box?"

"It was in my trunk when I went to bed. The next morning it was gone."

"Did you hear anybody in your room?"

"No."

"Was your door locked?" There was a sound on the gravel. "I really think petunias are hardier than pansies," William Crane said. "We had an early frost in our garden one fall, and do you know it killed every single pansy. We felt very badly. . . ."

A neat, medium-sized man was approaching on the path. He bowed to Miss Van Kamp. His face was long and pale and thin: so thin that it seemed to be all bone and gristle, entirely without that soft layer of fatty flesh which distinguishes man from machine. His skin was taut over high cheek bones. His hair was black.

"Good-morning," he said. He bowed again.

The man's eyes were large and brown and set in a terrible stare, as though they had been focused at something distant by someone who had forgotten to change them back to normal.

"Good-morning," said William Crane. "Nice day."

Miss Van Kamp had withdrawn into herself. Her shoulders were hunched apprehensively, and she was trembling.

"Yes," said the man. His lips twisted in a smile, but his eyes did not change expression. "If you like the daytime." His voice was suave.

Crane felt his hair rise. The man smiled again and passed with leisurely grace into the rear of the garden. He left a rank odor behind him.

"I think I've seen that fellow before," said Crane.

Miss Van Kamp did not reply. She whispered, "Take me away."

Crane seized her arm, helped her from the chair, and started briskly for the gate. Miss Van Kamp's breath came in short jerks. The old man and Charles appeared from around the corner.

"I was just coming to get you," said Charles. He led the way through the outer garden to the door of the detention home. He opened the door, signaled for them to go through, and then lingered to fasten the catch.

"One more question," said Crane. "What does the box look like?"

"What does a box look like?" Miss Van Kamp marched off to her room with restored dignity.

Chapter IV

Dr. LIVERMORE touched the tips of his fingers together, minister fashion, and leaned back in his chair. His long face relaxed; his manner became expansive.

"I think that will do for today," he said.

William Crane sat and looked at Dr. Eastman, who was on a straight-backed chair beside the big desk. The room was angular with the amber rays of the afternoon sun. The splashing of the fountain, irregular and distant, mingled with the drowsy notes of small birds.

"Will he keep the same room?" asked Dr. Eastman. He scowled through black eyebrows.

Dr. Livermore turned to a large man at the opposite side of the room. "What do you think, Dr. Buelow? Same room?"

Dr. Buelow was youngish, with blond hair in a German pompadour, and a blond mustache. He looked as though he could have played on the Cornell football team in the days of the flying wedge. He took his time with the question. "I think not," he said at last. "I think he should be with the others."

"I don't agree," said Dr. Eastman. He thrust out his heavy lower jaw. There was a red mark on it where Crane had kicked him. "He's violent. We'd better keep him where he is."

"Now, Dr. Eastman," said Dr. Livermore. He raised a long finger. "You know what our policies are."

"Not to do anything sensible," said Dr. Eastman. He swayed on the edge of his chair, ape-like with his short legs, long arms, and barrel chest.

Dr. Livermore ignored the remark. "We'll give him the corner room. Eleven will do very well." He pushed one of the buttons on his desk. "If you will take him over, I will have Charles bring his clothes."

"All right." Dr. Eastman submitted angrily. "I know your policies." He stood up and looked at Crane. "Come on."

"Wait!" Dr. Buelow waved a muscular arm. "Mr. Crane, will you have the goodness to repeat this after me?"

"Repeat what?" asked William Crane.

"This," said Dr. Buelow. "The ragged rascal ran round the rugged rock."

"The ragged rascal ran round the rugged rock."

Dr. Buelow turned to Dr. Livermore. He said, "I don't understand it." His large face surrounded puzzled blue eyes.

Dr. Eastman led Crane to the large building he had

seen across from the detention ward. They entered through the porch, passed a huge living room, and climbed stairs, sided by a wrought-iron railing, to a narrow corridor on the second floor. Room 11 had windows on two sides. There were a three-quarter bed covered with a peppermint-stick spread, an easy chair, a desk, a straight chair, and a low bureau with a mirror halfway to the ceiling. The rug was pale green and covered the entire floor. There was a bit of lint on the part by the foot of the bed.

"This is your room," said Dr. Eastman. "Your clothing will be here in a minute."

Crane sat on the bed. He jiggled up and down. "Not bad," he said.

Dr. Eastman raised the two window shades. Sunlight engulfed the room. He walked to the door.

"You needn't bother with ice water," said Crane.

Dr. Eastman regarded him darkly. He said, "I wouldn't be too funny, if I were you." He slammed the door from the outside.

Crane went to the windows. One looked over the fountain to the detention building; the other over the large outside garden. He inspected the scenery until someone knocked on the door.

It was Charles. He had two bags and a bundle. His smooth face was covered with a fine perspiration, and his hair hung over his eyes. He put the bags down and pushed back his hair. "Anything else you want?" he asked.

William Crane took a five-dollar bill from his watch pocket. "I want a quart of that liquor they make up here."

Stepping backward, Charles closed the door. "You want some liquor?" His face was crafty. "You aren't allowed money here. How much have you got besides that bill?"

William Crane produced a handful of bills. "Sixty dollars."

"Hand it over," Charles demanded. "I won't let the doc know about it."

"What if I don't?"

Charles edged closer, sliding black shoes along the green carpet.

"How would you like me to tell Dr. Livermore that you've been in jail?" said Crane conversationally. "He might be glad to learn he has a stir-bug around the place."

Charles's eyes glinted through narrow slits.

"He'd be glad to know how serious the last rap was," said Crane. He held out the five-dollar bill. "Now, get me that stuff."

For a moment Charles seemed undecided. Then he took the money. "A guy's got a right to try to go straight," he said.

"It doesn't look as though you were trying very hard."

Charles's face attained the inscrutability, reposed and calm, of a choir singer during an intermission. He nodded and walked out.

Crane grinned at his battered reflection in the mirror over the dresser. "As a good guesser," he said aloud, "C. Auguste Dupin had nothing on me."

The closet was large, with hangers for his clothes, and he began to unpack his pigskin suitcase. He was putting a pair of rubber-soled golf shoes in the closet when there was a knock on the door. He closed the closet, pushed the suitcase under the bed, and walked to the window.

"Come in," he said.

Miss Clayton entered with towels and two cakes of Palmolive soap in her hand. She put these on the dresser. "Anything else you need?" she asked.

"Some cracked ice and a bottle of White Rock."

Miss Clayton showed her small regular teeth. "Have you anything to go with them?"

"Why should I tell?" asked William Crane. "You're probably a G-girl."

Miss Clayton was puzzled.

"G-girl," he said. "Snooper, prohibition officer, revenuer."

"Well, I like that." Miss Clayton was really injured.

"I don't think there's anything wrong with liquor."

"Good girl," he said.

"Of course, you are not supposed to have liquor in here."

"I haven't."

"I advise you to keep it well hidden if you have some."

"I haven't any."

"I said if you have some."

"Do they send people around to look for it?"

"No," said Miss Clayton, "but Miss Van Kamp is liable to find it. She's always going through everybody's things."

"What's her idea?"

"I told you last night. She thinks she has lost something. But she won't tell anybody what it is."

"It can't be her virginity?"

"You're nasty," said Miss Clayton. "Nice people don't say things like that."

"Maybe that would account for Miss Van Kamp's reticence."

Miss Clayton mingled her indignation with a smile.

"I am just one of the local wits," said Crane.

"Half-wits!" Miss Clayton moved toward the door. "Dinner is at seven downstairs."

"Do you have to dress?"

"You really ought to wear something." Miss Clayton started to leave.

"Wait a second," said William Crane. "Did you happen to notice the fountain last night? I thought it stopped for a while after they locked me up."

"I heard it stop, too. It was the first time it stopped since I've been here."

"I just wanted to be sure I wasn't beginning to hear things."

The light from the afternoon sun was heavy bronze. There was already outside the faint haze of evening, odorous of leaves and pine and smoke. The air was still and peaceful. Vines partially shaded the windows of the room, filtering the darkness with soft veins of metallic light. Crane removed his shoes, the candy-stick cover from the bed, and lay down. A moment later he got up, locked his door, and went back to bed.

He was awakened by a subdued but persistent tapping. He swung out of bed and opened the door. Charles stood there with a bundle of towels hung over his bent arm.

"I've got too many towels now," said Crane.

"Not this kind," said Charles. He stepped inside and pulled the towels off his arm and put two quart bottles on the dresser. The bottles were of white glass, and the liquor in them was a pale yellow, like medium-priced white wine.

"That's good stuff," said Charles.

"I didn't expect you to get so much," said Crane. "What did it cost?"

"Four bucks," said Charles. He smirked disarmingly. "You got a dollar coming."

"You didn't have to spend that much," said Crane. He drew another bill out of his pocket. "Here's a fin. Keep it."

"Thanks. Say, if you don't like that stuff, I can take it back."

"Let's try it." Crane got two glasses from the bathroom. He pulled the cork from one of the bottles and filled each glass to the brim.

"I got to work around here." Charles made an alarmed gesture. "That'll knock me."

Crane handed him the glass. "Here's how," he said. He drained the glass.

He was all right for a moment, and then Crane thought he was going to die. He felt as though he had stepped under a cold shower and had swallowed a pint of molten iron at the same time. Then it was all right again.

Charles looked at him with awe. "God!" he said. "No wash?" He had taken a sip from his glass.

Crane waited until his vocal cords had stopped

fluttering. "Not bad," he said. He wedged the bottle behind the dresser. "Finish up."

Charles slowly drank the rest of his liquor. "You certainly can take it," he said.

"I don't hate the stuff."

Charles took his glass into the bathroom. Over the noise of running water he said, "You certainly started something between Dr. Eastman and the boss."

"How do you mean?"

"I wouldn't be surprised to see those two having a battle pretty soon."

"Why?"

"Over Miss Evans."

"So?"

"They're all nuts about her," said Charles. "Even that Dr. Buelow is gone."

"How about you?"

"She ain't a bad-lookin' dame," said Charles, "but too skinny." He cast a look at the bottles behind the dresser.

"All right," said Crane.

They had another drink.

"That's the McCoy," said Crane.

Charles edged toward the door. "How'd you know I'd been in stir?" he asked.

"Nine by two. Three steps one way, one step across, three steps back."

Swift comprehension lit Charles's eyes. "You ain't so dumb."

"No," said William Crane. "I'm not."

He waited until the door had closed, and then he took the glass Charles had used carefully by the bottom and wrapped it in an old newspaper. He put the package in his suitcase

It was dusk when Crane awoke. The room was dark, and the windows emitted grayness through the loosely woven vines. An imperceptible movement of air, intermittent and impersonal, was gradually cooling the room. In the distance there was a sound of dishes being moved about and the steady rush of running water. He got up and switched on the lights. After a short drink, he washed and shaved, carefully avoiding the bruises on his chin and lips. He noticed with satisfaction that his eye was progressing from a gala red to a somber blue. He closed his good eye and experimentally regarded the effect in the mirror.

He descended the stairs into the huge living room. At the opposite end there were two divans at right angles to a large fireplace. Other comfortable chairs were around the sides, and a large mahogany table in the center was covered with magazines. There were filled bookcases built into the walls. Two men were talking in front of the fireplace.

"How do you do?" said one of these, advancing out of the gloom. He was a middle-aged man with steel-flecked hair and kindly wrinkles. "You're the new guest?"

"Yes. My name is Crane."

"Mine is Pittsfield. I'm a lawyer. And this is Richardson."

Richardson moved slowly forward, approaching without pleasure. He was powerfully built, about forty years old, but still in good condition His face was tanned. His mouth drooped in a sullen pout. "Hello," he said.

"I've been asleep," said Crane. "Is dinner over?"

"It hasn't started yet," said Pittsfield. His blue eyes twinkled. "The invigorating air here gives one an excellent appetite. So much better than Washington."

Crane nodded. He was surprised to detect a warning look from Richardson. "I hope the food is good," he said.

"It's really first rate," said Pittsfield. "It is simple, but it is delicious."

Crane nodded politely.

"My dear friend John Hay," said Pittsfield, "had a fine taste for proper food. His perfect dinner was composed simply of a clear soup, a steak cooked over charcoal, a fresh vegetable, a touch of potato, a salad and cheese and biscuits. That, with a bottle of burgundy, and a port with the cheese, leaves a man ready for a bit of conversation."

"You have quite spoiled my appetite with your talk of gourmandizing." A large, flabby man with bad teeth and a yellow complexion stood regarding Pittsfield with a mocking smile. His small brown eyes glowed with a golden inner light. He had on a dress suit.

"Hello there," said Pittsfield. "Blackwood, this is Crane. He's planning to stay with us."

"Delighted," said Blackwood. He sank into a chair and put a fleshy hand on his hip. "I do hope you have some interests outside of football and law. Football, you know, is the resort of thugs who are afraid of compromising their gentlemanly position by following a career of saloon brawling."

Richardson snorted and moved away.

Blackwood bared his yellow teeth. "But you haven't told us what you are interested in," he said, watching Richardson's retreating back.

"Murder," said William Crane.

Blackwood turned toward him and blinked his golden eyes. "Murder?"

"Murder," said William Crane.

"Now you are joking," said Blackwood.

"I am perfectly serious."

"How are you interested in murder?" asked Pittsfield. "Actually or in the abstract?"

"Actually," said Crane.

"You mean you commit them?" Blackwood asked. He watched Crane alertly.

"No. I catch those who commit them."

"You mean you are a detective?" asked Pittsfield.

"That's right."

"I haven't heard of you," said Blackwood.

"You would have, if you knew my right name," said William Crane.

"Ah, yes, you must have your alias," said Blackwood. "An alias is to a sleuth what a nom de plume is to a third-rate author. It conceals his identity without hiding his mistakes."

"Good-evening, gentlemen." A deep, timbrous voice indited the words. Crane turned to see a tall, jeweled lady standing behind one of the couches She was poised, as if she had halted in the middle of a step. She was about fifty. She was dark, her face was long and tragic; her eyes were huge and heavily mascaraed.

"Ah, Miss Queen!" said Blackwood. He did not rise. "May I present—what did you say your name was?"

"Crane."

Miss Queen moved majestically from the couch to Crane. She held out a hand covered with rings. "So pleased," she said.

William Crane saw the jewels were imitations.

"We were talking of murders," said Pittsfield. "Mr.
Crane investigates them."

"How horrible," said Miss Queen. "Can't you talk
of something more interesting—say, love?" She managed to draw her long face into a coquettish smile.

"That's just as illegal," said Blackwood.

Pittsfield said, "In some cases."

"I mean adultery," said Blackwood. "That's the only
interesting form of love."

"Oh, really now! Do you consider adultery such a
crime?" asked Miss Queen. She unfurled a fan and
peered over it at William Crane.

"Oh yes," said Blackwood. "Much worse than
murder."

"Why?"

"You see murder only gives pleasure to one party.
Adultery gives it to both. Therefore it is more reprehen-
sible."

"Mr. Blackwood, you are shocking," said Miss
Queen, tapping him delightedly with her fan. "In
London, I should say to you——"

What Miss Queen should have said to Mr. Blackwood in London was never said. Miss Van Kamp
marched into the room. With her was an even smaller
lady of slightly less age. This lady had natural brown
hair and soft white unwrinkled skin and blue eyes.
She had on a black dress with a frilly white collar and

cuffs. Miss Van Kamp had on a black dress without frills. Crane wondered if the Dolly Sisters would look like them in 1984. Miss Van Kamp made directly for his group.

"Mr. Pittsfield," she said, "I would like to have a word with you."

"Certainly. Pardon me, please." Mr. Pittsfield moved off with Miss Van Kamp. The other lady followed.

"Have you been in London recently?" Miss Queen asked William Crane.

"Not since 1929."

"That was a delightful year. Did you ever go to the theater?"

Crane nodded.

"What did you see?"

"I saw Tallulah Bankhead."

"What sort of an actress is she?"

"She's a stripper."

"What do you mean?"

"She kept taking her clothes off in the show I saw. She finally got down to a negligee and a pair of black silk stockings. I expected her to take them off any time. But she never did. I went back three times."

"You didn't try going backstage, did you?" asked Blackwood.

"No." William Crane saw Miss Van Kamp beckoning him. "Excuse me."

Miss Van Kamp put her mouth close to Crane's **ear**. "Mr. Pittsfield has a clue," she said.

"What is it?"

"I'll tell you later," said Pittsfield. He looked about him. "We are facing an implacable enemy." The two old ladies were impressed. "It may be I shall have **to** summon my marines from Washington."

"Marines from Washington?" said Crane. He caught a look from Miss Van Kamp. "I don't think you'll have to do that."

"I trust not." Pittsfield moved away.

"You haven't told anyone else about me?" asked Crane.

"Nobody but Nellie here," said Miss Van Kamp. "She won't tell a soul. She and Mr. Pittsfield have been trying to help me."

"You mustn't tell anyone else."

Both women nodded solemnly.

"Who is Miss Queen?" Crane asked.

"She was a noted English comedy star," said Miss Van Kamp. "She had a series of nervous breakdowns and was forced to give up her career."

By the door, Crane caught sight of a tanned, aristocratic young lady in a blue evening dress. "Who's that?" he asked. The lady crossed over to where Richardson stood alone.

"Mrs. Patterson Heyworth," said Miss Van Kamp. She and Nellie walked from him.

Richardson regarded Mrs. Heyworth possessively. He leaned over and said something to her. She smiled and looked around the room and caught sight of Crane. Her eyes were passing over him casually, as over a stranger, when suddenly their expression changed. The new expression was of recognition, of intimacy, of joy; such as a woman might use to greet a lover. It was a look outside the bounds of sanity, a transcendental look. Crane stared at her. Suddenly she put a warning finger to her lips. She turned to Richardson.

Crane sat down in a chair. "What the hell," he said. "What the hell."

A musical chime rang. He sat up in his chair.

"Dinner," said someone.

"Sure," Crane said. He got up and started to walk.

"Not that way," said someone. "That's the garden."

Dr. Livermore took Crane's arm. "I'll show you," he said. He looked curiously at him. "You seem to have been preoccupied."

Crane said, "That's right."

They went into the dining room.

Chapter V

BY THE TIME the coffee was served, Crane had them pretty well placed. He was seated between Miss Queen and a small man who hadn't said a word all evening. He had been introduced as Horace Penny, a manufacturer of ladies' underthings and he had acknowledged both facts with a faintly ribald droop of the right eye. Mr. Penny was really amazing. During the dinner he had indicated his desire for celery with a motion of his little finger; he had intimated the fish that was not all it should be with a slight twist of his lips; he had delicately urged Crane to try some of the chutney with a movement of his left eyebrow. He got along quite nicely without speaking. Across from Crane was a blowsy blond lady with a large bosom and sparkling teeth. She talked continually at the top of her voice. Her name was Mrs. Brady. She was interested in the finer things of life: gambling, race horses, prize fighting.

The table was chastely sophisticated with fine silver and linen, and Dr. Livermore sat at the head like the czar of all the Russias. He ate ponderously, chewing his food carefully but not cautiously. Every now and then he would sweep his napkin across his beard.

Crane tried his coffee and then put some camembert on a cracker. "What does everybody do in the evening?" he asked. He inserted a piece of the cracker in his mouth and eyed Miss Queen.

"This is movie night," she replied, looking a little pointedly at the small piece of cracker left in his hand.

"Movies?" He put the piece of cracker in his mouth. "Do they really have movies here?"

"You'll see," said Miss Queen.

Mrs. Brady caught Crane's eye with her overbright blue ones. She shouted across the table, "Do you like horses?"

"What kind of horses?" asked Crane.

"Race horses," said Mrs. Brady. "The kind my husband used to own."

"I didn't know your husband."

"Oh, Mr. Crane!" Mrs. Brady was convulsed with some emotion. Crane didn't know whether it was amusement or rage. "I *mean* all race horses."

"I think they are wonderful."

"Oh, you do," cried Mrs. Brady. "So do I."

That seemed to end it. William Crane returned to his cheese. At the end of the table opposite Dr. Livermore, Blackwood was talking to Pittsfield.

"There is no beauty in a legal document," he was saying. "It is like a maiden lady who has been raised under Victorian standards, stiff, stilted, repressed."

"I suppose you are right," said Pittsfield; "but you can't deny that lawyers are able to write fine prose."

"But I can," said Blackwood. "And I do. No lawyer ever wrote anything of real artistic value. His training precludes that possibility, just as does that of the journalist."

"Lawyers framed the Constitution of the United States."

"Fine prose that is."

Pittsfield was pale. "I am supposed to have written some good prose myself. Take the Gettysburg address. Critics call that a gem."

"Now, gentlemen," said Dr. Livermore. "I think posterity had the final say as to the quality of prose."

"I'll have you deported—" Pittsfield glared at Blackwood—"just as soon as I get back to Washington."

Blackwood's puffy face broke into a smile. He winked at the rest of the table. Pittsfield sank back in his chair. His face became blank. Dr. Livermore returned to his food.

"Poor fellow," said Miss Queen. "That Blackwood can always infuriate him." Her face lengthened in sympathy.

"Why does Blackwood try?" asked Crane.

"They hate each other. I think it is because of their different natures. One is so simple and honest, and the other is so complex."

One of the two colored maids poured fresh coffee into Miss Queen's cup. Crane looked toward Mrs. Heyworth. She was talking to Richardson. The light slid brownly from her boyishly cut hair and shadowed her dark curling eyelashes. Conscious of his look, she turned and stared into Crane's eyes. Her glance was warm and intimate. He hurriedly returned to his cheese. He reached for a knife, knocked over a water glass, pushed the knife on the floor, and dropped a cracker on his lap.

Miss Queen said, "It will be easier just to push the table over."

"Huh?" said Crane. He removed the cracker from his trousers.

"All we need is a drink to top off this meal," declared Blackwood. His small eyes shone maliciously. "You haven't any port wine, have you, Dr. Livermore?"

"Alcohol?" Dr. Livermore's beard quivered as though there were animals running through it. "Poison on top of a fine meal? Mr. Blackwood, how can you ask?"

"It's the only way to end a dinner. As for its being a poison, many drink it and live."

While Blackwood was speaking, Crane looked at Mrs. Heyworth out of the corner of his eye. He was relieved to find she was talking to Richardson.

"I cannot express too strongly my disapproval of alcohol," said Dr. Livermore to the table. "It is one of the chief causes of human trouble. It lowers the morale, the resistance of the body to disease, and destroys the nervous system."

Crane had a startled impression that the doctor was talking to him. He took a hasty drink of coffee on the theory it would kill the smell of applejack on his breath.

"You take rats," said Dr. Livermore. "If you feed rats alcohol, their offspring are weak and far below the intellectual standard of normal rats. And if you feed the offspring of an alcoholic rat alcohol, it will be stunted for life."

"You take the rats," said Blackwood; "I'll take the alcohol."

Dr. Livermore continued: "As for cancer, experiments have shown that rats with cancer die much more quickly when they are fed alcohol than when they are not."

"So much the better for the drunkard rats," said Blackwood. He looked around the table for approval.

"Science has exploded the myth of alcohol." Dr. Livermore was not to be stopped by any futile attempt at humor. "In the instance of snake bites, it has long been assumed that whisky would materially help in the cure. It has been proven that the alcohol aids the venom."

"Interesting, if true," said Blackwood. "But how do

you account for the fact that whisky is taken along on every expedition into wild country?"

"Merely misguided zeal on their part. Now, you take rats that have been exposed to very hot or very cold——"

Miss Van Kamp rose stiffly from her chair. "I don't care for rats." Her voice was thin. "Particularly at dinner." Nellie stood up, and the two turned and walked from the table. Dr. Livermore muttered something that was lost in his beard and pushed back his chair. There was a general burst of conversation. Pittsfield brushed by Crane as they walked into the living room. He whispered, "I'll tell you about the box after the movies." Crane nodded.

Dr. Livermore glanced at the brass clock over the mantel. It was eight o'clock. "Well, well," he said cheerfully. "Time for the evening's show."

He led the way out into the hall into a large room at the end. This room had a screen at one end with lines of chairs reaching to the rear wall. Projecting a few feet from the wall was a stand, and on this was a strange, bulky instrument of steel and shiny chromium. A large nurse sat composedly on a tall chair beside the machine. She was about thirty. She had very large breasts, and she gave the appearance of being held in an S-shape by a series of tight rubber abdominal bands. She was very stiff and proud.

Everybody came into the room and took seats, in most cases so that at least one chair separated each from the other. Only Richardson and Mrs. Heyworth and Miss Van Kamp and Nellie sat together. William Crane took a seat near the door in the back row. Dr. Livermore stood behind him.

"I want you all to remember to relax," said Dr. Livermore. "It is important to relax. You are going to have complete repose; deep, complete repose; deep, deep repose for one hour."

The lights were turned off. It was black and so still that Crane could hear the breathing of Dr. Livermore behind him and the faint rustle of the nurses' starched clothes from the platform. He became aware of a soft radiance emanating from the screen. It was delicate and weird and at first barely perceptible. Soft greens and blues floated across the screen in combinations of pastels; then came darker colors, sea blues, purples, mauves, heavy greens, and even a suspicion of red, so that there were yellow and faint gold. The colors formed patterns on the screen; clouds and dark hills and lakes and strange ghostly shapes that moved slowly from right to left.

The effect was soothing, and it was some time before Crane realized that music was being played by a phonograph in subtle harmony with the colorama. The music was confusing. It seemed to have a smell attached to it.

In fact, there were smells attached to it. William Crane recognized some of them. There was new-mown hay, rose, old lavender, a curious acid smell, a sort of manure smell, licorice, pine, mint, cinnamon, and some others that touched his memory but which he could not identify. These odors, too, were very subtle and he let his mind and body relax in the luxury of utter nothingness. He felt suspended in the state which is reached only just before falling asleep or just after waking. He would have fallen asleep if he had not caught a rustle behind him on the carpet. He turned his head slowly toward the lesser shadow of the door and saw a faint movement as a dark shadow slipped across the opening. A second later another shadow, smaller and quicker, followed.

Crane waited a moment and then tiptoed out into the hall. He looked up to the living room, but there was nobody in sight. The living room was empty too. The brass clock read eight-fifteen, which meant at least a half hour more of the movies, and he decided to look around upstairs. He went first to his room and secured a flashlight from a compartment in his pigskin suitcase. Cautiously he crept out into the hall again. The first door was unlocked, and he stepped inside. The room was like his except that the two windows were together at the end opposite the door. It was a man's room. There were a pair of white trousers across the bed, and underneath, an orderly row of men's shoes. They were small and he decided they must belong to Mr. Penny. He was not interested in Mr. Penny, so he tried the next room. This was also obviously inhabited by a man. He passed on to the next.

It was a surprising room. Instead of a bed, there was a studio couch gay with colored pillows. The curtains on the windows were of red and brown batik; the rugs were red and black. Two red and black moderne chairs and a chromium writing desk of curved pipe were under the windows. He opened the closet door and disclosed with his flashlight an array of dresses. The floor of the closet was covered with shoes. In a corner stood a tennis racquet. He closed the closet and went back to the writing table. He found a photograph of Mrs. Heyworth, a tall man, and a baby. He thought the man looked slightly familiar. His light flashed onto an object by the head of the couch. At first Crane thought it was a tea wagon. He flashed the beam squarely on it and discovered it was a baby carriage, painted gray, with rubber tires and a silvered handle. He bent over it and looked into the interior. His light was reflected by a pair of staring blue eyes and rosy cheeks of colored enamel. He saw it was a large doll, neatly tucked in under blue bedclothes of wool. Beside the doll was a bottle half filled with milk. It was uncomfortable being stared at by those unmoving blue eyes, and he decided to leave the room. He snapped off his light and turned the knob of the door, pulling it slowly toward him. As he edged out into the dark hall he heard a rustle of cloth. Someone hurried by him and turned down the stairs.

After several minutes he stepped out into the hall and continued his search. He tried three more rooms. Two belonged to men, and the other obviously was lived in by a woman younger than Miss Van Kamp, if black lace lingerie was any indication. A fourth room proved to be vacant. The fifth was the object of his search. The bed was covered with an elegant patchwork quilt with a date, 1812, sewn on the middle of it in some heavy white material.

William Crane wondered if it was Miss Van Kamp's class numeral at Vassar. He pulled a heavy mahogany rocking chair against the door to prevent being surprised and laid his flashlight on the bureau so that the rays were directed away from the windows at the end of the room. In the reflected light he examined both shades carefully, and the catches on the windows, but he could detect nothing unusual. On the edge of the sill of the right-hand window, he was surprised to find a series of fresh holes about the size made by a thumb tack. There were nearly one hundred of them. He examined these closely and then turned to the rest of the room. It was hard trying to pick up something on a theft that had happened nearly three weeks before, but he hoped he might find something.

The closet, partially filled with dark dresses, black petticoats, dressing gowns, and two dark coats, yielded nothing of particular interest. Neither did the bathroom, which was hung with robes-de-nuit and an enormous series of neatly coiled rubber tubes, the purpose of which Crane did not like to surmise.

A writing table furnished nothing noteworthy except a savings deposit book with a balance of $26,384.31. He studied this enviously for some time. A pincushion on the top of the dresser he gave only a glance, but he carefully emptied out a box filled with small pieces of jewelry, rings, cameos, a shilling piece, a silver medallion inscribed, "Sunday-school Attendance—First Prize," three pennies, and a large thumb tack. The top left-hand drawer in the bureau was filled with handkerchiefs, silk and embroidered. The right-hand drawer contained a neat pile of silk and woolen stockings. There were also some pieces of black lace. In the first big drawer were careful piles of fine silk petticoats and wool underwear, a gray silk dress of webbed texture, a few pairs of gray silk stockings, and a fine paisley shawl. There was a strong smell of lavender in the drawer, and William Crane thought of the movies downstairs. He pulled open the next drawer and found nightgowns and more wool underwear jumbled together in a haphazard mess. He flashed his light over the tumbled contents and carefully felt through them with his left hand. He encountered only matted clothes. He softly closed the drawer, opened the bottom one, and saw that it was in order, and promptly closed it. He returned to his inspection of the mussed drawer. Finally he shut it for the second time and flashed his light around the bottom part of the bureau. Underneath, on the side away from the door, the heavy Wilton rug was partially turned over in a firm crease. He pondered over this for some time. Then with a sigh he stood up and flashed his light around the entire room. Everything else was in perfect order. He walked over to the green waste basket and looked in it. It was empty. He moved toward the door, but in passing the bed he bent down and turned his light under it.

The clear, white rays shone on an agonized face, staring out into the room with redly protruding eyes. The skin was a liver-blue and from a distorted mouth hung a swollen tongue like a misplaced velvet necktie. Around the corpse's neck there was an angry crimson welt.

After a time William Crane managed to breathe. He saw the body was that of Pittsfield. He reached under the bed to the dead man's vest and found the heavy gold watch was in place. The wallet he found in the hip pocket of the trousers was empty, but two rings were on the fingers of the man's right hand. There was a diamond stick pin in his tie. A pocket in the wallet contained nothing but a book of postage stamps and a photograph of a painting of Abraham Lincoln. He put it back in the hip pocket, smoothed out the rug where he had knelt, and quickly let himself out of the room.

He hurried down the dark hall to his room, feeling a sudden uplift of relief as he closed the door behind him. He found a glass in the bathroom, filled it halfway with moonshine, and drained it in a single gulp. He felt better immediately. He put the flashlight back in the grip, washed out the glass, and stuck the bottle behind the dresser. He reflected that whatever Pittsfield had to tell him would go untold. He thought it was a hell of a way to die, strangled and stuffed under an old lady's bed.

He went down to the living room. There was nobody there, nor in the dusky corridor leading to the room where the movies were being held. The door to this room was still open and he slipped into his seat. In the room the only sounds were the irregular noise of breathing and the faint whir of the color machine. He settled back in his chair, but his nerves were taut, and he was unable to feel the earlier compulsion to relax. The colors, seething in polychromatic vistas across the screen, were garish; the music was false, the succession of odors as cheap as those from the perfume machines in a penny arcade. Behind him, his ear caught the noise of a soft footstep on the heavy rug, and he became aware that someone was coming into the room. The steps progressed to the machine and then merged with its regular purr.

A second later the colors disappeared from the screen, and the electric lights shone brilliantly. Crane blinked in their glare and turned to look at the machine. The nurse, composed and bland, was seated on the platform. Dr. Livermore was nowhere in sight. Around the room, Crane saw all the others with the exception of Pittsfield. The patients looked like drowsy birds disturbed in sleep. The nurse said, "Good-night, everybody."

As if hypnotized, the patients started toward the door. Crane found himself beside Blackwood. "What do we do now?" he asked.

"We go to bed. Everyone must be in the gentle arms of Morpheus by ten o'clock."

"What time is breakfast?"

"From seven-thirty to noon. It's come as you please."

They were now in the living room. "Do you have to have breakfast?" Crane asked.

"Yes, decidedly. That's one of Dr. Livermore's ideas. He is convinced that breakfast is as beneficial to humanity as alcohol is bad." Blackwood lowered his voice. "But I finished him tonight, and Pittsfield, too."

"Huh?" said William Crane.

"You heard me at dinner, didn't you?" Blackwood

smirked triumphantly. "I certainly had the best of both arguments."

"Oh."

"Don't you think so?" Blackwood persisted.

"Sure," said William Crane. He watched the slim silk ankles of Mrs. Heyworth precede him upstairs to the bedroom hallway. She was with Richardson, and she turned to the right toward Crane's end of the hall. Richardson nodded to her and walked off in the opposite direction. At the top of the stairs, Crane turned after Mrs. Heyworth, and Blackwood followed him to the fourth door from the end.

"This is my cell," he said. "Good-night."

Crane watched Mrs. Heyworth disappear into the room with the doll.

"Good-night," said Blackwood again.

"See you in the morning," said Crane. He went on, and as he passed Mrs. Heyworth's room he saw the door was open a crack and noted the lights had not been turned on inside. He opened his door, closed it loudly, and then opened it a crack. He heard Mrs. Heyworth's door click, and he closed his again.

He turned on his lights and undressed in the bathroom. He put on a pair of brown pajamas and opened the windows. In the moonlight, the garden was brilliant and serene. There were tiny pinpoints of flame where the heavy dew reflected the moon, and he could see stars in the pool of water below the fountain. The fountain seemed to be running all right. He went to the bed, looked under it, and then climbed into it. He fell asleep wondering if Miss Van Kamp would look under her bed before she climbed into it.

Chapter VI

IT SHORTLY BECAME OBVIOUS that Miss Van Kamp had looked under her bed. The quiet cloth of the night was torn by a thin screaming which persisted grimly and evenly until it was joined by another and shriller voice. William Crane listened to this duet from the harbor of his bed for some time and then threw on a bathrobe and advanced into the hall. He reached Miss Van Kamp's room immediately after Richardson and Penny. They halted at the door, bulking darkly in the jaundiced light, but he could see over their shoulders. Like a figure in a waxworks, Miss Van Kamp knelt unnaturally on her floor in an attitude of agonized supplication. Under the heavy white nightgown her body was formless. Crane was startled to see that she was nearly bald. She was still screaming, but no sound came from her mouth. Beside her in a lavender nightgown stood Nellie, her small body shaking convulsively as she filled the room with noise. The cover on the bed was thrown back, and underneath Crane could see the face of Pittsfield. He looked no better than he had before.

As the three stood in the doorway, footsteps clattered

on the stairs and Dr. Eastman pushed by him with the proud nurse of the movies. Her low, rubber-soled shoes moved silently as she took the old women out of the room, urging them with relentless arms. Dr. Eastman moved the bed out into the middle of the room and bent over the figure on the floor. "He's dead," he announced.

"Oh, Doctor!" a voice exclaimed from behind Crane. "Not really?" It was Mrs. Brady. Her full figure was revealed in a gold and red kimono, and her pink face was shining with curiosity and cold cream. She had on Japanese sandals over bare feet.

"It looks as though he had been strangled," Richardson said.

Mrs. Brady said without conviction, "Isn't that terrible."

Dr. Eastman nodded. He pulled the quilt from the bed and laid it over the corpse so that the 1812 came directly over the dead man's chest. At once the room seemed less crowded.

"What'll we do?" asked Richardson.

"You wait until I get Dr. Livermore," said Dr. Eastman. "Don't let anyone touch the body."

The three men moved into the room. "Who did it?" asked William Crane.

With a delicate movement of his shoulders Mr. Penny indicated he had no idea. He expressed sympathy and depreciated the idea of violence with a twist of his mouth and a wave of his hand. He made it apparent that he could throw no light on what was to him a shocking crime.

Richardson said, "I think it was Blackwood. If he didn't do it, why isn't he here?"

Mr. Penny lifted his eyebrows.

"He's the sort of a snake who would do something like this," Richardson said. His voice was filled with conviction. "He's been at odds with Pittsfield for months. He's been trying to pick a quarrel by goading him with all sorts of insults. Now he's killed him."

"He picked a funny place to do it," said Crane.

"He probably carried him in here to escape suspicion." Richardson's tone intimated that nothing was beyond Blackwood.

"Maybe he wanted to throw suspicion on Miss Van Kamp," Crane suggested.

"She couldn't have done——" Richardson turned and peered at Crane. "You're quite a joker, aren't you?" His jaw was thrust out.

"No," said Crane. "I'm not."

"A punch in the jaw is no joke," Richardson said.

"No," said Crane. "It's not."

"Neither is murder."

"I see your point," Crane said. "What shall we do in a serious way?"

"We'd better search the room. The murderer may still be here." Richardson opened the closet door and poked his head into the orderly orchard of clothes. Mr. Penny drew away, his face alive with fearful anticipation. The closet and the bathroom were equally empty. Richardson appeared to have exhausted his ideas.

"It seems as though the fellow got away," he said, looking at the corpse with disapproval. "When do you think it happened?"

"Dr. Livermore ought to be able to tell us," said Crane.

"It must have been while we were at the movies."

Crane nodded. He was watching Mr. Penny as he meticulously searched the room.

Richardson said, "I say! That means someone from the outside did it."

"Why?"

"Nobody could have gotten out of the movies without having been missed."

"Maybe."

"I've got an alibi. I was with Mrs. Heyworth. She'll back that up." Richardson's jaw demanded agreement.

"What alibi have you got?" Crane demanded of Mr. Penny.

Mr. Penny shrugged his shoulders. He closed his eyes for a second and let them understand that he had had the misfortune to sleep through the greater part of the movie.

"I'm in the same boat," said Crane.

Presently Dr. Eastman returned with Dr. Livermore. "What a terrible thing!" Dr. Livermore said. His beard was stiff with horror. "Where is the body?"

"Here," said Dr. Eastman. He pulled aside the quilt like a magician at the end of a Woman-Sawed-in-Halves trick, only Mr. Pittsfield did not sit up. "He's evidently been strangled," he added. "I wonder what the murderer used?"

Mr. Penny held out a black woolen cord with a purple tassel at either end. "Where did you get that?" Richardson demanded.

Mr. Penny made a slight gesture toward the floor beneath the bed. Where else would you find a cord that had just killed a man than beside the corpse? his wink at Crane intimated. Dr. Eastman seized the cord. He said, "If we can find the bathrobe that goes with this, we will probably know who killed Pittsfield."

Meanwhile Dr. Livermore had made a quick examination of the corpse, flexing the arms and feeling the chest with the palm of his hand.

"He hasn't been dead long," he said. He rose from his knees. "Less than two hours."

"Have any of you seen someone prowling through the dormitory?" Dr. Eastman demanded.

Richardson said he hadn't.

"How about you?" Dr. Eastman scowled at Crane. "If you're so smart, you ought to know something about this."

"I don't."

"Please, please!" Dr. Livermore's hands trembled. "Let's not have any accusations in this unfortunate accident."

Dr. Eastman said, "Accident? Murder is no accident."

"Please!" Dr. Livermore's voice was oily. "I think it would be well to have these three gentlemen go downstairs while we discuss what is to be done."

On the stairs their feet raised dull echoes, which were suddenly flung back in their faces as Charles and the driver rushed upward past them. From the downstairs hall Crane saw the figure of a man lurking on the porch. There was a cigarette in his mouth, and when it glowed Crane saw he was Joe. In the living room were Miss Queen and Mrs. Heyworth. The former comedy star had on a garment of black silk which clung to thin shoulders. Mrs. Heyworth wore a tan polo coat over blue pajamas.

"Have you seen him?" asked Miss Queen. Her white nostrils quivered. "How did he look?"

Crane said, "Dead."

Mr. Penny plumped down in an armchair like an

anemic Buddha, his eyes closed and his face passive. Richardson moved over to Mrs. Heyworth.

"Was he murdered?" Miss Queen asked eagerly.

"It looks that way," Richardson said. "He was strangled."

"Who did it?"

"We don't know," Richardson said, putting his hand on Mrs. Heyworth's arm. She was watching Crane with wide, curious eyes.

Miss Queen moved closer to the men. "Who will be next?" She spoke in a loud whisper. "Who will it be?"

"Now, Miss Queen. They'll find out who killed Pittsfield before morning." Richardson spoke soothingly.

Miss Queen's face was funereal with foreboding. She shook her head sadly and smoothed her strange black outer garment with a hand the color of white lead. "There are things happening here," she said. "And they will continue."

"What do you mean?" Crane asked. "What things?"

Cold air shook the shade on an open window by the porch so that it made the noise of a person breaking through bushes. There was a noise, too, upstairs. There were a thudding on the floor and the creak of boards.

Crane repeated his question.

Miss Queen answered reluctantly. "Someone prowls

through this place at night. I do not think it is a human being."

Mr. Penny's eyes gleamed for a brief instant and were veiled again. Dr. Livermore came into the room. Behind him, carrying the body of Pittsfield on a hospital cot, shuffled Charles and the driver. They were followed by Dr. Eastman.

"I would like to find out all I can about this terrible tragedy," Dr. Livermore said. "I wish you would help me."

"We are perfectly willing," said Richardson. Dr. Eastman departed. Crane saw that Joe was still standing on the porch, watching them through the open window.

Dr. Livermore said, "The others will be down in a minute." Soon the others came. Miss Van Kamp and Nellie were together, looking very fragile and frightened. The large nurse and Mrs. Brady closely and protectively followed them. They arranged themselves in the room so that all the women and Richardson were together and Crane and Mr. Penny were quite separate.

"Has anyone anything to say about this tragedy?" asked Dr. Livermore.

Nobody had anything to say.

"It took place while the movies were being held," said Dr. Livermore. "Did anybody leave during them?"

Except for the delicate tap dancing of a moth against a window, there was silence.

Dr. Livermore said, "Somebody must have left the show."

"Somebody did," Crane said.

"Who?"

"Pittsfield."

The exposed portions of Dr. Livermore's face reddened. He glared out of small eyes. The proud nurse regarded William Crane indignantly and snorted angrily.

"How about you? Did you leave the room?" Dr. Eastman demanded in a choked voice.

"No," Crane lied.

"Can you prove it?"

"No."

Dr. Livermore nodded in satisfaction. "How about you, Penny?"

Mr. Penny shook his head.

Other questions revealed that Miss Van Kamp and Nellie vouched for each other. Miss Queen denied she had left the room, but she had no one to give her an alibi. Mrs. Brady was in a similar position. Richardson repeated what he had said upstairs. Mrs. Heyworth did not appear to hear him, but stared at Crane with her sleepwalker's eyes.

Crane said, "You might ask the nurse where she was."

The nurse threw out her magnificent bust. "Well, I never," she said.

"Go ahead," said Crane. "Ask her."

"I don't see why anyone should be left out of this investigation," Dr. Livermore stated. "Miss Twilliger, did you leave the room at any time?"

Miss Twilliger started to answer but thought better of it. She looked contemptuously at Crane. "You heard me, didn't you?" She spoke bitterly. "And you had to tell, you sneak."

"Miss Twilliger!" Dr. Livermore exclaimed.

"That's all right. I was out for a while."

"Where did you go?"

"I met the driver out by the garage. I wanted to tell him something . . . I wanted him to get something . . . for me when he made his next trip to New York. I suppose we talked about fifteen minutes."

"Very well," said Dr. Livermore. He made a motion to indicate the questioning was over.

"Wait a minute," Richardson said. "Where's Blackwood?"

Dr. Livermore was surprised. "I'll go and get him." He hurried up the stairs.

Richardson said, "That fellow will throw some light on this."

Blackwood had to be led downstairs. His flabby body hid under a green robe, and his eyes rolled in terror.

His breath came in gasps, his face was covered with sweat, and his legs shook so under him that he was forced to slump onto a chair. "Is it gone?" he moaned.

"Is what gone?" asked Crane.

"The corpse. I can't bear the sight of a corpse. It would drive me insane. Is it gone?"

Those in the room felt a sympathetic terror. Miss Queen shuddered perceptibly and clenched her hands and rocked back and forth on her feet. Miss Van Kamp and Nellie huddled together, their eyes kindled with renewed horror.

"It's gone," Dr. Livermore said. "But how did you know there was a corpse?"

"I heard them talking out in the hall after that terrible screaming. I lay there in bed trembling, expecting to be killed at any moment. I was so frightened." Blackwood rubbed his face with his hands, tenderly.

"Why didn't you come out?"

Surprise widened Blackwood's eyes. "To see a dead person? Oh! Oh!" He began to breathe again, very loudly.

"What we want to know," said Dr. Livermore, "is where you were during the movies?"

Blackwood's reply was halted by a muffled wail from Mrs. Heyworth. She was staring with hypnotic directness at a window in the back of the room. Framed within the open lower rectangle was a grinning demented face with bared fangs and flecks of saliva on the lips. It was the wolf-man of the previous night. The face slid away, and there was left only the screaming of the women, frantic and urgent.

Dr. Livermore ran to the porch and bellowed into the silver air. "Help! Charlie! Joe! Help! Help!"

There was a distant answering shout, and presently there came running Charles and Dr. Buelow. They halted on the porch. Dr. Livermore faced Charles. "I thought you had L'Adam locked up in detention."

"I have," said Charles.

"No, you haven't. He's loose outside. He was here a moment ago."

"He can't be."

"We'll have to get him at once. Get the driver to help us."

The three hurried off in the direction of the main hospital building. Mr. Penny walked across the room and shut the open porch door. Miss Twilliger had succeeded in soothing the women so that only Nellie made any noise. She was crying in a minor key. Blackwood had pulled a pillow over his chest for protection, and from behind this he watched the others apprehensively. Crane felt the attention of all upon him. It was as though he possessed a cue without which the play could not go on. He felt uncomfortable and walked to the window which overlooked the garden. Outside there was the excited noise of shouting. This gradually increased in fury and then died to nothingness. There followed the familiar mournful howling, sad and lonely as gypsy music. It made him shudder. "My God!" he said aloud. "What sort of a place is this?"

He felt warm air upon his neck. "Didn't you know?" whispered a woman's voice. "It's a madhouse."

The speaker was Miss Queen. She was looking at him through eyes luminous with compassion. "You poor boy, she said.

Crane got the hell out of there. He got out on the porch. He wished he were back in New York. He thought about Mr. Pittsfield, trying to have his mind fasten upon someone as the murderer. His mind was no good at this, and he tried it out on the missing box. It was no good on this, either; although he realized that one of the three doctors might have taken it. For the money, anyone could have taken it. Still thinking, he walked off the porch and into the garden, but as he reached a small cluster of trees someone seized him from behind. He struggled and was struck heavily on the head with something hard and blunt. He fell forward on the gravel path, his face against the pebbles, and someone knelt on his back, choking him strongly.

A man growled, "What did you do with that box?"

Crane tried to get his face out of the ground so that he could answer, but the fingers tightened on his throat.

He reached out an arm and seized a leg. It was thin and covered with sheer silk. Someone stepped sharply on his wrist. He let go. The fingers released his neck, and there was a noise of running. He discovered he couldn't get up.

Light from an electric torch fingered him and in its reflected rays Crane saw that a number of persons surrounded him.

"Is he dead?" asked a voice. It sounded hopeful.

A hand was laid on Crane's breast. "No, his heart is beating."

Crane decided he was among friends and struggled to his feet. Dr. Buelow was holding the flashlight. Around him were the patients, their faces opalescent in the milky light of the moon. Miss Twilliger peered into Crane's face. "What happened?" she asked.

"I don't know."

"I heard a woman scream," Miss Twilliger said accusingly.

"I didn't," Crane said. He found he had a nose bleed.

"You go to your room, Mr. Crane," said Dr. Buelow. "I'll get some dressings for your cuts. You can tell us what happened later."

Followed at a respectful distance by the patients, Crane went up to his room. He got a towel, wet it, and applied it to his nose. He stretched out on the bed with his head hanging over the side so that the bleeding would stop.

The bleeding had stopped when Dr. Buelow arrived with Miss Clayton. He dressed the cuts made by the gravel on Crane's face with precise gentleness and felt around his head for a possible fracture. There was none, but the place where he had been hit was tender.

"Never mind," Dr. Buelow said. "See, I do not hurt you." He washed the spots with alcohol. "So, I do not need even to bandage it."

Miss Clayton deftly pulled the covers over him. She arranged the pillows comfortably.

"Can you tell us what happened?" asked Dr. Buelow.

"Somebody hit me from behind. Somebody tried to choke me. I grabbed somebody's leg, and I guess somebody screamed. That's all I know."

Miss Clayton asked, "But why did they do it?"

"I don't know."

"Have you any idea who could have done it?" asked Dr. Buelow.

"I have a clue," said Crane.

"What is it?"

Crane held out his wrist. "Somebody stepped on that with the high heel of a shoe. See the mark?"

"But what good is that?" asked Miss Clayton.

"To catch the criminal," said William Crane very solemnly, "all I have to do is to find out the heel that made this mark."

Chapter VII

NEXT MORNING it was colder. The sun shone bravely
enough, but it didn't seem to do any good. It was
windy, and the air smelt of snow and of the usual pine
and of wood-fire smoke. There weren't enough covers
on the bed and, after an internal struggle, William Crane
forced himself to get up and close the windows. Then
he went back to bed and lapsed into a comfortable doze.

About an hour later Miss Clayton knocked, entered,
and looked at him severely. "Do you know what time
it is?" She had a bottle marked "alcohol" and some
cotton.

Crane modestly pulled the blankets up to his chin.
"No," he said.

"It's after eleven o'clock."

He made a clicking noise of surprise and regret.

"We decided to let you sleep after your . . . unfortunate experience with that lady last night."

"That lady?" asked Crane. "Do you know who she
is?"

"You should ask who she is!" Miss Clayton wiggled
her nose.

"You don't think I assaulted her?"

"I wouldn't know."

"If I decide to assault anybody it won't be a lady wrestler."

Miss Clayton laughed. "I'm going to bathe your battle scars."

"By the end of the week I'm not going to have any face left. There'll just be pebbles."

The alcohol pin-pointed the cuts, but soon the skin felt better. Miss Clayton was gentle.

"Do you know, they say poor Mr. L'Adam did it."

"Beat me up?"

"No, you silly! Killed Mr. Pittsfield."

"Why don't they keep him chained up?"

"They do. But he gets away every now and then. They think he crept into the guest house and killed Mr. Pittsfield."

"Who thinks that?"

"Dr. Eastman and Dr. Livermore."

"Well, maybe he did."

"I don't think so," said Miss Clayton. "He might bite somebody, but he wouldn't strangle them with a cord."

"That sounds logical." He sat up a little higher in bed. "But who did it, then?"

Miss Clayton's face was tense with concentration. "I've tried to think, but I can't figure it out."

"Did Pittsfield have any particular enemies?"

"I don't think so. He was kind and good. He thought he was Abraham Lincoln."

"Ah!" said William Crane. "I know who did it."

"Who?"

"John Wilkes Booth!"

Miss Clayton dabbed some of the alcohol into his eye. He said, "Ouch!—Ow!"

Miss Clayton said, "You'll have to get up now. Dr. Livermore wants to see everyone in the living room at noon." She dropped the wet cotton in the waste basket and put the glass stopper in the bottle. "He wants to question you."

"Me?"

"He thinks the attack on you can be explained in connection with the murder . . . if there was an attack."

"He must think I am a circus contortionist if he believes I did this all by myself."

A smile dimpled Miss Clayton's face. "You can hardly expect him to believe you would resist a woman as vigorously as you say you did."

Miss Clayton had a nice way of making her exits.

Crane was so astonished at his raffish reflection in the mirror that he took several extra minutes shaving to admire himself from all angles. The bruises of last night were still fresh and crimson, contrasting well

with two earlier blobs of purple on the side of his face
and the mournful aspect of his eye. His nose had a
skinned place on its bridge, and his neck was blue at
the points where fingers had pressed it.

He finished the rest of his toilet, splashed in the tub,
and dressed. When he reached the living room, he
found Miss Van Kamp seated in front of a lazy fire in
the stone fireplace. She motioned him to sit beside
her.

"How do you feel after your unpleasant encounter
last night?" she asked. She was knitting, and she did
not look up.

"Pretty bad."

Miss Van Kamp leaned toward him. "So do I," she
said. "I hardly slept a wink."

"I pretty nearly froze to death."

"It was quite cold. There was such a sudden change
that they decided not to give me my bath."

"Your bath?"

"I have a special steam bath three times a week in
the large bathroom upstairs. It's good for my nerves."

"Oh! . . . I see now."

Miss Van Kamp rested the gray, loosely knit material
on her lap. "Do you know who killed Mr. Pittsfield?"

"No."

"Will this make any difference in your looking for
my strong box?"

"I don't think so." He stretched his legs toward the fire. "What was it he had to tell me?"

The knitting needles stopped. "I'm not sure. I think it was about Dr. Livermore. I think Mr. Pittsfield saw him in the corridor late on the night my box disappeared."

"That might be a help." Crane leaned over toward the old lady. "What do you wear when you are given your bath treatments?"

"Young man, don't you think that's a bit personal?"

Crane disclaimed being personal. "I mean the key you have. The one the holder of the other key would need before he could open your safety-deposit vault in New York. You don't wear that around your neck when you are having a bath, do you?"

"No, but I have a perfectly safe hiding place for it."

"I don't think hanging it by a string out the window is so hot. Anybody can see those thumb-tack holes on the window sill."

"You've been in my room." Miss Van Kamp became unyielding and isolated. "When were you in there?"

"Last night."

"When Mr. Pittsfield was killed?" Her voice was accusing.

"After he was killed. After you found him. Didn't you see me?"

"Oh, yes!" Miss Van Kamp drew a long breath.

"I'm a suspicious old lady. Did you find anything else there?"

"We found the cord that killed Mr. Pittsfield."

"Where?"

"Under the bed."

"Who has it now?"

"Dr. Eastman, I suppose."

"If we can find who owns the cord, we'll have a clue, won't we?"

"Sure."

"I don't see why he doesn't show the cord to everybody. Maybe someone might know to whom it belongs."

"That's probably why Dr. Livermore wants to see us all here at noon."

"Oh! I forgot to tell you. He has decided to have us meet him here before dinner instead. About four o'clock."

"All right." Crane stood up. "Would Pittsfield have any reason to be in your room while you were away last night?"

"None at all."

"When do we have lunch?"

"We don't eat together. Just ask Maria. She'll get you what you want."

Maria was one of the two colored maids who had served dinner the night before. Crane had orange juice, coffee, soft-boiled eggs, and toast. On his way out of the dining room he met Dr. Eastman.

"How's your face, Crane?" asked the doctor.

"Pretty bad."

"We have suspended all treatments for today," Dr. Eastman said, "so you can do whatever you please."

"Swell."

Crane went out onto the porch and walked down the path to the point where he had been attacked. Someone had carefully smoothed the gravel all around there. At the entrance to the closed part of the garden where he and Miss Van Kamp had met, he found the old guard seated on a stool and whittling. His hair blew in the wind sparsely. There was a bald place on the top of his head. He looked up at Crane with no smile of welcome.

"Hello," said Crane. "A little cool?"

"Some would say so," said the old man.

"Where were you last night? Lots of excitement at the house."

"I was tending my own business."

"So was I," said William Crane, "and I got a sock in the head for it."

The old man said, "I was busy watching Her."

"Oh, Her!" Crane said. He nodded his head. "Her, eh?"

"She don't like it," said the old man. Saliva dripped

from his mouth, and he looked suddenly at Crane with electric-blue eyes. "She's possessed. She's got the devil hanging around her, urging her on to sin. I seen him, too."

The old man stood up and pushed his face close to William Crane.

"I'll catch her, harlot and daughter of wickedness that she is. They tried to stop me by having me transferred, but it won't do them no good."

"Transferred?"

"I have to work at nights now. I kin no longer watch her for the Lord. Work at night!" He clenched his bony hands. "O Lord! How they persecute Thy servant!"

Crane bent over the old man. He said, "Therefore also said the Wisdom of God, 'I will send them prophets and apostles, and some of them they shall slay, and some they shall persecute.'"

"Glory! Glory!" shouted the old man. His lips trembled and his blue eyes stared toward the sky. "Will you watch in my place?"

"Verily," said William Crane.

"She comes at night by the garage. But I've never been able to catch them."

"Them?"

"She meets him there."

"Who? The devil?"

"That's what I bin tryin' to find out." The old man spoke disappointedly. "But they always disappear, and now I kin watch no more."

"What does She look like?" Crane asked.

"She has hair of gold."

"Fear not, then," said Crane. "I will gird my loins and watch with eyes sharper than the swords of Damascus."

The old man's face was cunning. "And when we catch them in their unholy intercourse, we'll smite them in righteous wrath." The old man rubbed the back of his hand against his nose. "You take the devil and I'll 'tend to Her." He chuckled.

"O. K.," Crane agreed.

He moved away toward the garage and the servants' quarters. It was colder now, and the wind was blowing quite hard. The elm and oak trees flickered in the bright cold sunlight like early motion-picture films. Flowers bent convulsively toward the ground, and the pool below the fountain, as he passed, shook itself until its surface bristled with tiny waves.

The servants' house was of frame, painted a dull gray and adorned with square green shutters. Past it and a little to the side was a stone two-car garage. He walked into the garage. Inside there were two automobiles: the ambulance and a large Packard sedan. The sedan was dark blue, and on the right rear door were the initials,

"W. L.," stenciled in gold paint. The garage was filled with oily tools and rubbish and boxes, and he was examining these things when he heard voices. He climbed into the back of the ambulance.

"I got it here," said a voice he recognized as that of Charles. He heard a heavy object being moved. "It's potent stuff." Charles laughed. "This is the commission on some I got for a guy."

"That's just what I need." The voice was Joe's. "I don't go in for wrestlin' with loonies. I can't get used to them." He drank noisily.

"Don't take it all." This was the driver. "I can use some, too." Charles said, "There's plenty." There was the noise of another drinking.

"What kind of a joint is this, anyhow?" Joe asked. "Do they kill a lot of 'em off up here?"

"This is the first that died in nearly a year," the driver said.

Charles said, "They think that wolf guy killed him."

"Don't you?" asked the driver.

"I don't know," said Charles. "I don't think he'd do it that way if he was to murder someone."

"If they are satisfied, I am," said the driver.

"You ought to be," said Joe.

"Why?"

"I see you back here with a nice babe last night."

"Aw," said the driver. He giggled embarrassedly.

"Ho!" Charles said. His voice was sharp. "Who was it?"

Joe said, "That nurse with the big deze and doze." He sounded as though he were talking over a bottle.

"That's Miss Twilliger," said Charles. "She's really got 'em."

"How is she?" asked Joe.

The driver giggled again. "Now, boys, I'm a married man."

"Sure you are," said Joe. "But that don't answer my question."

"We're just gettin' acquainted," said the driver defensively. "She came out to get some air while the movies was going on."

"I'd like to get acquainted with her," Joe said.

"She's a nice girl," said the driver.

"Just another frail," said Joe. He and Charles laughed again. "It'd take a piano mover to throw her over."

"Never mind, ol' pal, ol' pal," said Charles. "Let's have another drink."

There was a moment of silence as they had another drink.

The driver said, "It don't feel so cold outside."

"It don't feel so cold inside," Joe said.

"Say," said Charles, "what the hell are you supposed to do around here?"

"Damned if I know," said Joe. "The doctor keeps me by him ever since I gets here and then he says about half hour ago, 'You may take an hour rest, my man.' If he's afraid someone's goin' to bump him off, why don't he keep me around all the time?"

"Unless the guy he's afraid of is busy," said Charles.

Joe said, "If he knows who he's afraid of, why don't he tell me?"

"That's a tough one," said the driver.

"I'd better put this stuff away," said Charles. "I got to go get L'Adam and put him indoors."

"Alone?" asked Joe.

"He don't make any trouble in the daytime. It's only at night he gets wild." Crane could see Charles deposit the bottle in back of a box, which he pushed close to the wall. "I got to be going," Charles said.

"Don't forget, the boss wants us all in the guest-house living room just before supper," said the driver as they moved away.

"I'll be there," Charles said.

Their voices faded into the rustle of leaves and the asthmatic breathing of the wind, and Crane got out of the ambulance and walked over to the box by the wall. He picked up the bottle, pulled the cork, and tried its contents. It was the same kind of moonshine he had in his room. He took a long drink and sat down on the running board of the ambulance.

He decided that cleared the big nurse, the driver, and Joe. This was nice because it narrowed the number of suspects down to fifteen or so. He thought that ought to be a cinch for C. Auguste Dupin. He looked at his watch. It was nearly five. He took another drink and put the bottle away. He noticed on his way back to the guest house that it was warmer.

He went to his room and washed and changed his shirt. He had a leisurely drink. Then he went down to the living room. Everyone was there except Dr. Livermore and Joe. On one side were the patients, seated on the couches and on easy chairs. Richardson was standing behind Mrs. Heyworth, who smiled at William Crane as he hesitated by the door.

Miss Van Kamp, Nellie, and Mrs. Brady sat on a couch; Blackwood was slumped in an armchair. Miss Queen sat in another. Mr. Penny was perched on the arm of a couch. Opposite them, by the door, stood Charles, the driver, Dr. Buelow, and Dr. Eastman. The three nurses leaned against a long table. Crane looked at Miss Evans. It was the first time he had seen her since the opening night. She had on a white nurses' costume, and her hair was the color of Bass's ale. Her face was pale, and her lips, full and turned down sultrily at the corners, were red. She was very seductive. Crane crossed the room and sat down close to Richardson and Mrs. Heyworth.

He said, "Cold, isn't it?"

Richardson stared at him dubiously. "I suppose so." His heavy face was impassive. "You've been out?"

"Took a little walk," said Crane.

Richardson asked, "You didn't get beat up again?"

Crane tried to smile, but it hurt, and he compromised by screwing up his face into what he thought was a humorous look. "This must be my day off," he said.

Mrs. Heyworth smiled and looked up at Richardson. "I'm cold, Dick," she said. "Will you get my coat? It's on the bed in my room."

Richardson moved away eagerly, and when he had left the room Mrs. Heyworth leaned toward William Crane. Her face was a lovely tan, the skin firm and smooth and soft over delicate bones. She was quite patrician and he thought of newspaper photographs he had seen of society girls at Palm Beach and Bermuda. She was looking at him with wide brown eyes.

"I'm so sorry you were hurt," she said.

"It was nothing." Crane was gallant.

"You must take care of yourself."

"I always do when I can. Things seem to get out of hand around here, though."

"Yes, they do, don't they?" She bent closer to him, her eyes compassionate. "You'll let me help you, won't you, dear?"

Crane had trouble swallowing. He blushed. He

coughed. "Sure," he said. He saw with relief that Richardson was returning with the coat. He stood up.

Richardson helped Mrs. Heyworth on with her coat, tenderly as with a child. He brought up a straight-backed chair and sat down on the other side of Mrs. Heyworth. His face was suddenly pleasant.

"What do you think about Pittsfield?" he asked.

"You mean who do I think killed him?" Crane noticed Miss Queen's melancholy eyes upon him.

"You don't think L'Adam did it?"

"No."

"Neither do I."

"Nor I," said Mrs. Heyworth. She was looking at Crane, too.

"Who was it, then?" Crane asked.

Richardson said, "Blackwood. I still think he did it."

"But he said he didn't leave the movies."

"I know he did leave them." Richardson spoke fiercely. "I remembered this morning. He was in a different seat when the movie was finished than he was when it begun."

Crane nodded his head. He looked across the room. Miss Evans was regarding him intently, her face triangular with scorn. Richardson said, "You don't change seats in a show like that. The view is the same from all over."

"Maybe his seat was broken."

"I looked them all over this morning. They're all the same."

"Just because he went out doesn't prove his guilt. Maybe he had to . . . get a drink," said William Crane delicately. He looked at Mrs. Heyworth. She smiled into his eyes. She had not been listening to what they were saying.

Richardson said, "No, but if he had an innocent reason for being out, why did he lie?"

"He didn't want to bring any attention on himself."

Dr. Livermore, followed by Joe, came into the room. He had a paper parcel in his hands.

"Listen," whispered Richardson. "Suppose you ask Blackwood about it. You can do it."

"All right," said William Crane.

Joe remained with the driver and Charles, while Dr. Livermore strode to the center of the floor. He put the parcel on the table. He said, "Ladies and gentlemen, I am sorry to have inconvenienced you, but there are several things I want to tell you. One of these is that we have solved the misfortune of last night."

He paused dramatically.

"We found that L'Adam had secreted a key to his door in the detention building under his bed. It was found there this morning. With this he released himself last night, entered here while all you were at the movies, and made his way upstairs."

Crane noticed that the three women on the couch were leaning forward breathlessly. Miss Van Kamp and Nellie had their hands clasped.

Dr. Livermore continued: "Outside Miss Van Kamp's room, Mr. L'Adam encountered Mr. Pittsfield. What went on there I shall not attempt to describe, but when L'Adam came out of that room he left the dead body behind him."

Crane said, "Boloney."

Dr. Livermore turned and looked at him. "What was that?" he asked. "What did you say?"

"Boloney."

Dr. Livermore looked away from him. "Mr. Pittsfield's body will be removed in a day or two. You need have nothing more to fear from L'Adam." Dr. Livermore pulled at his beard. "He will be kept locked up in a safe place. Dr. Eastman will have personal charge of him."

Everyone looked at Dr. Eastman. He did not appear pleased.

"Aren't you going to call the police?" asked Crane.

Dr. Livermore said, "That won't be necessary." He looked at Dr. Eastman. "Don't you think so?"

"They won't be any help," said Dr. Eastman.

Dr. Livermore said, "I have just one more thing to

bring to your attention. This was found in Miss Van Kamp's room last night. It is undoubtedly what caused Mr. Pittsfield's death." He picked up the package and unwrapped it and displayed the bathrobe cord with the purple ends which Mr. Penny had found under the bed. "Does anybody recognize this?"

For a moment there was silence. Slowly Nellie rose from her place beside Miss Van Kamp, hoisted upward by a force utterly outside her own volition. She gasped, "Oh, my God! It's mine!"

It was the first time Crane had heard her speak.

Chapter VIII

AFTER NELLIE, sobbing with restraint and embarrassment, had been convoyed to her room by Miss Clayton
and Miss Twilliger, Richardson stepped over to Dr.
Eastman and whispered something. Dr. Eastman looked
sullenly surprised and nodded his head reluctantly.

Dr. Livermore held up his hand. He said, "I think
we can do nothing further until we question Miss Paxton
about the bathrobe."

"Just a moment," said Dr. Eastman. His voice was
harsh. "I'd like to ask a question."

Dr. Livermore nodded benevolently.

"You say none of you left the movie." Dr. Eastman
scowled at the patients. "I know at least one of you
did."

The patients stared at the doctor's menacing figure
in silence.

Miss Van Kamp straightened in angry defiance and
cleared her throat. Miss Queen fingered her neck with
nervous hands. She glanced at Crane, and her lips
fluttered.

Dr. Eastman demanded, "Which one of you left the

room last night?" He moved closer to the huddled group. There was no answer.

"It will be better to tell," he said with ominous restraint.

Those at Dr. Eastman's back watched interestedly: Joe with cynical approval, the driver with awe, and Charles with an oblique snicker. Miss Evans's face was a delicately carved mask: composed, inscrutable, and cruel. The room was noisy with apprehension.

Dr. Eastman repeated, "One of you went out."

William Crane had a conviction that the attention of the doctor was centered on him. He wondered who could have seen him.

"So you won't talk?" Dr. Eastman's black eyebrows met in the center. "All right. Blackwood, I know it was you."

Blackwood started convulsively, as though he had been cut with a pair of Mexican rowels. He cried, "No! No one saw me!"

Dr. Eastman said, "I know you left."

"No!" Blackwood squirmed fatly in his chair. "No! No! No!"

Dr. Eastman looked at him with disgust. He turned to the attendants. "Boys, take him down to the hospital and see if you can get him to talk."

Joe and the driver moved toward Blackwood. Joe was contained and grimly pleased; the driver reeled and hiccoughed gently. He was drunk again. They seized Blackwood's arms and pulled his flour sack of a body to its feet and started it toward the door. Joe called to Dr. Livermore, "All right, boss?"

Dr. Livermore nodded.

Blackwood cast an agonized glance of appeal at Crane. "Please," he said. "Please." Then, as he was pulled forward, "Oh no, oh no, oh no!" His voice was a child-like treble. The three disappeared out the door.

"Now we may get somewhere," said Dr. Eastman.

Crane asked, "Why bother with all this when you are sure Mr. L'Adam did it?"

"I didn't say I thought L'Adam did it," Dr. Eastman said.

Dr. Livermore was bothered with his hands. There seemed to be no place for them. He clasped them behind him; he held them in front of him; he put them in his beard. He said, "Everything points to L'Adam."

"Nothing points to L'Adam," Dr. Eastman said. The two nurses who had gone upstairs with Nellie returned. Dr. Eastman looked at them questioningly.

"We put her to bed," said Miss Twilliger.

Miss Clayton supplemented, "She'll have to stay there for a while. She is quite hysterical."

In the distance, faint and muffled, there was a slender

noise of screaming. Everyone listened, but it was not repeated.

Dr. Buelow broke the silence: "Somebody ought to ask Miss Paxton about the cord. She might be able to remember who took it."

Dr. Eastman swung toward him. "No," he said. "Wait until she has time to calm down."

Dr. Livermore said, "Yes, indeed. There is plenty of time to question her."

"I think we ought to ask Crane about the attack on him," said Dr. Buelow.

"All right," said Dr. Eastman. He faced Crane. "Who attacked you?"

Crane said, "I wouldn't know."

"What motive would they have for an attack?"

"I wouldn't know that, either."

"Have you made any enemies here?"

"Enemies? I should say not."

As Crane shook his head he heard a noise in the hall. He saw Joe, the driver, and between them Blackwood. His puffy face was a map of crimson splotches. His nose was bleeding slightly; there was a nasty cut under his right eye; his right ear was oddly twisted, as though it had been torn off and carelessly pasted back on. His breath was coming in sobs, and his eyes wavered crazily.

Joe announced, "This guy came through all right." He daintily wiped sweat off his brow with a silk handkerchief stained with blood. "He spilled his guts." He thrust Blackwood forward. "He's soft."

"He admits he left the movie," said the driver. He blinked drunkenly at his audience. "He was out for half an hour."

"But that ain't all, by God," Joe said, giving Blackwood's arm a pull. "He's got something else to tell you." Blackwood quivered in terror and looked apprehensively at Crane. Joe pulled his arm again. "Ain't you got something to tell them, buddy?"

Blackwood forced himself to nod. He raised his free hand and pointed a finger at Crane. He swallowed with an effort.

"Go ahead and tell them, buddy," Joe said. His hands tightened on the arm. The driver pressed close on Blackwood's other side. He said, "Don't be scared."

Blackwood spoke with difficulty. "It . . . was him . . . Crane . . . I saw him upstairs." He tried to draw back, but Joe held him firmly. "I saw him, really," he said. He shuddered and wrenched his arms free and covered his eyes.

"That's what he told us," the driver said. He let go of Blackwood's shoulder and backed toward the door. Blackwood sprawled heavily on the red-and-brown carpet.

"My God!" said Dr. Buelow. "What did you do to him?"

"Aw," said Joe. He smiled whimsically and made a horizontal and depreciatory gesture with his hands. "We just cuffed him around a little."

Once again in his room and with only a few minutes before supper, Crane sipped yellow moonshine and reflected upon the developments of the afternoon. He decided ruefully that he had not been as careful in slipping out of the movie as C. Auguste Dupin would have been. However, he now knew of three others who had also slipped out: Miss Twilliger, Blackwood, and Dr. Livermore. That was something. He wondered what questions the three doctors would have for him tomorrow. Dr. Livermore had said there was no time to question him now. Dr. Eastman had wanted to lock him up, but the other two had decided against it.

It was still cold outside, and he went to close his windows. It was noisy, too: trees yammered under the blows of the wind and branches roared approval. It was almost dark, and storm clouds raised hostile heads on the horizon. In the garden he saw a trace of sunset gold on the water in the pool. A smart gust of wind sent chill air into the room, and he slammed the two windows. He returned to the bed and picked up his drink.

It still seemed to him that almost anybody might have killed Pittsfield, but he thought of those who would have been likely to do it. There were, first on his mental list, Blackwood and Dr. Livermore. Blackwood could have done it for hatred; Dr. Livermore because he had said nothing about leaving the movies. Then came Dr. Eastman and Dr. Buelow: because of the box. William Crane felt certain that the box and Pittsfield's murder were connected. After all those, he decided, came Joe, Charles, and the driver. He felt that probably the proud nurse and the driver had a good alibi, but he wasn't so sure that Joe couldn't have seen them and still committed the crime. Two others, he felt, were excellent possibilities. These were L'Adam and the religious guard. This made ten high-grade suspects, and he added Richardson for good measure.

As for the women, he decided that none of them were strong enough to have strangled Pittsfield with the woolen bathrobe cord.

His thinking and his liquor finished, Crane slid off the soft bed with a groan and reluctantly washed his face and hands. His bruises were no better, but all were darker and more the same color than they had been in the morning. He looked at his watch. It was nearly time for dinner, and he hurried with his washing and took out a clean shirt from the dresser drawer. The soft broadcloth felt good against his skin, but it still hurt where the collar pressed the bruises on his neck. He selected a dark blue tie and fastened it loosely. He put on his coat and opened the left-hand top drawer of the bureau for a handkerchief. On top of the neatly folded linen squares in the drawer was a white envelope. On it was printed in ink:

MR. NOSEY

Crane lifted the envelope cautiously and turned it over. There was no writing on the other side, and the flap was not glued down. He opened it and pulled out a piece of writing paper. It read:

If you got any sense you will pack up get out a here quick. There are some folks who dont like they way you do your hair and they are thinking of parting it in the middle with a 38. They are people who dont miss. You take that box and put it under the front steps of the help building. There is a loose board on the third step and no one will bother you further if you lam out right after you leave that box and whats in it.

A Friend.

He thoughtfully put the letter on top of the glass he had wrapped up in a newspaper. He poured himself a long drink and finished it without haste. He had another, and then he had a glass of water. He felt pretty good.

He thought, This is a hell of a restful place. He put the bottle away and crept out into the hall. Miss Clayton was just emerging from a room near the stairs.

She said, "Miss Paxton seems to be better."

"Fine," said Crane heartily. "How's Blackwood?"

"He's asleep in his room."

As Crane started down the stairs, Miss Van Kamp came out of the same room as had Miss Clayton. She paused at the door.

"I'll send you up some tea and toast," she said to someone in the room.

A feeble wailing came up from inside. It was Nellie. She moaned, "Don't leave me." Miss Van Kamp snorted. "Nonsense!" She started to close the door. "Somebody will bring your food in a few minutes."

"I'll bring it up," said Miss Clayton. She and Miss Van Kamp and Crane descended the stairs together.

Mrs. Heyworth, slim and brown and athletic in an informal evening dress of printed material, left Richardson on the couch by the crackling fire and came over to Crane.

"I believe in you," she said simply. She took his right hand and pressed it and looked into his eyes.

Crane blushed. "Thanks," he said. He looked at his feet.

Mrs. Heyworth pressed his hand again and returned to the couch.

Crane was conscious that Richardson was inspecting him furiously. He turned and bumped into Miss Queen. He seized her waist to support her.

"Ooo!" Miss Queen's mouth was only a few inches from his. "Oh!" She panted and pushed his arm away and backed off.

"I'm sorry," said Crane. Miss Queen did not reply. She sidled to a seat by Mr. Penny, her startled eyes on William Crane.

Crane thought, What the hell? He felt for his tie and found it was there, and he could see that his pants were still on. He sat down in a corner. Dr. Buelow appeared at the dining-room door. "Dinner will be ready in a minute." He caught sight of Miss Van Kamp, placidly knitting under a lamp. "How's Miss Paxton?"

"Much better, thank you." Miss Van Kamp's parchment hands continued their lively concentric movements. "She'll be all right by morning."

Dr. Buelow's large face was kindly sincere. "That's fine. She's naturally upset." He sat down in a straight chair. It creaked under his weight. Miss Clayton stepped in front of him.

She said, "I'll come back in a few minutes and take Miss Paxton up some food."

"That's fine," said Dr. Buelow. "Some food will do her good."

From his seat, Crane glanced around the room Mrs.

Heyworth was still regarding him with her warm eyes.
Mr. Penny's small humorous eyes were friendly. Miss
Queen was peering at him with a sort of shuddering
horror. For a time he fastened his eyes on Mrs. Brady,
who had on a black evening gown and a lot of powder,
and then he peeped at Miss Queen. She became rigid.
She turned her head away from him. She trembled.
She stood up. She sat down. William Crane felt nervous
sweat on his brow, and he reached in his pocket for
a handkerchief. He had no handkerchief. He self-
consciously walked to the stairs and up them to his own
room.

He was aware of a chill in the hall and wondered if a
window were open anywhere. It was warm in his room,
and he got a handkerchief from the dresser. He had a
drink of moonshine. He wished he were in New York.

Once at the dinner table, the patients became vi-
vacious. Mrs. Brady plunged into a description of the
time her husband and she were insulted by a manager
in the finest hotel in Louisville.

"Do you know to whom you are speaking?" she
quoted herself as having told the manager.

The manager had admitted he did not know.

"I told him very simply: 'You're talking to R. J.
Brady, you fool,'" Mrs. Brady said. She illustrated this
point with her butter knife.

She continued: "You should have seen that manager. He said: 'Not R. J. Brady, the great horse fancier?'"

"I said: 'None other.' After that nothing was too good for us in that hotel. He sent up a quart bottle of thirty-year-old bourbon and said we could throw that out the window, too, if we wanted. Of course, I just pushed that first bottle out as a joke." Mrs. Brady giggled reminiscently. "How was I to know it would hit the chief of police?"

While Mrs. Brady vigorously pursued her anecdotes, butter knife in hand, William Crane ate reflectively. Directly across from him sat Miss Queen, and he peeped secretly and curiously at her during the corn soup and the broiled chicken. It was not until the tomato and cucumber salad that he noticed her chest was moving spasmodically, as though she were riding a bicycle. He raised his eyes suddenly to her face, met her eyes. She was pale, and she rose from her place, letting her napkin slide off onto the floor. She cried, "I can stand it no longer!"

She pointed a long finger at Crane and swayed against the table. Her dark hair hung limply over mad eyes. "I know your evil intentions," she croaked. "But you can't seduce me." She backed away from the table, upset her chair, and reeled out of the room. She could be heard going slowly up the stairs. Crane felt a blush creeping over his face, and he had difficulty swallowing a piece of cucumber. He pretended to be absorbed in his salad, but he knew the others were watching him.

"Never mind about her, Mr. Crane," Dr. Buelow said unexpectedly. "She has had similar delusions before." Crane looked up from his plate, and Mr. Penny caught his attention. By introducing an abnormally large piece of chicken into his mouth, the little man conveyed a humorous recognition of the unbalanced state of all women and at the same time dismissed the incident as being of no importance. Crane smiled in spite of his embarrassment, and, delighted, Mr. Penny smiled back at him.

Maria was removing the salad dishes when Miss Clayton came in from the kitchen.

"Would it be all right for Miss Paxton to have some soup and toast and tea?" she asked Dr. Buelow.

"Anything she cares to eat," Dr. Buelow said. "Give her stomach something to do, and her mind won't be so busy."

Miss Clayton said, "I'll take up Mr. Blackwood's dinner later."

Dr. Buelow indicated that would be all right, and presently Miss Clayton passed through the room with Nellie's tray.

"I'd like to have my breakfast served in bed," Mrs. Brady announced coyly.

"That's the quickest way to ruin a woman," Miss Van Kamp snapped. "Any woman who can't get up for breakfast, and make it, too, is a slut." Her teeth clicked on the final "t."

Mrs. Brady should have known better than to disagree with Miss Van Kamp. She said defiantly, "I always used to have my breakfasts in bed."

Miss Van Kamp's logic was exact. "Then you are a slut," she said.

Miss Clayton ran into the room. Her face was flour white. There was blood on her hands.

"Did you cut yourself, Miss Clayton?" Dr. Buelow asked.

"No. Oh no!" Miss Clayton looked at her hands with horror. "It's Miss Paxton. She's been murdered."

Crane followed Dr. Buelow's broad back out of the room and up the stairs. He was right behind him when they entered the congealed interior of Nellie's room.

It was a remarkably neat room. The dresser was covered with an amber toilet set, each piece placed in exact mathematical relation to the others. Two colored etchings of Paris scenes, one showing golden pumpkins for sale in a market place, and the other a lavender branch of the Seine flowing under a stone bridge, balanced themselves on either side of the opposite wall. An easy chair, with a brown-and-white doily fastened on the back, was precisely in the middle of the wall with the two large windows. The plain blue rug was flat and spotless. Miss Paxton lay on the bed. Her curiously neutral hair pour_d from the pillow in two careful braids. Her face was calm and composed. The bed was perfectly smooth. Miss Paxton might have been asleep except for the dagger which protruded wickedly from her thin neck. It was a large dagger such as hunters use, with a brown bone handle. Crane thought the murderer had displayed nice taste to murder the old woman with a dagger which so nearly matched her toilet set.

Dr. Buelow bent over her, his ear to her mouth, his hands to her breast. "She's dead," he said after a few seconds. He straightened his back. He gazed stupidly at the blood on his hands. "Warm," he said. "Warm!"

"My God!" said Richardson from behind Crane. "I'd better keep the women out." He blocked the doorway.

Dr. Buelow looked at Crane apologetically. "There is nothing we can do." There were sudden wrinkles at the bottom corners of his eyes.

William Crane pressed against the bed. He felt Miss Paxton's arm. It was small and smooth and warm. He touched the dagger with the back of his hand. The bone handle was cold and hard. The steel of the blade was icy. "I guess not," he said. "But how about Blackwood?"

Dr. Buelow was off again like an anxious Percheron,

galloping down the hall and almost through Blackwood's door. By the time Crane got there he was coming
out.

"Thank God," he said. "He's alive and doesn't know
what's happened." He rubbed his forehead with his
blue serge coat sleeve. They went back to Miss Paxton's
room. Outside were Mrs. Brady, Miss Queen, and Mrs.
Heyworth; all questioning Richardson. Miss Van Kamp
and Mr. Penny, who looked like a small owl, were inside.
Miss Van Kamp was hopelessly smoothing the covers
over her dead friend as she peered into the tranquil
face.

"Don't you think you'd better go to your room?"
asked Dr. Buelow.

"No! No!" said Miss Van Kamp fiercely. "She was
all I had left." She resumed caressing the sleek covers.
"I should have stayed with her."

While Mr. Penny watched, Dr. Buelow and Crane
looked around the room. Nothing seemed to be unusual,
and Crane opened the closet door. Within there hung
orderly rows of dresses, coats, and other garments, all
either black or gray. There was a gray bathrobe on the
hanger, and he saw that the loops for the belt were of
the same woven black wool as the cord which had been
used to strangle Mr. Pittsfield. He brought the robe into
the room for a better look. It seemed to be in good con

dition, and the wool was firm and unfrayed. There was a yellow label in it: *The Brockmann Woolen Mill, St. Paul, Minn.* "Whew!" said Crane. "It certainly smells of naphtha." The pockets were empty, and he put the robe back in the closet. He looked at the shoes. Only one pair, black and new, had very high heels. He closed the closet door just as Miss Clayton arrived with Dr. Eastman.

"Murdered?" Dr. Eastman asked. His dark face was outraged.

Dr. Buelow pointed to the dagger.

"What are all these people doing in here?" Dr. Eastman was savage. "They can all get out." He pressed his fists against his chest, then jerked them outward. "Get out, do you hear?"

Even Miss Van Kamp, her crow's-footed face at once grim and tragic, had to leave. Crane went to his room and waited until he had heard them carry the body down the stairs and out on the front porch. There were still people talking in the living room when he tiptoed to the head of the stairs. By standing on the banister, he was able to reach the light fixture on the ceiling. He took a penny out of his pocket, unscrewed the hot bulb, and balanced the penny on the metal contact point. Then, very carefully, he screwed back the bulb so that the penny was carried up into the socket. At the last turn there was a flash, and all the lights in the building were extinguished. There was excited talking downstairs. He went to his room and undressed and climbed into bed, and fell asleep listening to futile attempts being made downstairs to fix the lights.

Chapter IX

WHEN WILLIAM CRANE awoke creamy sunlight washed the sills of his two windows, and sparrows chirped irregularly and shrilly in the vines on the wall of the guest house. There were also bees and flies and other insects enjoying the change around his windows. He was unable to sleep, so he took a shower. After this, he dressed slowly, examining the bruises on his face. They were darker, and he was surprised to notice that some of them were green. He had heard of people turning black and blue, but never black and green. He wondered if he had Irish blood in him. He hoped not.

Downstairs he discovered from the clock on the mantel that it was a minute before eight. He felt a surge of admiration for himself. No hour was too early for him to get up and begin his deductions. Maria was in the dining room, dusting the cupboard.

"Good-mornin'," she said loudly. "What d'you want for breakfast?"

"What have you got?"

"We got melon an' orange juice an' cereal an' eggs an' bacon an' buckwheat cakes an' codfish balls an' potatoes an' toast an' coffee. Of course, if those don't jest touch your fancy, we could get you sumpin' special."

"Those'll do," said William Crane.

"What do you mean, those, Mistah Crane?"

"I mean those things you mentioned."

"All o' them?"

"All of them."

Maria's eyes were two china saucers on a mahogany table. "Lawd!" she declared, "you sure must be hongry."

"Maria," said William Crane, "I have to prepare myself for some important deductions today. You know what a drain deductions are on the system?"

"Yes sir!" said Maria. "Lawdy me!"

Crane had just placed a fried egg and two pieces of bacon on a pile of buckwheat cakes and was pouring maple syrup over them when Dr. Eastman and a man in blue overalls came into the living room.

"I don't see how you got here so soon," said Dr. Eastman. "It usually takes three or four hours for an electrician to get here."

The electrician was a well built man of medium size. He had salt-and-pepper hair, and his green eyes were hard with experience. His face was covered with dirt. He said, "I was working at a place near here, and when I called the shop to order some parts for a Delco, they told me to come over here." He plopped his bag of tools on the floor. "This where it is?"

"I don't know what's the matter," said Dr. Eastman. "We were talking down here last night when the lights suddenly went out. I thought it was a fuse, but each time we put in a new one it would blow out. I think there must be a short circuit somewhere."

"We'll see," said the electrician. He knelt by his kit and began pulling out wire and tools.

Dr. Eastman called, "Maria."

"Yes sir." Maria popped out through the swinging kitchen door and stopped in back of Crane.

"This is the electrician," said Dr. Eastman. "Show him where the fuse box is in the kitchen."

"Yes sir."

Dr. Eastman said, "If you want me, I'll be in the building right across the way."

"O. K.," said the electrician. He followed Maria through the dining room into the kitchen. Crane was trying the codfish balls when he emerged.

The electrician said, "Feed you pretty good, don't they?" He snapped the light switch two or three times. Nothing happened.

"You can have anything I leave," said William Crane. He forked the last codfish ball, poured cream sauce on it, and pushed it into his mouth. The electrician watched, entranced. William Crane drained his coffee cup. He stood up, folded his napkin. "You know, I think that light trouble started in my room. The cord on the reading lamp is broken."

The electrician followed him upstairs and into the room.

Crane closed the door.

"What in hell they been doing to you?" asked the electrician.

Crane said, "They got some guys around here who can't keep their hands in their pockets. They gotta always be sticking them in somebody's eye."

"Sluggers, eh?" said the electrician.

"That isn't all," said Crane. He pulled the nearly empty bottle of moonshine from behind the dresser. The electrician's predatory eye glistened as the heavy liquid gurgled in the glasses. "They bumped off two since I got here," Crane added.

"Jesus!" The electrician tentatively fingered one of the glasses, picked it up, and held it to the light. "Why don't somebody call the police?" He drank and smacked his lips. "Nothing like moon that's been properly aged."

"Not unless it's turpentine," said Crane. "The only phone is in Dr. Livermore's office, and he doesn't seem anxious to have the constabulary drop in."

The electrician emptied his glass and rolled his eyes until only the whites showed. "Can anyone hear us?" Crane shook his head. "Tell us about it, then. Was there anything to the dope old Van Kamp had from his sister?"

"Was there? Say, this Van Kamp dame had a little tin box in her room, and in it was four hundred grand in negotiable securities. Somebody stole the box."

The electrician was kneeling on the rug, busy with the reading lamp. "Go on," he said. He pulled off the red shade with a flourish.

"The securities weren't as important as the key to Miss Van Kamp's safety-deposit vault in New York. It was also in the box. This key and another, which Van Kamp has still got, are necessary to open the vault and in the vault is eight hundred thousand dollars in cash, jewels, and bonds. The old dame was foolish enough to tell one of the docs about the box and the keys."

"What a setup! What a setup!" The electrician waved his pliers. "All the guy that stole the box has to do is to get the second key off Miss Van Kamp, and then he has a million, two hundred thousand bucks to carry him to South America." He lingered over the numbers with a loving tongue.

"You probably got to bump off Miss Van Kamp before you can get that other key," said Crane.

"All right, then," said the electrician. "Bump her off too."

"You aren't so dumb for an electrician. A lot of people around here seem to have the same idea. There also seems to be a feeling that it isn't so healthy for anybody around here. The head doctor, Livermore, has got a guy up from Brooklyn to guard him, a gun by the name of Joe Kassuccio. He came up when I did."

The electrician had the lamp in pieces. "Who do you think has the box?"

"My guess right now is that Livermore took it and then somebody got it from him."

There was a knock at the door. Crane seized the bottle and the glasses and put them back of the dresser. "Come in," he said.

Miss Twilliger came in. She had a roll of tape and some gauze. She halted abruptly when she saw the electrician on the floor. She raised her nose several inches. "Oh, I didn't know you had company."

Crane said, "Not exactly company. This is the electrician. He thinks this lamp has caused the trouble with the lights. Miss Twilliger: Mr. . . . ?"

"Williams," said the electrician savagely.

Miss Twilliger did not acknowledge the introduction. "Dr. Livermore sent me up to see if your cuts were healing. I have some fresh bandages."

"You needn't bother," said Crane. "I am quite all right."

Miss Twilliger hesitated and then backed to the door. "I believe I smell liquor. You know how Dr. Livermore feels about liquor."

·No," Crane said. "No, I don't. How does Dr. Livermore feel about liquor?"

"He has forbidden all his patients to drink. I am afraid he will have to take measures to keep you away from it."

Miss Twilliger vanished.

"Some dame," said the electrician with enthusiasm.

"You should see some of the other babes," said Crane. "You'd think Earl Carroll ran this place."

"Hot dog, have you got it soft! Why does the boss always fix you up like this?"

"Yeah, I got it soft." William Crane was bitter. "I only get beat up once a day."

"Don't let it get you down, Bill. Even the best people get beat up now and then." The electrician pulled out his glass and the bottle. He filled his glass. "But about this box: you think one of the doctors got it?"

"You asked me that one before."

"Well, I figure it out this way. That Livermore has probably had the box and then lost it. He wants to get it back: that's why he hired the gun. In the meantime the other guy, having heard about the dough in the vault, is making a play for the other key on Van Kamp."

Crane said, "Either that, or Livermore is trying to get the key from the old lady, either because he has the first key, or to force whoever's got it to dicker with him. Then he'll have that cheap gunman knock him off."

"Sure. But who were the two that got killed?"

"A fellow named Pittsfield was strangled on the second night I was here. Last night somebody stuck a knife in an old girl named Nellie Paxton. They were both patients, and they were both friendly with Miss Van Kamp."

"Who are they goin' to pin the murders on?"

"I think they got me in mind."

"So what?"

"So what," said Crane.

"I better give the sheriff a call."

"That's a good idea. But before you go I want to give you these things." Crane brought out the glass he had wrapped up in a newspaper. "There are some prints on the glass," he said. "They belong to an ex-con who works here. I'd like to get his record and anything else you can find out about him. His first name is Charles. I think he's a New York boy."

He also handed the letter to the electrician, who read it quickly. He said, "Nobody seems to like you around here."

"Oh, I don't know," said Crane. "Anyhow, you might have Doc Owens look that over. He ought to be able to tell us something about the person who wrote that. He's pretty good with handwriting."

"O. K.," said the electrician. "How about another drink?"

William Crane had filled one glass and was emptying the bottle over the other when he became tense. He put the bottle down and leaped for the door and swung it open. There was nobody in the hall.

"Kinda jumpy, aren't you?" said the electrician.

"Who wouldn't be in this place?" Crane filled the glass. "They got me thinkin' I'm daffy."

"You may be right," said the electrician. He held up the glass. "Here's how." They drank.

The electrician said, "Look here." He pulled a thick red stick with a piece of fuse on the end out of his kit bag. "Me and Tom Burns are in one of those tourist trailers about a mile up the hill. That was the Colonel's idea. He said we were to stick around if you seemed to be in trouble. And you seem to be in plenty."

Crane accepted the red stick gingerly. "What's this for?"

"It's a Roman candle. It shoots out balls that explode with a hell of a bang in the air. You can hear them for miles around. If you want us, just shoot it off, and we'll be along in no time at all."

"The Colonel is full of good ideas," said William Crane. "If they lock me up, all I got to do is to ask a guard to get my Roman candle for me because I want to call my friends. Or else I carry it everywhere with me. I suppose the best place is in my mouth, like a pipe."

The electrician did not seem disconcerted. He grinned. "It's the Colonel's idea, and we got to do it." He closed up his bag. "His ideas are pretty good. He was the one who thought of having you put the lights on the blink and us tapping the phone wires so we'd know when they called for an electrician. That got me in here, anyway." He moved toward the door. "I'll be back either tomorrow or the next day."

Crane said, "You'd better fix those lights before you go."

"What d'you do to them?"

"I stuck a penny in the light at the head of the stairs. All you got to do is to remove the bulb and then go down and put in a new fuse."

"You're not so dumb." The electrician elaborately admired William Crane. "Say, who beat you up?"

"A couple of guards on the first night. On the second night I don't know."

"Got any ideas?"

"Plenty. It was probably the same guy that wrote the letter I gave you. At least, they both think I swiped the little tin box, and both would like to get it."

The electrician scanned Crane's face. "He did a very artistic job." He cocked his head, closed one eye. "I think the color scheme is swell."

"Nuts," said William Crane. "You're drunk."

"Can't have too much color," repeated the electrician. "Can't have too much liquor, either. Too bad it's all gone."

Crane produced the full bottle from behind the dresser.

The electrician put down his kit bag again. "If you insist . . ." He accepted another drink. He had a whole tumbler full. Crane had another drink. Then they both had another drink.

"Where does the doll that was in here sleep?" asked the electrician.

"I don't know," William Crane said.

"What! You been here three days and you don't know where she sleeps?" The electrician located his kit bag with some difficulty. "What have you been doing with yourself?" He edged up on the door and seized the handle. "What *have* you been doing with yourself?"

William Crane said, "Aren't you going to fix my lamp?"

"Fix it yourself," said the electrician. "Remember, if you need us, just light that candle. I'll be back in a couple of days anyway." He opened the door, stepped into the corridor.

A few minutes later, as he was putting his dismantled lamp together, William Crane heard the electrician's voice in the hall. "These rural lighting systems are lousy," he was shouting. He was apparently carrying on a conversation with someone downstairs. "Always out of order, by God!"

There was a silence, and this was followed by the crash of a heavy object at the head of the stairs and the report of an exploded bulb. There was a muffled cursing.

"Hey! You down there," the electrician suddenly bellowed. "Send up another bulb, this one was defective as hell."

Crane could hear doors in the hall being opened, and from the sound of conversation downstairs he judged that a crowd had assembled. After a moment someone climbed the stairs.

"That's the kind of a bulb, old boy," the electrician announced to his audience and to whoever had brought it. "We'll have everything fixed up now, ole boy, ole boy."

Crane suspected the electrician was addressing Dr. Livermore.

"Now," the electrician hollered, "some of you mugs put a new fuse in the box down there."

After another interval the lights in Crane's room gleamed palely.

"Hey! Hey!" The electrician was jubilant. "If Williams can't fix 'em, they can't be fixed."

Crane heard the electrician march down the stairs, win a brief and bitter argument over his pay, and then, outside, he heard him noisily and affectionately bid his audience good-bye. Finally a car roared out of the driveway with a series of metallic whoops and climbed up the hill past the part overlooked by one of Crane's windows. As silence frightenedly crept back into the house he watched the black touring car disappear and reappear around bends in the gravel road.

It was now very warm, and the noise of the birds had diminished to sporadic cheeping. The day was poised and assured, its maturity untroubled by wind. William Crane was admiring the sky as it was reflected in the pool, when Dr. Livermore and Miss Evans strolled by toward the trees in the north end of the garden. Through some obscure metallurgy, the sun was pale in Miss Evans's hair. She walked with a feline undulance that was not quite feminine. Dr. Livermore was talking to her with great earnestness. Watching them with interest, Crane was surprised to see Dr. Eastman come around the corner of the house and, with elaborate indirection, start after them. His face was sullen. Crane felt he did not like Dr. Eastman.

"Hi, Doc," he called from his window. "Swell day, isn't it?"

Dr. Eastman started and looked up at Crane. He did not answer, but he reversed his direction and returned around the corner he had just left. Crane tittered and went to get another drink. As he wavered in front of the dresser mirror, pouring the liquor into a tumbler, he winked at himself. It was really excellent liquor.

Chapter X

CRANE APPEARED at the luncheon table quite blithe with optimism and whisky. He found a number of others seated at the table. "It's certainly a nice day," he announced.

Dr. Livermore, in his place at the head of the table, nodded. "It's more like summer than fall," he said pontifically.

"Indian summer," Crane said.

"St. Martin's summer," Dr. Livermore said.

"St. Raphael's summer," Crane said.

Miss Van Kamp was buttering toast at the other end of the table. She said in a sepulchral voice, "Who is to be next?"

"St. Christopher's summer," William Crane said.

The others regarded him furtively. He suddenly realized they were no longer friendly, with the possible exceptions of Mrs. Heyworth and Mr. Penny. And it was certain none of them thought him funny any longer. Miss Van Kamp regarded him with grim distaste.

"This is no time for humor," she said. "There is a murderer among us."

Miss Queen said, "Who knows but one of us is about to go!" She avoided looking at Crane.

Mrs. Brady's face was flat and lifeless above an orange frock. She said, "Isn't there something we can do?" She spoke to Dr. Livermore.

"Won't you call the police?" asked Miss Queen.

"They certainly should be notified," Miss Van Kamp said. Her voice was harsh, but it was appealing.

Dr. Livermore coughed in his beard. "That is out of the question." He broke a piece of toast between his fingers. "**Dr.** Eastman and I have the situation well in hand."

There was a defeated silence, and Crane felt a surge of sympathy for the patients.

"Listen," he said. "None of you are involved in these things unless it is the Doc here."

Richardson asserted, "It's Blackwood."

"Oh, I wish my husband were here," said Mrs. Brady. Her eyes were moist, and she trembled violently.

Crane said, "It's not Blackwood. It's not one of you. I know that."

"Sure," Richardson said. "You're C. Auguste Dupin, the great detective. Why don't you tell us who did the murders, then?"

"I don't know."

"Then what makes you so certain it wasn't Blackwood?"

"Please, Mr. Richardson," Dr. Livermore said, "don't excite Mr. Crane on the subject of detection. Let him have his little opinions."

Crane said, "I'll keep my little opinions to myself until the proper time."

"I am sure Mr. Crane could catch the murderer if he wanted," said Mrs. Heyworth. He looked at her suspiciously, but her brown eyes were sympathetic. She smiled at him. Richardson explosively pushed back his chair.

"Thank you," said Crane.

Mrs. Brady's hands jerked at the neck of her dress. "They strangled Mr. Pittsfield, and now they're going to strangle me." She lurched to her feet, ran unsteadily from the room.

All through the luncheon, Miss Van Kamp and Miss Queen were strained and fearful. They left together. William Crane didn't blame them for being afraid. Now that the whisky was beginning to wear off, he didn't feel any too good himself.

Mr. Penny followed the two ladies out. He seemed chastened. He tried to wink at Crane, but as an expression of confidence it was a failure.

"Where is Blackwood?" asked Crane of Richardson as he and Mrs. Heyworth prepared to leave.

"Still in bed," Richardson snarled. "The coward! He knows they will get the truth out of him when he recovers from his sudden illness." He escorted Mrs. Heyworth to the door, but she halted him there.

She said, "Mr. Crane, you know you are the image of my husband?" She watched him intently with her brown eyes.

"Is that so?" said Crane politely. Mrs. Heyworth seemed disappointed. She turned and pulled Richardson out of the room.

Dr. Livermore was dipping his nervous hand into a green finger bowl when Dr. Eastman came in from the living room. "The sheriff is here," he said without emphasis.

Dr. Livermore rose abruptly. He forgot to dry his hands.

"Dr. Livermore?" boomed a deep voice.

Dr. Livermore stepped out into the living room. He held the napkin behind his back.

"I'm Sheriff Walters, Peter Walters," said the deep voice. "This is my boy, Cliff. We heard you had some trouble up here."

Dr. Livermore had stopped just inside the living room, and William Crane could still see him.

"Sit down, gentlemen." Dr. Livermore put his napkin in his hip pocket, but a part of it hung out. "I see you have already met my assistant, Dr. Eastman."

"You bet we did," said Sheriff Walters heartily. "He wouldn't let us in at first. But we fixed it up all right."

Dr. Eastman said, "Purely a misunderstanding."

"Shorely," Sheriff Walters said. "But what about this trouble up here?"

"What have you heard?" Dr. Livermore was diplomatic.

"I heard something about a fellow named Pittsfield. You got a patient here by that name?"

"Yes, we did have. But he's dead."

"That's just what I heard. But wasn't there something funny about the way he died?"

"Strictly speaking, yes," said Dr. Livermore. "He was strangled by another patient."

"That's murder," said the sheriff severely. He sounded like a large man. Crane wished he could see him. "You know you can be held as an accessory after the fact for failing to report a murder."

Dr. Livermore's voice was alarmed. "But, Sheriff Walters, it was done without malice. I fail to see any necessity for a report. The crime, if it can be called a crime, was committed by an insane man. There is no way he could be punished."

"Well, I don't want to have any trouble with you, Dr. Livermore. I am willing to overlook that, but how about this other death?"

Crane could see Dr. Livermore's back straighten. "What other death?"

"The woman. That Mrs. Hackstone."

Crane decided that Mr. Williams must still have been drunk when he called the sheriff.

"Oh," said Dr. Livermore. "You must mean Miss Paxton."

"I don't know who I mean, but have you or have you not got a murdered woman here?"

"Yes," Dr. Livermore said wearily.

"Who killed her?"

"I don't know. I suppose another patient."

"You suppose another patient?" The sheriff's voice was sharp. "Do you know the law of the state of New York, Dr. Livermore?"

"More or less."

"Do you know you are supposed to notify the coroner every time there is a death which you cannot certify is natural?"

"Yes."

"But you didn't. Do you realize you have committed two very serious offenses?"

"I'm afraid I have, but I assure you——"

"Never mind. I don't suppose I'll be forced to arrest you." The sheriff's voice was not unfriendly. "I want to know who you think did the first murder?"

"Mr. L'Adam must have done it. He is very violent at times. He was found loose immediately after the body of Pittsfield was discovered."

"So! And the dead woman?"

"Just a moment, please," Dr. Eastman interrupted suavely. "I must disagree with my colleague. I believe both murders were committed by the same person."

"Who is that?"

"I'd like to have you look the patients over first before I tell you. I wouldn't want my opinion to influence you in any way."

"You think it was a patient?"

Dr. Livermore said, "Oh, yes. It must have been. No one employed here would have anything to gain by killing the patients."

"This is a good case to work on," said Sheriff Walters. "As soon as we catch the murderer, we got to let him go because he is insane." He chuckled. "That's about all the reward a sheriff gets anyway."

"I imagine the work is not always pleasant," Dr. Livermore said.

"It's not so darn bad. How about talking to some of these patients?"

"All right. Should we have them in here?"

"Good a place as any."

Dr. Eastman moved over to Dr. Livermore and into the square of Crane's vision. He bent over and whispered to Dr. Livermore, who nodded enthusiastically. While they were standing together, William Crane heard the screen door close with a thud.

It was Miss Van Kamp. Her voice said, "I beg your pardon. I believe I left my knitting here."

"Are these little ladies patients here?" asked the sheriff.

Dr. Livermore said, "Miss Van Kamp has been here more than a year. Miss Van Kamp, this is Sheriff Walters. And this is our chief nurse, Miss Evans."

Sheriff Walters added, "And this is my boy Cliff."

"How de do," said Cliff without enthusiasm. His voice was reedy.

"I was taking Miss Van Kamp up to the steam room for a shampoo," explained Miss Evans. Her voice sounded nice.

"Why can't we begin on these ladies?" asked the sheriff. "They look very intelligent indeed."

"You can," said Dr. Livermore.

"Miss Evans," said Sheriff Walters, "have you any idea about these—aha—deaths?"

Miss Evans said, "None."

"Where were you when they occurred?"

"I was with Miss Clayton, listening to the radio, when Mr. Pittsfield was killed. Last night I was in the servants' house."

Dr. Eastman said, "That was when Miss Paxton was killed."

"Was there anyone with you last night?" asked the sheriff.

"I'm afraid not. I did see Charles. He went into the men's bathroom for a bath as I passed him in the corridor. I heard him in there for almost an hour."

"And that's all you can tell us about these—aha—deaths?"

"That's everything I know."

"Well, thank you, miss." The sheriff's voice sounded very friendly. "That certainly eliminates you—and Miss Clayton and Charles, whoever he is, for that matter."

"He's one of the attendants," Dr. Eastman said.

"Now about this other lady." The sheriff's tone was forcedly gallant. "I'm sure you can tell us something of these terrible crimes, can't you, Miss Van Kamp?"

Miss Van Kamp said, "I certainly——"

"I wonder if I could leave," Miss Evans's voice interrupted her. "I have so many things to do."

"Why, certainly, miss," said the sheriff. "Though we'll be sorry to lose you, miss, won't we, Cliff?"

"Sure," said Cliff.

After the screen door had closed, Miss Van Kamp said, "It's about time they called the authorities. I can tell you a great deal." She spoke rapidly. "Both Mr. Pittsfield and Miss Paxton were friends of mine. My only friends. Through them the murderer hoped to get my key."

"What key?" asked the sheriff.

"The key in my box. You know they stole my key when they stole my strong box."

The sheriff's voice was bewildered. "Strong box?"

"The box with the four hundred thousand dollars in it." Miss Van Kamp spoke sharply. "Somebody stole it from my room. And now they are trying to kill me." Her voice quavered.

Crane saw that the sheriff must have glanced at the two doctors. Dr. Eastman pointed his finger to his temple and shook his head significantly.

"Miss Van Kamp, you've been a mighty great help to us," Sheriff Walters said. "Don't worry about being killed; we're here to protect you, aren't we, Cliff?"

"Sure," said Cliff.

Miss Van Kamp said, "But my box with——"

"If it can be found, we will find it," said the sheriff. Cliff said, "Sure."

When Miss Van Kamp had gone, protesting bitterly, the sheriff wanted to know who else he could question. "Let's get somebody with more sense," he said. "We won't get anywhere with them as batty as that."

"You're quite right," agreed Dr. Livermore.

"We got to get at the bottom of this," the sheriff asserted. "Cliff, you go tell Ty and Tom to wait outside. The doc here will get us another witness to question."

Presently Dr. Eastman brought in Richardson.

"I told the others to stay in their rooms alone until we sent for them to question them," Dr. Eastman said. "I was afraid they might talk to each other. I have one of our nurses watching in the corridor."

"That's good," boomed the sheriff. "Where's that Cliff at? Hey, Cliff! We got another daffy to question."

"All right, all right, Pa. I was jest talkin' to Ty out here." The screen door banged petulantly.

Sheriff Walters said, "What is your name?"

"Richardson."

"What is your address? I mean, where do you live on the grounds?"

"I have a room in the south wing of this building, near that of Miss Van Kamp."

"What do you know about these crimes?"

"Nothing." Richardson's voice was morose. "But I got a good idea who did them."

"Who?"

"A patient named Blackwood."

Dr. Livermore said, "I am sure Blackwood could have had nothing to do with the murders."

"Never mind what you're sure of," said the sheriff. "I want to hear this fellow." Sheriff Walters cleared his throat. "What makes you think Blackwood killed these people?"

"He had the opportunity and the motive. He killed Pittsfield because he hated him. They were always quarreling. And he killed Miss Paxton because—well—because he did not like her either."

"What do you think, Doc?" asked the sheriff.

Dr. Eastman replied, "I think he's wrong."

"Richardson, where were you at the time the first murder was committed?"

"I was with Mrs. Heyworth. She can verify that."

"Cliff."

"Yeah?"

"Take a note of that."

"Yeah."

"All right, Richardson. We'll look into this Blackwood angle."

"Aren't you going to arrest him?"

"Not just now."

Richardson's disappointed footfalls receded heavily.

Sheriff Walters asked, "How about another man? We'll save the women for dessert." He chuckled again.

"There is Mr. Penny," Dr. Livermore said, "but he doesn't talk."

"What's the matter?"

"He can hear, but he doesn't talk at all. He hasn't uttered a word since he came here nearly four years ago."

"He isn't much use to us, then. Who would you suggest?"

"We might call Miss Queen."

"All right. Bring her in."

Dr. Eastman again left the room.

"Pa," said Cliff, "what's the good of questioning all these bats? You can't bring nothing they say into court; it ain't admissible as evidence."

"Now, Cliff," said the sheriff. His voice was placating. "We got to get at the bottom of all this. If a loony done these murders, we had best see them all before we decide which one."

Cliff said, "It would be smarter to question some of the help around the place. If you want me to ask some of those nurses we saw when we came in——"

"You stay right here by me. We'll question them nurses later."

Footsteps descended the stairs.

"This is Sheriff Walters: Miss Queen," said Dr. Eastman. He walked into William Crane's narrow field of vision and sat down beside Dr. Livermore.

Sheriff Walters said, "Miss Queen, I wish you would tell us what you know of these murders."

"Oh, Mr. Sheriff, they are so tragic. I can hardly bring myself to talk about them. Two people well and happy on one day and on the next—dead. It is terrible! As Mrs. Brady said, which of us is doomed to be next?"

"Now, now, Miss Queen. Everything is all right. We are here to take care of you."

"Oh, Mr. Sheriff." Miss Queen's voice was opened at

the tremolo stop. "We women do so need the help of a fine capable man like you. You can't imagine what we have been through."

"Miss Queen!" The sheriff sounded pleased. "I guess I have the reputation of being a real man. Don't you worry. Just help us out by giving us anything you know about these deaths."

"I think I know who did them." Miss Queen spoke with hushed importance. "It was a newcomer among us."

"Who is that?"

"It's Mr. Crane. Everything was all right until he came. He is such a strange man, too. The way he looks at me. I am sure he has marked me for death."

"Who's this Crane?"

"He's one of the patients," said Dr. Livermore. "He's been here only three days. He came very well recommended."

"What's the matter with him?"

"I'm not altogether sure. He suffers from delusions. He has a fixation that he's a great detective. He becomes quite violent when he is doubted."

The sheriff said, "Miss Queen, what makes you think he had something to do with these crimes?"

"When Mrs. Paxton was killed, Mr. Crane was upstairs getting a handkerchief. He could easily have killed her, and Mr. Blackwood admitted seeing Mr.

Crane out in the hall on the night poor Mr. Pittsfield met his end ¨

"Hm," Sheriff Walters meditated. "He's a good prospect. But what about motive?"

Miss Queen suggested, "Perhaps he did the murders so as to have the fun of pretending to try to solve them."

"He's the one I suspect," Dr. Eastman said. "He has been acting very mysteriously all the time he has been here."

"I think Mrs. Brady knows something about him, too," Miss Queen said. "Why don't you ask her?"

"Send for her," Sheriff Walters ordered.

"I'll get her," said Dr. Eastman.

His feet hurried up the stairs, and after a moment Crane could hear him loudly pounding on a door.

"Mrs. Brady, we want you below." Dr. Eastman's voice easily carried downstairs.

There was another pause. Dr. Eastman pounded on he door again.

"Mrs. Brady? Can you hear me?"

The voice of Miss Twilliger mingled with his. "Mrs. Brady, they want you to come downstairs." The knocking on the door was redoubled.

Dr. Livermore said, "I know she's in there. She went up to her room during lunch. She couldn't have gone out."

Miss Queen glided into the part of the living room

which William Crane could see. She clasped her hands prayerfully in front of Dr. Livermore. Her long face was tragic.

"She's dead," she said. "She's dead."

The sheriff said, "Now, Miss Queen."

Upstairs the din grew. Somebody was now kicking on the door.

"Mrs. Brady," called Dr. Eastman. "Wake up."

Dr. Eastman essayed again.

"MRS. BRADY! WE KNOW YOU'RE THERE."

"Hell," said Cliff. "That guy could win the county hog-calling contest in a whisper."

"Now, Cliff," said the sheriff.

"SAY, DR. LIVERMORE." Dr. Eastman's voice echoed down the stairs, "HAVE YOU THOSE PASS KEYS? MRS. BRADY IS EVIDENTLY ASLEEP, AND WE SHALL HAVE TO OPEN HER ROOM."

Dr. Livermore entered into the gala spirit of the occasion. He replied:

"I'LL BRING THEM RIGHT UP."

The windows in the dining room rattled.

Dr. Livermore stood up and bowed to the sheriff. "You will excuse me for a moment?"

He nodded to Miss Queen and moved toward the door but halted as there came a sound of feet pounding on the porch. The screen door slammed, and there was a noise of heavy breathing in the living room.

"Jesus, Sheriff," said a strange male voice between gasps. "There's a neked woman getting ready to jump from a window out here in the front yard . . ." The man's voice apparently gave out.

"What's that?"

"A woman . . . window . . . jump."

Cliff asked: "A naked woman?"

"Neked as hell."

Cliff departed through the front yard on the run.

"That must be Mrs. Brady," said Dr. Livermore. He wrung his hands.

"Don't make no difference who she is," said Sheriff Walters. "Somebody's got to catch her."

"Ty's still out there," said the strange male voice. "But I don't reckon he'll catch her. She's past the squab stage."

Sheriff Walters said, "Come on! We better get out there and figure some way to stop her, if she ain't already jumped."

The party, including Miss Queen, hurried to join Ty and Cliff in the front yard. Crane followed.

Chapter XI

IN THE GARDEN Cliff and a tall elderly man with an unshaven red face and an Adam's apple were gazing skyward. In a vine-bordered window above them stood Mrs. Brady. The reports about her had been accurate. She was quite naked. She was grasping the edge of the window behind her, and her body was leaning outward, as if she were poised for a dive. The sun was high overhead, and the shadows of the ivy were patterned on her white skin. Her face was calm. A diamond-and-ruby pin gleamed in her hair.

"Lady," the sheriff shouted, "don't jump. Nothing is going to happen to you." The sheriff was a stocky man. He had cobalt-blue eyes, and a straw-colored mustache stained with tobacco juice. There was an Elk's tooth hanging from a gold chain on his vest, and his pants were too big for him.

Mrs. Brady gave no sign of having heard him. Her face seemed to express a secret and tranquil satisfaction: perhaps at the fine audience she was drawing. This expression changed suddenly as the knocking on her door was resumed. Her eyes appeared startled and she leaned farther out over the window ledge.

"Mrs. Brady," called Dr. Eastman from inside, "wake up!"

"Hey, you," shouted Sheriff Walters. "Cut out that damn knocking."

Crane could not tell whether they heard each other by way of Mrs. Brady's windows, or whether their voices went back and forth by way of the living room and the stairs.

Dr. Eastman shouted, "We got to get this door open." He knocked defiantly.

The driver, Charles, and Miss Clayton arrived at a run.

"Whooee!" said the driver. "Nekid, eh?"

Dr. Livermore said, "I'll take the keys to Dr. Eastman. We'll open the door and hold her." He turned toward the house.

"Tell him to cut that knockin' out," said the sheriff. "Somebody down here get a ladder and we'll climb up to her."

"I'll get it," said the driver.

As he ran off, Dr. Buelow, Joe, and Miss Evans arrived. Miss Clayton moved over to Crane. "What's the matter with her?" she asked.

"I think she's afraid they want to murder her," he said. "She's been funny all day."

"Poor thing."

William Crane said, "Whoever tries to catch her will be a poor thing, too."

Presently the driver returned with a ladder. He placed it under Mrs. Brady's window and stepped back.

Sheriff Walters asked, "Who's going to climb up there?"

No one volunteered.

"She wouldn't hurt nobody," said the sheriff.

The pounding on the door resumed and then stopped. Dr. Livermore had arrived.

The sheriff said, "How about you, Ty?"

"No, sir," said Ty. He was the man who had reported the presence of Mrs. Brady in the window. He was firm about it. "No, sir." He was a sawed-off man, and his back muscles bulged under a shiny blue coat that did not match his pants.

"She's just a harmless old lady," said the sheriff. "She won't hurt nobody."

"She's not so old," said Cliff.

"Now, Cliff," said the sheriff.

"I got eyes," said Cliff.

Joe Kassuccio swaggered before the sheriff. "Coppers are all alike." His mouth was an ugly scar. "They're all yellow. I'll go up and get that dame."

He started ponderously up the ladder, but before he was halfway up the window Mrs. Brady, with an agility surprising for her size, stepped inside. She slammed the window and fastened it. She disappeared within the room. There was a concerted movement toward the guest house, with William Crane and Miss Clayton well in the lead. In front of Mrs. Brady's door stood a group which included the two doctors, Miss Twilliger, Mr. Penny, Miss Van Kamp, and Richardson and Mrs. Heyworth. They looked at the approaching rabble with startled eyes.

Dr. Livermore stepped back of Dr. Eastman. "What's the matter?" he asked. "Has she jumped?"

"She's back in her room," said the sheriff. "We got her blocked from the outside."

Dr. Eastman said, "All we have to do is open the door, then." He took a bunch of keys from Dr. Livermore and tried the lock. The fourth key fitted. The door swung open. Crouched in a corner by the windows was Mrs. Brady. Her hands were crossed over her breasts, and her eyes were like nickel lollipops.

"Who's going in to get her?" asked the sheriff.

"You're the one who wants her," Dr. Eastman said. "Don't you think you ought to get her yourself?"

"Not me," said Sheriff Walters. "I'm a married man."

Deputy Tom Powers moved up to the door and took off his cap. "Lady," he said, "we don't mean no harm. We jest wanta talk with you."

"That's right, lady," Sheriff Walters supplemented. "We're here to help you."

Mrs. Brady crouched farther back in her corner.

"No!" she said. "No! You want to kill me like the others. I know." She began to scream in a subdued manner.

"Oh, my God!" said Sheriff Walters. "Tom, you better go in and fetch her out."

"All right," said Tom. He had to bend his long body to get in the door.

He advanced into the room and gingerly took hold of Mrs. Brady's fat arm. She shrieked and leaped at him. There was a swirl of figures, and the door was knocked shut, and there could be heard sounds of pounding, running feet, slaps, and breaking furniture. Finally the door was opened and Deputy Tom Powers staggered out. His face was red and scratched, his shirt was torn, his ear was bleeding, and he was nursing a hand in which Mrs. Brady had left the imprint of her teeth.

"What's the matter?" asked the sheriff.

"Did you ever try to grab a greased pig?" asked Deputy Powers bitterly. "Well, this dame is a greased tiger."

He retired with Miss Twilliger to have his wounds dressed. Mrs. Brady had resumed her crouching position in the corner of the room. Around her was the wreckage of two chairs. The bureau was tilted against the wall. The rug had slipped under the bed, exposing brown hardwood floor.

Dr. Buelow made his way through the crowd. "I have

an idea," he said. "Miss Evans, haven't you a portable phonograph in your room?"

Miss Evans nodded her blond head.

"Could we have it for a moment?"

"Certainly." Miss Evans was bewildered. "I'll send for it, if you want it. Charles, will you get my phonograph?"

Charles made off at a dead run.

"What's the idea?" asked the sheriff suspiciously.

"You'll see," said Dr. Buelow.

In a few minutes Charles returned with a red leather case. He handed it to Dr. Buelow.

"If everybody will please stand back," said the doctor. He placed the phonograph on the hall floor in front of Mrs. Brady's door, cranked it, and placed the needle on the record. "Please be quiet."

Someone clasped William Crane's hand. It was Mrs. Heyworth. She pressed up close to his side, but her eyes were intent on the scene in front of the door. William Crane did not know how to move away.

The phonograph emitted a few grating noises and then began to play the "St. Louis Blues." Dr. Buelow stood beside it.

> "*I hate to see that evenin' sun go down,*
>   *That evenin' sun go down,*"

sang a negroid voice.

Dr. Buelow moved slowly into the room. The voice sang on:

> *"I've got forty-nine women,*
>   *and all I need's one more.*
> *I've got forty-nine women,*
>   *and all I need's one more."*

Dr. Buelow moved a step further. Mrs. Brady huddled against the wall, her back toward him. Her buttocks were smudged with dirt.

> *"If you don't like my peaches,*
>   *why do you shake my tree?*
> *If you don't like my peaches,*
>   *why do you shake my tree?"*

Dr. Buelow waited. Over her bare shoulder, Mrs. Brady's eyes were bright.

> *"And when the big dog comes home,*
>   *tell him what the little dog's done.*
> *And when the big dog comes home,*
>   *tell him what the little dog's done."*

The music continued, hot and throbbing and primitive. Saxophones moaned, trumpets slobbered, drums beat a barbaric tattoo. The air was filled with rhythm.

Dr. Buelow asked, "May I have this dance, Mrs. Brady?"

Mrs. Brady advanced toward Dr. Buelow. He clasped her in his arms, and they swung off to the music. They turned around the room, Mrs. Brady's bare feet, padding across the smooth wood, followed by Dr. Buelow's black shoes. As the record neared the end, Miss Clayton knelt and set the needle at the beginning. She turned the handle quietly. Presently the pair appeared at the doorway, hovered grotesquely over the jamb, and then swayed down the hallway before the outraged eyes of Sheriff Walters.

The guttural voice with the orchestra announced:

> "*I'm goin' back to Chicago,*
> *to have my hambone boiled.*
> *I'm goin' back to Chicago,*
> *to have my hambone boiled.*
> *Because those New York Gals*
> *have really got it spoiled.*"

Down the hall the couple gyrated, whirling clumsily, backing spasmodically, pushing forward, halting, sidestepping, and reeling to the tune. Mrs. Brady's face did not notice the audience: it was serene and rapt and oblivious. Dr. Buelow frowned in concentration. They turned into a door marked "Steam Room" and were suddenly lost from sight. Miss Clayton bent over the phonograph.

> "*I hate to see that evenin' sun go down,*
> *I hate to see that evenin'* . . ."

Miss Clayton lifted the needle from the record, and the hall was silent.

"Well, I'll be damned," said Sheriff Walters. He took off his hat and scratched his head with a knobby forefinger. He looked at Cliff. "You better not tell your ma about this," he said.

"I ain't going to," said Cliff. He wet his lips with his tongue.

Deputy Powers asked, "What are they going to do with her in that steam room?"

"They'll give her a hot bath. She'll be all right in three or four hours," Dr. Livermore said. "It soaks the nervousness out of them."

"I'll be God-damned," said Sheriff Walters.

Cliff walked over to his father and whispered in his ear. "No," said Sheriff Walters. "We'll talk to them nurses later." Cliff whispered again. "That's all right," said Sheriff Walters. He faced the crowd in the hall.

"I would like to have everybody except Dr. Livermore and Dr. Un-huh here wait for me in the big room downstairs. Deputy Powers will go with you."

Sheriff Walters was very serious a half hour later when he came into the living room. Cliff and Deputy Ty Graham sniffed at his heels like puppies after a blood hound bitch. Behind them came the three physicians Dr. Buelow's face was worried.

The sheriff asked, "Which one's him?"

There was a gleam of triumph in the small eyes of Dr. Eastman as he pointed toward Crane. "That's your man," he said.

"You William Crane?" the sheriff demanded.

Crane nodded. The sheriff turned to his deputies. "Bad-looking customer," he said.

The deputies assumed menacing attitudes; their legs thrust far apart and their shoulders hunched forward. Nobody was going to get around them.

"Mr. Crane," Sheriff Walters said. His voice was polite. "I have reason to believe that you are connected with both these murders. The doctors have been telling me something about you while we were upstairs. Is there anything you want to say in your defense?"

Crane said, "I'd like to know what makes you think I have something to do with these murders."

"It looks pretty bad for you. You were about the only one who had an opportunity to kill this Miss Paxton. You were up in your room getting a handkerchief at the time."

"You don't arrest people for getting handkerchiefs, do you?" Crane asked.

"No, but we got more than that on you. You were seen leaving Miss Van Kamp's room just before Pittsfield was found." The sheriff nodded chidingly at him.

"You don't believe what that Blackwood was forced to tell last night?"

"I don't have to," said the sheriff triumphantly. "Someone else saw you too."

"Who was that?"

"Dr. Livermore."

"I thought he'd be the one." Crane stared viciously at the doctor. "He's no better off than I am. Why don't you ask him where he was when either murder was committed?"

The sheriff said, "We're interested in you. What reason could Dr. Livermore have for killing one of his own patients?"

"Plenty," said Crane.

"What is it?"

"I'll let you find it out."

Cliff said, "If you know anything it would be better for you to talk." He was a pool-room boy. His face was white and unhealthy, and his black eyes were lacquer bright.

"It would be better for you to stick to your nurses," said William Crane.

"Listen," said the sheriff. "We are ready to hear anything you have to say."

"How about Blackwood? Or Dr. Livermore? Why don't you ask them some questions? Why specialize on me?"

"We'll ask them when we get good and ready," said Sheriff Walters. "You get so goddam fresh and you'll get locked up. What we want to know is what you were doing in Miss Van Kamp's room when Pittsfield was murdered?"

"How do you know Pittsfield was murdered at the time I'm supposed to have been in the room?"

"That's easy," said Cliff. "Dr. Livermore says the fellow was dead before the time you were seen coming out of the room."

"That's certainly interesting."

"Yeah, it is," said Cliff. "And now maybe you'll tell us what you were doing there?"

"I haven't said I was there."

The sheriff said, "This ain't going to get you anywhere."

"It looks as though he was the guy," said Cliff.

"That's deductive reasoning for you," said Crane. "Because I don't admit I did the murder, that makes me guilty. If I confess, I suppose you'd set me free."

"This attitude ain't helping you none," said the sheriff. "What do you know about deduction?"

"Everything," Crane said. "I'm a great detective."
The sheriff and Dr. Eastman exchanged glances. "There
are two types of deduction: elementary and advanced.
The first type, such as your surmise that I must be the
guilty party because I am supposed to have had the
opportunity to commit the crimes, leads to no conclusion. The second type often provides definite information to the investigator. For instance, Mr. Sheriff,
I notice a yellow stain on your shirt front and I surmise
you had eggs for breakfast this morning. That is an
elementary deduction. But I also notice that your neck
is dirty and that causes me to alter my original deduction. From your neck I gather that you have not bathed
recently. I know you would not change to a clean shirt
without bathing. So I say to myself, the sheriff has had
eggs for breakfast recently. That's an advanced deduction."

Deputy Tom Powers asked, "Should we take him?"

"Wait a minute," said Crane. He stepped closer to
the sheriff. "Before you do anything rash, I want you
to think of a few things. What motive would I have in
killing Pittsfield and Miss Paxton? What motive would
any patient have? He couldn't get out of here, anyway."
William Crane waved his arm for the benefit of the
patients and employees, who were standing in back of
him. "What is usually the motive of a murder that is
done carefully and secretly? It is personal advancement,

isn't it? That isn't the way a crime of passion, of hate, or of violent emotion is done. They are covered up afterwards. At least one of these, that of Miss Paxton, was carefully planned. The murderer was careful to wait until we were all at dinner. You see that, don't you?"

"Yeah," said Cliff. "But what does it prove?"

"It proves that you should look for someone who is able to leave here whenever he or she wants."

Cliff said, "I don't see any motive anyway." His father regarded him admiringly.

"You already heard a lady tell you the motive, but you didn't pay attention."

"Ah, Mr. Crane, your analysis is subtle." It was Dr. Livermore, and his tone was derisive. "Of course, you can tell us the guilty party?"

"Of course not," said Crane, "but it looks as though you might answer the description."

"You're sure the glove doesn't fit you?"

"Positive."

"This still ain't gettin' us anywhere," said the sheriff. "I don't want to arrest you, but I think it might be a good idea to give you a rest in your room for a while, just in case anything else is planning to happen around here."

"I don't want to go to my room."

"It's either that, or I'll take you down to the courthouse and throw you in a cell."

Crane said, "If you put it that way, I'll take my room."

"Ty, you'd better go with Mr. Crane." Sheriff Walters indicated the stairs with a red hand. "See that he don't get out. I'll send someone up to spell you about dinner time."

Ty shambled over to Crane and, seizing his arm, propelled him toward the stairs. Crane was aware that the eyes of the patients and the nurses and the attendants were watching him. Only the brown eyes of Mrs. Heyworth and the black ones of Miss Clayton were sympathetic. As he passed Mrs. Heyworth, she pulled gently on his coat sleeve. "It's all right," she whispered. Her voice was low and set his spine tingling.

As he climbed the stairs he heard Cliff say, "He's not so dumb."

Dr. Livermore explained, "Some of these borderline cases are very deceptive."

"Often more dangerous than those known to have certain tendencies," Dr. Eastman added. "They are hard to guard against."

Ty walked right into the room with Crane. "You ain't got a gun?" he asked.

"No."

"Any weapons?"

"No."

Ty crossed to the windows and looked down from

first one and then the other. He fastened them both.

"Pretty good jump," he said, "but I ain't taking any chances." He examined the room briefly, then looked in the closet, and then in the bathroom. He pulled the chain tentatively and listened to the roar of water with obvious pleasure.

"Damn fine plumbing," he observed.

"Damn fine," William Crane agreed.

"I'm going to sit outside your door," Ty stated. "I don't want to hear you fiddlin' with them windows."

He took the small chair in front of the writing desk and carried it out into the hall and propped it against the wall. He returned for the waste basket, which he placed within easy expectoration. Then he closed the door until it was just ajar and climbed into the chair and began a steady and somber contemplation of the opposite wall. His jaws moved without particular emphasis over a plug of tobacco.

Crane sat on his bed and wondered whether he ought to summon Williams with the rocket. He finally decided he would remain where he was for a while and let events work themselves out. Time, he felt, was the detective's best friend. So thinking, he reached back of the dresser and secured the nearly full bottle of moonshine and poured himself a medium-sized drink. He drank this and another and was glad he hadn't set off the Roman candle. He heard Ty cough in the hall. He poured half a glass full of the light yellow liquor and leaned out the door.

"Care for a drink?" he asked. "It's good for what ails you."

Deputy Sheriff Ty Graham's eyes glistened and his tongue appeared for a second at the upper left-hand corner of his mouth.

"I don't hardly ever touch the stuff," he said wistfully.

"Come on." William Crane held the glass in front of his nose. "It's some of your local product."

"Well," said Deputy Graham. He looked quickly down the hall. "It's been a hard day."

In about an hour the bottle was empty

Chapter XII

WHEN WILLIAM CRANE awoke it was just passing to dark from dusk. His head ached, and he washed his face in the bathroom. He was still a little drunk. He opened the door to the hall a crack and found Ty asleep on the chair. He was breathing with alcoholic violence. It was dark, too, in the hall, and quiet except for the exhalations of the deputy. Crane slipped by him and crept down the hall and the front stairs. He reached the garden unobserved. It was not at all cold outside; the air was quiescent, and the thin poplars lining the detention building were like mourners beside a casket. In the translucent sky a few stars goggled at their reflections on the polished surface of the pool.

Crane walked carefully over to the hospital building and crawled under the bushes in front of Dr. Livermore's office windows on hands and knees. The lights were on in the office, but there was no one in the room. The huge mahogany desk was bare, and the cushions on the window seat in front of him were smooth and airy. The office was neat with the neatness of a hotel room waiting for a guest. William Crane was about to

try the window when he saw the knob on the door to
Dr. Livermore's bedroom turn slowly. He stepped
back into the shadow and watched. The door opened,
and Miss Evans slouched into the office. She was
wearing a close-fitting silk dress that was taut across
her small hind quarters and her breasts. It didn't seem
to William Crane that she had anything on under the
dress. She was applying lipstick to her mouth, turning
her head from side to side before a silver-framed wall
mirror, and thus giving herself, through the varied
angles of the light, many faces; all of them beautiful,
but some of them cold and reserved, some with a quality inscrutable and Eastern, and some quite wanton.
She was a remarkable woman with her high cheek
bones and her delicately hollowed cheeks and her
lovely skin and her mustard-colored hair and her
purple-shadowed eyes, and William Crane wondered
why the hell she was a nurse.

As Miss Evans was completing her lips, Dr. Livermore came out into the room. He had on a Chinese
silk robe and leather slippers, and his hair and beard
were disordered. His lips were a smeary red.

"Please don't go," he said. His eyes were pleading.
"Let's have dinner in here."

Miss Evans turned to him negligently. "For sixty
you're pretty good," she said. "But you haven't got
goat glands." Her voice was husky.

"Oh, I don't mean anything like that." Dr. Livermore's long hands were entwined. "I want, I need your company. This other thing," he gestured toward the bedroom, "is just incidental."

Miss Evans's laughter was mechanical. "Incidental. From the way you talk you'd think your life depended on it." She smiled derisively at Dr. Livermore, and then her face suddenly underwent one of those miraculous changes. "Never mind, Livy, you're no worse than other men, just a little older." But for the rasping quality of her voice, she might have been a nun.

"You don't understand," Dr. Livermore said. "This is something different. I love you, I want to marry you, I want——"

"You'd better consult your wife first."

"I'll divorce her. We haven't lived together for years."

"You won't get to divorce her if she ever hears about you having had all that money in Miss Van Kamp's box."

Dr. Livermore's voice dropped a few notes. "I've stopped worrying about that box."

"Why?"

"Even if it's stolen from me for good, it won't make any difference between us, will it?"

Miss Evans leisurely evaded his groping hands. "What do you think?" she asked.

"I don't know." Dr. Livermore was pathetic. "I can't lose you."

"If you got the box in your possession again, what would you do?"

"What do you mean?"

"Would you be able to put Miss Van Kamp out of the way to get the other key to her vault?"

"You mean . . . kill her?" Dr. Livermore's beard quivered, and his long, tapering hands quivered in front of him. "Oh, no! I couldn't do a thing like that. I couldn't think——"

"I thought you said you'd do anything in the world for me?"

"Oh, I would. I would. But I can't murder anybody."

"Somebody can around here."

"It must be that patient, Crane. It started as soon as he got here. He's a dangerous man."

Miss Evans laughed genuinely. "He's in a nice place right now. That stupid sheriff will be taking him off to jail tomorrow morning, black eye and all."

"It's very strange. Who could have given him that second beating? He must have incurred the enmity of someone here."

"I think it was probably the new guard. He doesn't seem to like Mr. Crane at all."

"Another thing I can't understand is who called the police? If they hadn't come we could have buried Mr.

Pittsfield and Miss Paxton without any notoriety at all. I'm afraid the sanitarium is ruined."

"That's why you ought to think of Miss Van Kamp," Miss Evans said savagely. "She's an old lady. She is due to die in a year or two anyway, and——"

"I couldn't. . . ." Dr. Livermore held up his hand. "Why won't you come away with me? I have nearly forty thousand dollars. We could live on that for a long time in Europe. A quiet little town on the French Riviera, or an Italian island. Sunshine and good food and——"

"Not for me." Miss Evans was as vivid as a poinsettia. "I want complete independence and everything that goes with it. Can't you see that I'm not made for work? Giving old ladies enemas, carrying trays, taking temperatures, being sweet and kind and good and gentle. No!" She was walking rapidly up and down the room. Her flat hips ducked in a quarter-circle each time she pivoted. "I want clothes and travel and a maid. I want music and gayety and admiration. I want to be able to order people around. I want—— Oh, you can't understand!"

Dr. Livermore watched her in silence, his face apprehensive.

"I know it takes money to have these things," Miss Evans said. She spoke slowly, as if to herself. "I'm going to get it some way."

The couple's eyes met for a second. Then the man's wavered, rolled downward. His beard pressed against the silk robe, and his fingers moved restlessly again. Miss Evans studied the top of his head speculatively. She drawled, "See you later, sweetheart." Her voice was flat, without inflection. She moved gracefully around Dr. Livermore. At the hall door she looked back, unsmiling, and was gone. Dr. Livermore sat down behind his desk. He had on nothing under his shiny dressing gown. His face was suddenly tired.

Crane ducked below the window, crawled to the shadow on the other side, and started around the house. From a window halfway down the other side, a band of yellow light made grotesque animals of the shrubs and rosebushes in the garden. Far out in the paleness a man was digging in the grass, moving a small spade with erratic eager movements. It was the religious guard. He was lifting small pieces of earth with the spade, peering into each indentation, and then carefully replacing the sod; bending down to tuck in the edges. He was completing a circle about six feet in diameter, and as he reached the end of the untouched soil, he groaned loudly, and then, appalled at the noise, clapped both hands over his mouth. Without stopping for the fallen spade, he hurried off into the dark.

From the lighted window came a murmur of voices, and Crane moved along to it. Miss Evans was standing in the room leaning against a desk behind which sat Dr. Eastman. His shirt was rolled up to the elbows, and his arms were black with hair. There was a livid bruise on his jaw where William Crane had kicked him. Miss Evans's eyes were open wide; her face was demure.

"Why, George, you know I went in to talk to Dr. Livermore just because you suggested it," she said. Her voice had moved up to a more feminine key. "You remember you——"

"I remember, all right," Dr. Eastman said; "but I didn't ask you to sleep with him."

"George!" Miss Evans fluttered her blue eyes. "I was in Dr. Livermore's room that night because I wanted to find out if he knew you had taken the box from him. You said you wished you knew——"

"You didn't have to go into his bedroom to find that out."

"I wasn't in his bedroom until they brought that Crane into the hall. Then I stepped into the bedroom because I thought it wouldn't be proper to be seen in Dr. Livermore's office at that hour of the night."

Dr. Eastman's face lost part of its ugly scowl. He was willing to be convinced. "How'd that smart guy know so much, then?" he asked.

"He didn't. Just because he was right about one thing, you assumed that everything else he said was right too." Tears ruffled the innocent and circular pools that were Miss Evans's eyes. "George, you must believe me. I haven't seen him alone since that night. What could I see in him after I had known you?"

For a brief moment Dr. Eastman's face was almost cheerful. Suddenly he stood up and walked toward the window. Crane dove to the ground and rolled into the shadows.

"Just a minute," Dr. Eastman said. His voice was a blade of suspicion. "How do you explain my losing the box? Who took it from me?"

"How should I know?"

Crane was back at the window in time to see Miss Evans shrug her shoulders delicately.

Dr. Eastman said, "You were the only one who knew I had the box."

"How do you know that?"

"I didn't tell anybody else."

"If you had kept it in a better hiding place," said Miss Evans, "it wouldn't have been stolen. Anybody might look in that desk drawer."

Dr. Eastman turned upon Miss Evans fiercely, his scowl menacing and immediate. "You didn't double-cross me with that old goat, did you?"

"You're crazy. He's a married man."

"You probably had a change of heart and took the box back to him."

"No, I tell you he hasn't got it back. He said he has given up worrying about where it is."

"I thought you said you hadn't seen him since that night."

"Not alone. He told me that when we were all at the guest house."

"I don't think you're telling the truth."

It was cold outside the window; the night was damp, and William Crane's hands and feet were smarting. He wished the conversation would end. Miss Evans looked as though she were getting angry.

"You're a fool," she said. "Anybody could have taken that box from you. It might have been Crane, or that Joe who is always hanging around Dr. Livermore. They both look capable of anything."

"I was sure at first that Crane must have taken the box, but I'm not so certain now. He's too crazy to find a thing like that on the day of his arrival."

"It was quite a coincidence, though, wasn't it?" Miss Evans's lovely mouth curled sardonically. "The day he arrives the box disappears. And maybe he isn't so crazy."

"I'd find out if I could get him alone. I'd beat the truth out of him if I had to kill him." Dr. Eastman's knuckles were white against his dark skin.

Miss Evans said, "You'll have a hard time getting at him now."

"Maybe the sheriff will beat it out of him. We finally got him to believe Crane did the murders."

"Maybe he did. Don't you think somebody is trying to kill Miss Van Kamp?"

"I'll bet it's Livermore. He's liable to do anything to get that other key." Dr. Eastman's shaggy brows nearly hid his eyes. "If I still had the first key, I might kill her myself."

Miss Evans moved nearer to Dr. Eastman and touched his arm. "Don't you believe me, George? I am just trying to help you. I wouldn't have helped you take the box from Dr. Livermore in the first place if I weren't, would I?"

Dr. Eastman wouldn't look at her. "I don't know what to believe. All I know is that somebody got the box from me."

"If you can't believe me, I might as well take my pin back." Miss Evans struggled to unfasten the gold arrow on his shirt. Her eyes were bright and moist. Dr. Eastman took her hands in his. "No," he said. "No. Give me time to think myself out of this."

"You must trust me, George," Miss Evans said. "You must." She patted his arm. Dr. Eastman caught her in his arms and kissed her passionately and then thrust her from him.

He said, "You'll drive me insane."

Miss Evans's face was mystical and wise. "That

will be nice, as long as you are insane about me," she said. She smiled wistfully, bit her lower lip with her teeth, and left the room.

Crane found he was still able to walk, and he hurried around to the front door of the building. He waited in the shadows until Miss Evans came out. She was humming the chorus of "The Last Round-Up," and he picked up a piece of wood and pursued her down the path and thrust the wood into the small of her back. "I've got you covered, babe," he said in a guttural voice, "and if you yell I'll blow your stomach out."

Miss Evans stopped humming, but she did not yell. "What do you want?" she asked. She was not frightened.

William Crane said, "Keep on walking. Into the garage."

Lights from the servants' house filled the garage with conflicting shadows. The ambulance was still there, and he forced Miss Evans to climb into the front seat. He sat down beside her. Her face was dimly illuminated by the reflected beams.

"So it's you," said Miss Evans. "I thought they had you locked up?"

"They have," he said. He looked at her in silence.

"What do you want?" Miss Evans was defiant.

"Just your company. I've long admired you from afar."

"This is a funny way to show your admiration."

"You have so many friends. This seemed the only way to talk to you alone."

Miss Evans was definitely hostile, but she was willing to fence. "I'd rather you'd ask for a date next time. This is so sudden."

"But, you see, I didn't know how you felt. You might have turned me down."

"Oh no, I admire you too."

William Crane said, "May I say that you also have a funny way of showing it?"

"What do you mean?"

He held out his wrist. "That black spot is where you stepped on me with your heel. You remember? The night you and Dr. Eastman beat me up? I seized you on the leg like this." He reached down and held Miss Evans's ankle. It was a nice ankle, and it was covered with silk. Miss Evans let his hand rest there for a moment, and then she moved the ankle away.

She asked, "What would you do if somebody had hold of your leg?"

"The same thing. I don't hold any grudge."

"But how did you find out that it was my heel?"

"Did you notice the other nurses all had on white shoes with rubber heels that night? They wouldn't be apt to change their shoes to commit a little assault and battery, and then change back again."

"How do you know Dr. Eastman was with me?"

"That was a fortunate guess."

"What makes you so interested in these things, anyway? Who are you?"

"I am really C. Auguste Dupin, the great detective," said William Crane. "I am a Doctor of Deduction. I am interested in everything. And even if I were not C. Auguste Dupin, I would be interested in finding out to whom I owe these bruises."

Miss Evans made an abrupt movement with her right hand. "You can drop that stuff with me." Her face was angry. "Talk plain English."

"All right," said Crane. "But I would like to know why you and the doc tried to beat me up."

"He didn't like the kick in the jaw you gave him. And I didn't like your talk about what I was doing in Dr. Livermore's office."

"He must have thought I kicked him with a box. Do you remember he expressed curiosity about a box just before he choked me?"

"I don't know anything about that."

"No?" He poked her in the ribs with the stick. "Well, Doc Eastman isn't so sure about that. I just heard him say that he thinks you and your vegetarian Romeo, old Doc Livermore, stole the box back from him."

"So!" Miss Evans's eyes were contemptuous. "You're just a Peeping Tom?"

"You might call it that, but I prefer to think of myself as Watchful William."

"Well, you didn't hear anything from Dr. Eastman and me that would hurt you."

"I heard plenty. But I'm not interested in your personal affairs except where they have to do with me."

"What's that box got to do with you?"

"I'm trying to find it."

"I haven't got it."

"No, but you helped Eastman steal it from Livermore after Livermore had told you of stealing it from Miss Van Kamp."

"Any girl would do as much for the man she loved.' Miss Evans's voice was righteous. "When I told him Dr. Livermore had it, he was afraid the doctor intended to steal it. So I helped him get it."

"Why didn't Dr. Eastman take it back to Miss Van Kamp?"

"You see, Miss Van Kamp has a weak heart. She might die any time. So George decided it would be best to keep the box in a safe place, where we would be sure nobody would steal it in case she died."

"Is a desk drawer a safe place?"

"You didn't miss much."

"I never do." Crane grinned at Miss Evans's sullen face. "And now you want Dr. Eastman to think I took it from him."

Miss Evans was silent.

"Well, I haven't got the box. All I've got is a terrible thirst." Crane climbed out of the seat. "You sit still, because I'm 'Dead-Eye' with a pistol." He walked over to the box in the corner, lifted out the jug of whisky, and returned. Holding the jug in his two palms, he took a long drink. After a second the liquor exploded in his stomach, sending warm, golden rays into his brain. "That's good!" He smacked his lips and turned to Miss Evans. "Have a shot?" She refused coldly. "Mind if I have another?" She did not seem to mind, so he drank again. He put the jug on the floor and said, "I want to ask you a few questions."

"I don't know what you have been doing for the last fifteen minutes," said Miss Evans.

"Do you know who killed Pittsfield and Miss Paxton?"

"I think you probably did."

"I think not. Are you sure it wasn't Dr. Eastman?"

"He couldn't have done it. He's not really as bad as he looks. He has a kind heart."

"That would go over big with a jury."

"I'm sure he didn't kill them. He'd have no reason to."

"They might have found out he had the box for a while."

Miss Evans was silent. The pale light barely touched

ner face, so that it was all in shadow except the white lines of her chin, her cheek bones and the aristocratic curve of her nose. She was lovely. William Crane jabbed the stick in her ribs again.

"You're sure you don't know who did the murders?"

"Yes."

"What do you know about Miss Van Kamp? Has she any enemies?"

"I don't think so."

"What doctor handles her case?"

"Dr. Buelow."

"Who gives her the steam bath she has three times a week?"

"I do."

"Doesn't she ever tell you anything? That she is afraid of somebody?"

"I think the only person she is afraid of is that poor Mr. L'Adam. Whenever he has one of his spells, she hardly sleeps at all."

"I don't blame her." Crane took another drink from the bottle. "That fellow scares me to death."

Miss Evans asked, "Is that your whisky?" Crane shook his head. He felt fine. "Somebody is going to be pretty darn sore at you," Miss Evans said.

"I don't care. Do you mind if I don't care?" Crane held the bottle up. "Won't you have one?" Miss

Evans nodded. She said, "Just one." She took the bottle in her hands.

"Listen," said William Crane. "If you try to bean me with that jug, I'll blow you to hell."

"Why, Mr. Crane! You don't think I'd do anything like that? I like you. I think you're such an intelligent man." She took a good drink from the bottle. "I could go for an intelligent man." She handed back the bottle, and he had a drink. As he placed the bottle on the floor, someone came into the garage.

"Oh, my God!" whispered Miss Evans. She seemed really frightened now, and he wondered why.

With a cautious shuffling step the figure had sidled toward the ambulance. Crane got a firm hold on the neck of the bottle. He wished he had a pistol. "Who's there?" he asked. He discovered his voice was hoarse.

The shadow bulked large against the wall, swaying slightly. A voice said, "I know you not, yet my gaze is upon you." It was the religious guard again, and Crane put the bottle back on the floor of the car. "Who are you and what do you do?" asked the old man.

"I am the Archangel Gabriel," said Crane. "I am waiting for them to come. I wait while you search."

The shadow on the wall seemed smaller. "You know I been searchin'?"

"No grain of sand on the beaches of the sea, no forest

acorn, no tick on a sheep's back can move without His knowledge," said Crane. "Have no fear of Us, but ask thyself: 'Am I faithful to my trust?'"

The old man chanted, "I have cast out all evil: I am pure and faithful."

"Have you been told for what you search?"

"I have seen it. It is a steel casket. I saw him take it to his room in the dead of night, but it is no longer there. He must have buried it somewhere, according to the Word."

"Who was it?"

"It was the bearded one."

"What is in the casket?"

"You should know."

"I do know. The Archangel Gabriel knows everything," William Crane hissed. "But I am testing you."

"It holds the missing scriptures. I have been chosen to find them."

Miss Evans moved her feet, and one heel struck the gear-shift lever.

The old man demanded, "Who is there with you?"

"Mary," said William Crane simply.

"What is She doing?"

"She is waiting for them, too."

"Then I'd better go about my search," said the old man.

William Crane waited until he had nearly gone.

"Should we need thy help, we will call Jordan. That will be the signal."

When the old man had departed, Miss Evans sighed. "I'm afraid of him. He's crazier than any of the patients. He watches me all the time."

"I don't blame him," said William Crane gallantly. He offered Miss Evans another drink. She accepted.

"You certainly know how to handle him," she said.

"I'm crazy too," said William Crane. "That's why we get along."

"You must have been talking with him before."

"I have, but this is the first time I have let him in on the fact that I am the Archangel Gabriel."

"I imagine that would astonish a lot of your other friends, too. I know mine would be surprised to know that I am Mary."

"You mean the Virgin Mary?"

"You don't have to be nasty."

William Crane said, "No, I want to be fair. I don't have to be nasty."

"No?" said Miss Evans.

"No," said Crane. "I can be nice or I can be nasty."

"Then why don't you be nice?" Miss Evans pressed a slender leg against Crane. "I like nice men."

"All right; I'll be nice." Crane was quite drunk. "I'll be very nice. I won't tell anybody what I saw in Dr. Livermore's window."

Miss Evans's leg moved away. There was a moment of tight silence, breathless and dramatic. The diffused light shone softly on Miss Evans's expressionless face, giving it a sort of internal glow independent of the external world. Her eyes were partially closed.

"Don't get excited," said William Crane apprehensively. "I won't tell. Not if you don't say anything about seeing me here."

Miss Evans laughed mechanically. Her voice had moved down the scale a note or two. It sounded as though she had tuberculosis. "You're a perfect gentleman, aren't you?" she said. It seemed to him that she was angry, very angry; but not at him. "I'll look under my bed at night before I turn out the lights."

Crane said, "Better look in your bed—that's where I'm more likely to be." For the first time he felt an admiration for her.

"You have an evil mind," Miss Evans said. "What did you really see in Dr. Livermore's office?"

"Plenty."

Miss Evans bent toward Crane and laid cool fingers on his hands. Her face was earnest in the subdued light. "You may not know it," she said, "but a girl has to eat. If I hadn't done what he wanted, I would have been dismissed. I can't afford to be dismissed."

"Why not?"

"Reasons . . . family reasons."

"Why don't you marry Dr. Eastman?"

"He won't have me until he makes some money."

"Doesn't he get paid here?"

"Oh, certainly." Miss Evans laughed again, bitterly. "But not as much as he thinks is necessary for a wife." She withdrew her hand.

William Crane changed the direction of the conversation. "Do you think Dr. Livermore has the box back again?"

"I don't know."

"I wonder if the key is still in the box."

"I don't know that, either."

"Have you ever seen the key?"

"No, I've just seen the box."

"You're sure Dr. Eastman has lost both the key and the box?"

"He said they were gone." Miss Evans's eyes were alert and bright. "You heard him yourself."

"He might be trying to make you think they were gone."

"I don't think so." Her lips were scornful. "He wouldn't fool me."

William Crane matched her tone. "You don't think he would?" He leaned toward her. "Did you ask him what was in Miss Van Kamp's New York vault?"

"He said there was just some old jewelry."

"He didn't mention there was cash worth eight hundred thousand dollars?"

Miss Evans pushed Crane's knees aside. She climbed over him and out of the ambulance. "The son of a bitch," she said. She marched off in the darkness.

Crane took a last drink from the bottle and put it back in its hiding place. He walked cautiously out of the garage and was slinking toward the guest house when a heavy figure loomed up a distance in front of him. Crane stepped back in the shrubbery. He felt a little giddy.

The figure was Joe Kassuccio. He emerged from the darkness cautiously and relentlessly. He was walking on the gravel path, and he stared suspiciously at the spot in the gloom where Crane stood.

"Who's there?" he demanded gruffly.

"Sheriff's office," said William Crane. He stepped quickly out onto the path and hit the man with a roundhouse swing to the cheek bone. Mr. Kassuccio grunted and fell on his back, his head a dark blob on the white pebbles in the path. Crane put his right heel in the exact center of the upturned face and threw his entire weight onto his right leg. Then he spun clockwise. There was a cracking sound, and under his heel it felt juicy. He stepped off the face, rubbed his heel on the grass at the side of the walk, and then walked swiftly to the guest house. On the front steps of the porch the sheriff was sitting. He was obviously waiting for dinner, and he had a cigar between his teeth. He did not see Crane.

One of the windows in the colorama room was partially open and Crane slid through it and walked unobserved up the stairs. But, as he was a few feet from his door, Deputy Ty Graham moved slightly in his chair. He was not quite awake, but he was sleeping lightly. Crane retreated to the women's steam bath near the other end of the hall. He picked up a small white enameled bath stool in one of the showers and carried it out into the hall and tossed it out the closed end window overlooking the front steps. As the pane of glass crashed, he uttered a piercing falsetto scream and stepped back into the ladies' bath. Deputy Graham awoke from his stupor with his feet already in motion. He raced past the ladies' bath and peered out the window.

"What's the matter down there?" he bellowed.

Crane was already down to his room when he heard the sheriff's indignant answer:

"What the hell's the matter up there? You trying to kill me?"

A few minutes later a much chastened deputy peered into Crane's room. From the tumbled condition of the bed it was clear that Crane had been asleep for some time. He was still asleep. He even snored slightly.

Chapter XIII

THE DEPUTY shook William Crane. He had been shaking him for some time.

"Huh?" Crane said. He pretended that he had been very deeply asleep. "Go away. I'm not well." He buried his face in the pillow.

The deputy shook him again. "Sheriff wants you downstairs." He turned Crane around. "You'll feel all right when you get up."

"Oh no," said William Crane.

The deputy led him into the bathroom and filled the wash basin with cold water. "Stick your head in that," he ordered.

Round his ears the water tingled, and in his nose and eyes it smarted. It was exceptionally cold, and it made William Crane's head revolve dizzily for several seconds. He did not know whether he was going to be sick or not, and then, suddenly, he felt fine. He dried his face and head with a rough bath towel and combed back his hair.

"That isn't such bad liquor," he assured the deputy.

Deputy Ty Graham's wrinkled face assumed an expression of injury. "You hadn't ought to have let me drink so much of that bottle," he said. "A little more and I might have fallen asleep. The chief don't like his men to drink." He looked at Crane intently.

"Neither does the doc," said Crane. "We don't have to say anything about it, do we?"

"I should say not. No sir! We'd best forget about it."

William Crane put on his tie, pulled on his pants, and reached for his shoes. Blood was still fresh on the heel of his right shoe, but he put it on anyway.

"What does the sheriff want?" he asked.

"Somebody tried to kill him with a chair. They threw it at him from the front end of the hall here."

"No!" William Crane was astonished. "Who was it?"

"That's what the chief is going to find out. Somebody up here did it, and they have to be here still. We got all the exits blocked. He's going to question every-body downstairs."

As they stepped out in the hall, William Crane asked, "Didn't you see who it was? You were out here in the hall, weren't you?"

"I was watching you all the time, not the hall."

"Oh!"

Sheriff Walters was seated in the living room. He was chewing tobacco vigorously, and his frosted blue eyes gleamed wickedly. Miss Van Kamp, Miss Queen, and Mr. Penny were perched on the edge of the lounge by the fireplace. There was a strained, frightened expression on their faces, and Miss Queen's fingers clutched nervously at the fringe of her black dress. Richardson sat on the arm of a chair in which was Mrs. Heyworth. She smiled reassuringly at William Crane, her teeth white against her delicate brown skin. She did not seem especially afraid. Cliff stood at the foot of the stairs, and at the top was the lanky figure of Deputy Tom Powers.

"How many more?" he called down to Cliff.

"There's that fellow Blackwood and your girl friend, Mrs. Brady," said Cliff.

"No more dames for me," said Deputy Powers. "I'll get the fellow, and if you want Mrs. Brady, come and get her yourself."

Sheriff Walters heard this mutiny without anger. "Get one of the nurses," he told Deputy Graham. "She'll get the lady down."

Soon Deputy Powers marched down the stairs with Blackwood. The latter was plainly frightened; his face was distorted, and his eyes were wild. His lips trembled with protest that he was unable to voice. He collapsed into a seat under a blue shaded lamp, his appearance that of a trapped animal. A few seconds later Deputy Powers returned up the stairs with Miss Twilliger. The sheriff turned to the assemblage.

"Look here," he said. "Somebody tried to kill me

by throwing a chair from the window on the second-floor hall. That's a serious matter. Now, what I want to know is: who done it?"

The patients looked surprised and faintly relieved. It was clear that the scream they had heard meant to them only one thing—murder.

"If nobody's going to tell me," the sheriff said darkly, "I'll find out for myself." He swept blue eyes bright with suspicion over the women. "It was a lady."

Behind him Mrs. Brady arrived on the arm of Miss Twilliger. Mrs. Brady was dressed in an evening gown with gold leaves sewn over a web-like material of brown thread. Her face was powdered heavily, her lips were bright, her eyes mascaraed; but she had forgotten to do her hair. It hung in two pigtails over her bare back. She nodded graciously to the sheriff, who had turned to glare at her, and marched to a chair by the fireplace. She evidently intended to ignore the dancing incident of the afternoon. Crane was astonished at the repose of her heavily made up face until he saw her eyes, which were like two frightened prisoners staring out the peepholes of a white adobe jail; waiting for daybreak and a Mexican firing squad.

"Is that everybody up there, Cliff?" Sheriff Walters demanded.

Cliff said, "I guess so."

"I'll take a look," said Deputy Graham. He looked slyly at Crane as he mounted the stairs. Crane remembered he hadn't told him the liquor was all gone.

The sheriff said, "Now, let's get back to business. Who let out that scream when the window broke?"

There was no response.

"It was a woman," Sheriff Walters continued. "It must have been one of you four. Nobody's come out of this house since that chair was throwed at me. Now, where were you, Miss Queen, when that window was broke?"

"I was with Miss Van Kamp," said Miss Queen without looking up. She was twisting a handkerchief in her hands.

"Is that right, Miss Van Kamp?"

Miss Van Kamp nodded; then thought better of it. "I don't see that it's any of your business," she said.

The sheriff took a deep breath. "You don't think it's any of my business to try to find out who's trying to kill me?" His face grew red. "Miss Van Kamp, was or was not Miss Queen in your room at the time of the scream?"

"She was not."

"She wasn't?" The sheriff seemed to grow in triumph.

"No. I was in her room."

"Didn't either of you scream?"

"No."

"How about you?" The sheriff scanned Mrs. Heyworth. "Where were you?"

"I was reading in bed." Mrs. Heyworth's voice was silky.

"Nobody with you?"

"Nobody."

"Did you scream?"

"No, but I heard it."

"How about you, Mrs. Brady?"

"I was dressing, and I didn't scream, but I was alone." Mrs. Brady spoke as though she were reciting a memorized piece. Her face did not change its effortful repose.

Sheriff Walters snorted. "Somebody's lying. Whoever threw that chair screamed, and whoever screamed was a woman." He turned savagely to Richardson. "What do you know about this?"

"Nothing. I was napping when I heard the scream, and by the time I got to the door there was . . ." Richardson's voice fell away to a stop, and he peered at the stairs in astonishment.

Deputy Ty Graham and Miss Evans were self-consciously coming down them, their arms locked affectionately together. Miss Evans was smiling, and her teeth gleamed under her full red lips. Her flat hips swayed as she stepped down each stair, giving her the exaggerated and bawdy walk of a honky-tonk lady. She was flower-like beside the blunt shrub of a deputy.

At the foot of the stairs they halted, and Deputy Graham reluctantly permitted Miss Evans to draw away from him. He addressed the sheriff:

"I found her upstairs."

Sheriff Walters fastened his ice-blue eyes upon Miss Evans. "Well, well. What was the little lady doing up there?"

"Hiding," said Deputy Graham.

"Where?"

Deputy Graham coughed embarrassedly. "She was . . . I mean . . . I heard her . . . it was in the . . ."

Miss Evans interrupted contemptuously: "Why don't you tell them? You were bold enough charging in." She looked haughtily at the sheriff.

"What were you doing upstairs? Why did you go up there?"

"I wanted to get things ready for Miss Van Kamp's steam bath. She has it three times a week, always just before dinner."

"Is that right, Miss Van Kamp?"

"Yes."

Sheriff Walters stepped closer to Miss Evans. "Did you hear someone scream?"

"Why, no."

"Did you hear the window break?"

"What window?" Miss Evans became indignant. "What is all this about?"

"You are upstairs," said the sheriff; "somebody screams, somebody breaks a window and tries to kill me with a chair, and you don't hear a thing." He looked like a turkey cock. "Are you deaf?"

"No. Not a bit deaf. But I had the water in the tub running. You can't hear much over that."

"Was there water in the tub, Ty?"

"Yeah, it was about half full," said Deputy Graham.

The sheriff looked suspiciously at Miss Evans. "It's damn funny, anyway. You ought to have heard something." He swung around again to Deputy Graham. "Ty, how near is that bathroom to the end of the hall?"

"Jest two doors."

"Whose room is next to the window?"

"Mrs. Brady's," said Miss Twilliger.

"And then who?"

"Miss Van Kamp on the same side."

"Who's across the hall?"

Miss Twilliger said, "There's Mr. Pittsfield and Miss Paxton . . . I mean there was."

"So." Sheriff Walters was lost in thought.

Cliff had been ogling Miss Evans from his place by the front door, and he moved closer to her. "Pa," he said, "why don't you find out where that chair came from?"

"That's a good idea. Tom, you got that chair?"

Deputy Powers brought in the white pieces from the porch. Sheriff Walters took them in his hands and turned to Miss Twilliger. "Ever seen these before, Nurse?"

"Why, yes," said Miss Twilliger. She looked happily at Miss Evans. "Those came from the ladies' bathroom."

"Aha!" Sheriff Walters scowled triumphantly at Miss Evans. "What have you to say to that?"

"Just because somebody took the chair out of the bathroom doesn't prove I threw it."

"No, but it makes it mighty likely."

Miss Evans said, "Well, I didn't throw it."

"How did you get in this place, anyway? I was sitting on the front steps all the time, and nobody passed me," said the sheriff.

Miss Evans smiled patiently. "I came in the back way, through the kitchen. There is nothing wrong in that, is there?"

"So you sneaked in?"

"I wouldn't call it that. I'd say I walked in." Miss Evans's face was innocent. "I often come in that way."

Sheriff Walters digested this, his eyes darkened by half-closed lids. "It was somebody upstairs," he said, "and it was a woman. Now, Miss Queen and Miss Van

Kamp have got a good alibi. So that leaves Mrs.—
er——"

"Heyworth," said Richardson angrily. "Mrs. Patterson Heyworth."

"Mrs. Heyworth, Mrs. Brady, and our little nurse,"
said the sheriff. "And I have no doubt that the same
person who tried to dispose of me is connected with
these murders." He was pacing up and down the room,
his face apoplectic in concentration. "I want all of you
to understand that any deception will be taken as an
evidence of guilty knowledge. You may be arrested as
accomplices after the fact, and liable to very heavy
punishment."

Sheriff Walters glared at William Crane and then at
Miss Evans. "At least two of you have considerable
explaining left to do," he said. "You'd better straighten
out your stories before the inquest."

Dr. Buelow came into the room from the front
porch. His face was a chalky background for eyes at
once frightened and angry. "May I speak to you privately, Sheriff Walters?" he asked.

"Sure," said the sheriff. They moved over to the
front door. Dr. Buelow whispered something to him.

"My Gawd!" Sheriff Walters said. "Cliff! Come with
me. Ty, you and Tom stay here. Don't let anybody
go."

With Dr. Buelow in the lead, the sheriff and Cliff

hurried clatteringly across the porch and out into the night. Everyone except Blackwood, who crouched in his chair, his hands covering his face, began to talk at once and to everyone else.

"What could have happened?" gasped Miss Twilliger.

"I'm going to leave this place in the morning," said Mrs. Brady. "I think I'll go to Louisville or New Orleans."

"It's another murder," said Miss Queen. "I feel sure it's another murder."

"I hope it's Dr. Livermore," said Miss Van Kamp. "As long as it couldn't have been that stupid sheriff."

"It isn't murder. It's nothing of the sort," said Richardson loudly. "Probably the coroner, or someone to see the sheriff."

"It couldn't be the coroner," said Miss Twilliger. "He's coming tomorrow."

Miss Queen said, "I feel sure it's another murder."

Crane and the two deputies had been watching the front door. "We'll find out in a minute," said Crane. "Somebody's coming back." Three figures could be seen coming down the gravel path. One had a flashlight. It was directed first at one side of the path and then at the other. A hand touched Crane's arm. It was Miss Evans. Her mouth was close to his ear.

"Are you going to play ball with me?" she said. "Or

am I going to have to tell them you've been out-side?"

Before Crane had time to answer, Sheriff Walters, Dr. Buelow, and Cliff came into the room. Their faces were grim.

Sheriff Walters announced, "Miss Clayton has been murdered."

"I knew it!" Miss Queen moaned loudly. "We are all doomed. All of us."

The others received the news in silence. They were doomed indeed.

"I want everyone to stay here." Sheriff Walters' expression was fierce, and he barked his orders. "Ty, you and Tom go out and take the body into the hospital and then bring everybody back here. Cliff, maybe you'd better help them. Get that wolf fellow, too."

Crane asked, "What happened?"

"Miss Clayton was stabbed from behind, in the neck. The poor girl died just as I found her," said Dr. Buelow.

"I told you so," said Miss Queen. She wreathed her face in a melancholy smile. "Another murder." She nodded her head up and down. "And who will be next?"

"Shut up, you," said the sheriff savagely. "There ain't going to be any next. I'll catch the guy that done this one if it takes me all my life."

William Crane moved beside Dr. Buelow. "Have you got any idea who could have killed her?" he asked.

Dr. Buelow shook his head. He looked ill. "The poor kid. She was the only decent nurse we had."

"Where was she killed?"

"Out in the garden just in front of the detention building . . . I nearly stepped on her." His voice trembled. "I'm sorry I'm like this, but it really takes you sometimes. . . ."

"I know," said Crane. "She was a swell girl."

"If I'd only come by an instant sooner . . . she was still alive when I found her . . . I might have got hold of the fellow who's doing all this. . . ." Dr. Buelow's strong fingers opened and closed. "I tell you he wouldn't be alive now." His voice became louder. "It's so unfair . . . a knife in the back of the neck. . . ."

Crane asked, "What kind of a knife was it? Was it like the one used on Miss Paxton? One with a bone handle?"

"By God! It was! Identical!"

Dr. Buelow gazed tragically and hopefully at William Crane.

"I don't know who did it," said Crane, "but I'm getting warm." He squeezed the doctor's arm. "What nurse took care of Miss Paxton?"

"Miss Clayton."

"One more question," said Crane. "Did she say anything to you before she died?"

"She was stabbed in the neck. She tried to tell me something, but the blood poured out of her mouth . . . I couldn't make out what it was."

"Couldn't you hear anything?"

Dr. Buelow was apologetic. "She said something that sounded like cleaning, but it didn't make sense. That's the only word I could distinguish."

"Cleaning?" said Crane. "Cleaning? Hmm . . . cleaning."

It took Cliff and the two deputies nearly fifteen minutes to find everybody. Dr. Eastman and Charles came in with Mr. L'Adam, whose black eyes shone with such a preternatural brilliance that even the sheriff drew back from them. The old white-haired guard came in by himself and smiled knowingly at Crane.

"The Lord's got 'em together," he observed.

"It's easier to smite them this way," said Crane.

"True," said the old man. "True." He sat down with folded hands to wait for the Lord to smite them.

With Dr. Livermore and Deputy Graham came Joe Kassuccio, his face, below his angry eyes, white with gauze and adhesive tape. Back of them was the driver, and bringing up the rear were Cliff and Deputy Powers.

"Now get them two colored ladies," said the sheriff.

Maria and Ulah, their eyes rolling, were brought in. Their plump figures shook visibly.

"Where you two been for the last hour?" Sheriff Walters demanded.

"Right here in this kitchen," Ulah said. Her voice was shrill.

"Doing what?"

"Cooking dinner."

"You haven't been out of the kitchen at all?"

"No sir!"

The sheriff looked questioningly at Maria.

"No sir," she said.

"Did anybody come in through your kitchen, like Miss Evans here?"

"Nobody been through our kitchen but her." Ulah was positive about it.

"All right." Sheriff Walters was pleased. "You can go back and get dinner." The two women vanished like a sleight-of-hand trick. "Now, before we question these people who have been outside, I want to know if any of you other people left this house within the last hour."

Miss Evans casually watched Crane. There was a faint air of triumph about her.

"How about you, Crane?" asked the sheriff. "Have you been out?"

Crane said, "The deputy can answer that."

"He didn't move an inch," Deputy Graham assured the sheriff. "I had my eye on him every second."

There was no change in Miss Evans's expression, but a film seemed to slide over her blue eyes. Crane winked at her.

"Sure none of you others have been out?" asked the sheriff.

The others were all quite sure.

The sheriff turned to Joe Kassuccio with interest. "How'd you get that?" he demanded, pointing a finger at the damaged face.

"You ought to know," Kassuccio said.

"What do you mean?"

"Either you or one of your smart guys give me the heel. An' I want to know what's the idea, see?" His voice was a rasp. "Nobody can get away with that stuff, even if they are hick dicks. When I find out who done this, I'll . . ."

"Wait a minute," said the sheriff sternly. "What makes you think I done that or one of my boys?"

For a moment Kassuccio was silent. "I know," he said after a time.

"Did you see him?"

"Naw. I would have conked him if I had." Joe's voice was hard with hatred. "He didn't give me no warning. But I heard him speak. I'll know him again."

"What did he say?"

"It was in the garden, he walked up to me in the dark and says, 'Sheriff's office,' and then he bashes me. What kind of a guy is that?"

"Whew!" the sheriff stared at Cliff and Deputy Powers. "Did either of you do that?"

"Don't be a damn fool," said Cliff. "Nobody'd be apt to say who they were just before they slugged somebody. It was the murderer who hit him. He'd probably killed that nurse and was making a getaway."

He turned to Kassuccio. "It's a lucky thing he didn't kill you."

"By God!" said the sheriff. "Maybe you got a clue as to who the murderer is."

"You're all nuts," said Joe sullenly. "Miss Clayton was alive then. She helped Dr. Livermore put these bandages on me."

"That's right," added Dr. Livermore. "She left us about five minutes before Dr. Buelow found her body."

"What did you two do?" asked Cliff.

Joe said, "I went back to my room to wash off my hands."

"How about you, Dr. Livermore?"

"I stayed in my room."

"You did like hell," said Dr. Eastman. "I saw you leave by the back door. You went out in the garden."

"I don't intend to have my word contradicted," Dr.

Livermore said sullenly. He pulled nervously at his beard. "I said I stayed in my room."

"You *said* you stayed in your room." Dr. Eastman imitated his tone. "But I followed you out in the garden."

The two doctors glared at each other. "Why did you follow him?" Sheriff Walters asked Dr. Eastman.

"I followed him because he'd been acting strangely for the last few days. I think he knows something about these murders. I wanted to see what he was going out for."

"Well, what did he go out for?"

"I don't know. I lost him in the garden."

Dr. Livermore said, "You lost me in the garden, did you? That means you were there when Miss Clayton was killed."

"So were you," said Dr. Eastman.

"It looks to me like all three of you got some explaining to do," said the sheriff.

"Not me," said Joe. "The driver here seen me come in my room."

"That's so," said the driver. "He was in there at least ten minutes before the deputies come and got us."

"That leaves you two doctors in kind of a mess," said the sheriff. "Either one of you might have bumped her off. Did you ever have any trouble with her? Either of you?"

"No," said Dr. Livermore. "She was a model nurse."

Dr. Eastman nodded his head. "A nice girl."

The glass doors to the dining room were opened, and a smell of tomato soup and roast beef invaded the living room. "Supper is served," said Ulah.

Sheriff Walters said, "I guess we'd better eat."

"How many places have you set, Ulah?" Dr. Livermore asked. "The sheriff will eat with us."

"Plenty of places," Ulah said. "Plenty for everybody."

"Cliff and me'll eat here," said Sheriff Walters. "Ty and Tom can eat with the help in the servants' hall."

"How about Mr. L'Adam?" Dr. Livermore spoke to Dr. Buelow. "Do you think it will be all right for him to eat with us?"

"I suppose so," said Dr. Buelow dubiously.

Mr. L'Adam's brilliant black eyes sparkled. "It would be a pleasure. It is very tiresome eating alone." His yellow teeth were bared in a smile. "I'd like some nice fresh meat."

Chapter XIV

IT WAS VERY SILENT at dinner. Night sounds, the calls of birds, the wind breathing through the dry trees, an occasional and distant howl from a dog drifted in through the windows to mingle with the civilized tinkle of glassware and silver. Quantities of roast beef and mashed potatoes and bread disappeared down Sheriff Walters and his son, but no one else ate much. There was a feeling of apprehension about the table, and of distrust. At the head sat Dr. Livermore, his face worried and white above his black beard. Opposite him was Dr. Eastman, flashing red glances at the others from sullen eyes. Dr. Buelow had gone to eat with the nurses and deputies in the servants' building.

Crane drank two cups of black coffee and wished Mrs. Heyworth would look at somebody else. Her eyes, affectionate and lonely, hungry and sympathetic, never left him. They were maternal, and they made him uneasy. He wondered what had happened to her husband and her child. Every time he glanced at her to see if she was looking at him, Richardson's pouty mouth would droop into a warning. The rest of the time Richardson watched Blackwood, who did not touch his food. Miss Queen, Mrs. Brady, and Miss Van Kamp whispered among themselves. Next to them was Mr. Penny, in serious thought. It was Mr. L'Adam, after the coffee had been poured by an unsteady black hand, who finally broke the silence.

"When do you expect to arrest the murderer, Mr. Sheriff?" he asked. He was seated next to Dr. Eastman, and he spoke mincingly over long yellow teeth.

Sheriff Walters abruptly halted a large piece of bread halfway to his mouth. "Huh?" He laid the morsel on his green plate with resignation. "Well, now, that's something I'd like to know."

"I once knew a detective," Mr. L'Adam volunteered. "He always maintained that the first thing to search for was the motive." Mr. L'Adam's bright doggish eyes sparkled with sinister politeness. "Have you found a motive, Mr. Sheriff?"

"No."

Mr. L'Adam's lips curved into a smile that pulled his skin tight over Indian cheek bones. "I should search for a motive, if I were you."

Richardson loomed over the white tablecloth. "He's got a motive, but he doesn't know it."

"So?" Mr. L'Adam arched fine eyebrows, and Crane discovered with some horror that the whites of his eyes were golden brown and interlaced with threads of blood.

Richardson continued: "He hasn't heard about Miss

Van Kamp's box and her bonds." He avoided looking at Miss Van Kamp. "I think someone ought to tell him."

"I did," Miss Van Kamp said. Her teeth clipped each word. "But he was too stupid to listen."

Sheriff Walters had difficulty in speaking. "Wait a minute. Wait a minute." He looked like a rooster. "You watch your language, or I'll send you upstairs."

"You and who else?" Miss Van Kamp wanted to know.

Crane so far forgot himself as to laugh.

"I really think the box is the clue to all this." Richardson was serious. "Anybody would like to get hold of the four hundred thousand dollars in bonds."

"The sheriff wouldn't," snapped Miss Van Kamp. "Not if it was a clue in a murder case."

Sheriff Walters appealed to Dr. Eastman. "What is this all about, anyway?"

Dr. Eastman did not answer.

"Ask old Doc Livermore," said Crane. "He knows all about the box and its contents—don't you, Dr. Livermore?"

"I suppose . . . in a way . . . I believe I do." The doctor's beard trembled. "But I can't see——"

Sheriff Walters interrupted him angrily. "Do you know there was a box?"

"Miss Van Kamp told me about it."

"Did you ever see it?"

"I don't recall . . ." Dr. Livermore closed his eyes in reflective pain.

"Oh, you don't, eh?" Each of Miss Van Kamp's words had the velocity of a shot from an elephant rifle. "You don't remember handling those bonds? You don't remember saying that I must have had very good advice on my investments?" Her voice became mellow and unctuous. "You don't remember: 'My dear Miss Van Kamp, I really think you should let me care for all these valuables. This box seems so—insecure.' You don't remember saying that?" Miss Van Kamp's bitterness was at high flood. "And then, because I wouldn't give it to you, you stole it and then murdered these people to cover up your crime."

Dr. Livermore's fingers fluttered in agony.

"You stole my box." Miss Van Kamp was calmer now. "But you'll never get anything more. I was going to leave most of my money to this sanitarium, but now I won't. Nobody here will get a cent."

"Now, wait a minute," said the sheriff.

"Let me talk to her," said Cliff. His licorice eyes were alert. "How did you come to show the bonds to the doc, Miss Van Kamp?"

"I wanted to let him know he needn't worry about the future of the sanitarium. He'd been troubled over the scarcity of patients. I felt grateful to him for what he had done for me (he made me feel so much better) and I thought I'd let him know I was going to leave him something to carry on his work. I'd have been glad to give him some if he'd come and asked me for it, but the coward had to steal it."

Crane intercepted an agonized glance sent by Dr. Livermore to Dr. Eastman and swung around in time to see the other nod perceptibly.

Dr. Livermore spoke hurriedly: "You must be careful what you believe, Sheriff Walters. You know Miss Van Kamp is naturally upset."

"She's been worried over the loss of her box for a long time," Dr. Eastman explained. "But I think we can find another for her, just as good."

"What do you mean, 'just as good'?" demanded the sheriff.

Cliff asked, "You mean she didn't have bonds in the box?"

Dr. Livermore tugged at his beard with nervous fingers. "I don't like to say this, but I feel I must, in fairness to you." He paused for a jerky breath. "Miss Van Kamp's wealth is a delusion."

"You lie! You are a thieving liar." Miss Van Kamp pointed a bony finger at Dr. Livermore. "This proves you stole my money. You wouldn't try to lie, if you didn't. You are a murderer and a thief and a——"

Swiftly the blood fled from Miss Van Kamp's face, leaving it the color of Holstein milk. Her distended eyes gazed in a frightened stare, and she slumped over on the table. Her face wallowed in her butter plate, and the hand that had been pointed at Dr. Livermore fell into a silver platter of cheese. A tumbler spewed water onto the linen, making a circle of damp grayness that widened and widened. . . .

"Oh, my God!" said Miss Queen. "She's been murdered under our very eyes."

Dr. Eastman was beside the limp body. His blunt fingers felt for her pulse, and he was tense for a second, his head held at a listening angle.

"She's only fainted," he announced. "Give me a wet cloth, somebody." He attempted to unloosen the tight neckpiece to her black dress.

Crane stood over him. "Keep your hands off her neck," he said. "Let Miss Queen undo that collar." He reached down and took Dr. Eastman's right thumb and twisted it back until it touched the wrist bone. At the same time he shoved the doctor away from the table. Dr. Eastman groaned with pain and hit Crane on the face with his left hand.

The sheriff stepped between them. "What the hell's the idea?" he demanded.

"That's what I'd like to know." Dr. Eastman was

furious. This bastard's going to get it." He moved toward Crane. His jaw was rigid.

"Cut it out," roared the sheriff. "You two behave, or I'll lock you both up."

Crane turned his back on Dr. Eastman. Under Miss Queen's ministrations, Miss Van Kamp was regaining consciousness. A blue vein squirmed in her temple, and moisture flecked her pallid lips. She looked ninety years old.

"We'd better send her upstairs," said Dr. Livermore. "Would you mind getting Miss Twilliger, Dr. Eastman?"

Dr. Eastman left, pulling at his right thumb. "I'll see you later," he said to Crane. "You'll answer for all this."

"Sure," said Crane.

Dr. Livermore held a glass of water to Miss Van Kamp's mouth. She pushed it away. "Leave me alone," she said. "I'm all right."

"Mrs. Brady and I will take her to her room," said Miss Queen. Her long face was almost cheerful. "We'll get her ready for bed. She may die yet."

Dr. Livermore said, "I'll go along."

Miss Van Kamp was able to walk slowly with the two women holding her arms. Dr. Livermore followed them out.

"See here, you." Sheriff Walters squinted blue eyes at Crane. "What's the matter with you? Trying to keep the doc from helping that old lady. Do you want to see her die?"

"No, I don't," said William Crane. "That's why I pushed him away."

Sheriff Walters appealed to his son. "What do you make of all this?"

"Nothing," said Cliff. "But I'm gettin' some new ideas." He blew his nose violently on a greasy handkerchief. "What makes you so sure the doc might want to kill the old lady?" he demanded of Crane.

"If you stole an old lady's money and nothing but her word is keeping you under suspicion, you might want to get rid of her. Especially if you could slip her something while she was having a stroke. Then it would look as though her illness had carried her off." Crane balanced a cheese knife on his hand. His face throbbed where Dr. Eastman had struck him. "And then, if you had one of the two keys to her safety-deposit box in New York, you might have a better chance getting the other with her dead than with her alive."

The sheriff's blue eyes expressed disbelief. "That's interesting if true," he said. He glanced around the table. "Say! Where's that wolf fellow?"

Mr. L'Adams's chair was empty, and his napkin was neatly folded in front of his plate. He had not touched his crackers, but his cheese was gone, all of it, even the rind.

"How'd he get out?" asked Sheriff Walters.

Blackwood shoved back his chair in panic, threw down his napkin, and half rose from the table.

Sheriff Walters turned a clammy eye on him. "Where you goin'?"

"Away." Blackwood's thumbs were bloodless against the table. "He may be under here, getting ready to bite somebody's leg."

The sheriff snorted, but he lifted the flap of linen. "Nothing there."

"I don't care." Blackwood's voice trembled. "I'm afraid. I'm going upstairs and lock myself in my room. Nobody can tell what will happen around here next."

"Go ahead," said the sheriff contemptuously. "But you needn't worry. One of my men will sleep in the hall."

Richardson stood up and stepped around to the back of Mrs. Heyworth's chair. He said, "I'll take you upstairs, too."

"I don't want to go to bed," said Mrs. Heyworth. She smiled at Crane. "I think this is fun. I'm so anxious to see who the murderer is. Do you really think it could be that poor Mr. L'Adam?"

Sheriff Walters relaxed visibly. "Well, now, ma'm, I'd like to be able to show you, and maybe I will in the morning, when you have had your beauty sleep."

Richardson said, "Come now, dear. It's been a very long day."

Mrs. Heyworth smiled at Richardson and then looked directly into Crane's eyes. "Good-night," she said. Her expression was tender and sad. She allowed herself to be led out of the dining room. Blackwood followed them at a discreet distance.

Cliff said, "Some bim!"

"Very pretty," Sheriff Walters agreed.

"With her and that Miss Evans I could put on a show."

The sheriff said, "Cliff!" He shook his head at his son. "We got to get to work."

Dr. Livermore appeared at the door. With him was Dr. Eastman, his glance sullen on William Crane.

"We put her to bed," said Dr. Livermore. "Her nerves were overburdened. Miss Twilliger will watch until she falls asleep."

"What I want to know," said the sheriff, "is how you happened to lie about that money box?"

Dr. Livermore's beard shook in easy laughter. "I didn't think it important. She's been worried about that box for months. She hides it and then pretends it has been stolen." He laughed again. "It wouldn't make much difference if it were. It is filled with bits of torn newspaper and cloth that she has picked up around the grounds. The whole collection isn't worth a penny."

"The hell it isn't!" said Sheriff Walters. "Why didn't you tell us that at supper?"

"I didn't want to speak before Miss Van Kamp. It

always throws her into a violent rage when anyone openly doubts her word. It has a very harmful effect upon her, as you saw."

Sheriff Walters absorbed these facts coldly.

"We should have told you all about the box before this," said Dr. Eastman, "but neither of us thought about it. We believed you understood she was insane on that subject when she tried to tell you about the bonds before."

"Then that clears it all up," said Sheriff Walters. He appeared relieved.

"We still got to look for a murderer," Cliff reminded his father.

Sheriff Walters brightened over the possibility of physical action. "That's right," he said briskly. "We'd better run down that L'Adam."

"What happened to him?" Dr. Livermore asked.

"He got out somehow."

"I suppose I'd better get Charles and somebody else to help me," Dr. Eastman said. He glanced at Crane. "You wouldn't care to help, would you?"

"No, I wouldn't."

"Do you want the others sent back from the servants' house, Sheriff Walters?" Dr. Eastman paused at the door.

"Yes, might as well send them back. Take one of the deputies to help you, if you like."

"Thanks." The doctor was gone.

Crane tilted back his chair. "I don't think it's so smart to forget that box altogether," he said. "Even if the doctors knew there was nothing in it, the help didn't. One of them might have stolen it, thinking it was full of bonds." He grinned ruefully. "You would, hearing her talk."

"I won't overlook anything," the sheriff promised. "Least of all that Joe fellow with the broken nose. He looks like a bad actor to me."

"I assure you he could hardly be responsible for these things," Dr. Livermore said hastily. "He's been here only three days."

"It don't take that long to murder anybody," said Sheriff Walters.

A murmur of voices, first faint and then quite loud, reported the arrival of the group from the other dining room. Dr. Buelow, Miss Evans, and Deputy Powers were in front of the others. Sheriff Walters walked over to them.

"I'd like to have practically everybody stay in this building tonight," he said. "Will there be room, Dr. Livermore?"

"Oh yes. Plenty." Dr. Livermore coughed politely. "That is, Miss Evans, if the beds can be made up?"

"I'll have Maria and Ulah do them at once." Miss Evans was formal, too.

Ulah was brought in. She asked, "Does that mean me and Maria get to sleep in here?"

Sheriff Walters undid the cellophane wrapping around a cigar. "I guess you two needn't sleep here. You make the beds, and then you can go back to your rooms."

"Mistah Sheriff," said Ulah, "we don't want to go back to our rooms. We'd like to sleep here. We'll sleep in the kitchen."

Maria agreed fervently. "Yes sir!"

"All right. Go ahead and make up those beds."

It was only a few minutes before everyone was settled. The sheriff decided that the doctors could sleep in their rooms in the main hospital building, and he delegated Deputy Powers to go with them as a guard. Dr. Eastman, his hand stained with dirt, arrived just as Dr. Buelow and Dr. Livermore were leaving. "We got him," he announced. "He's locked up in the detention building."

"Who's gonna' watch him?" Sheriff Walters asked.

"He can't possibly get out," Dr. Livermore said. "No one need guard him."

Sheriff Walters decided that was all right. "But where is that old fellow who guards the place at night?"

Dr. Eastman said, "He should be at the front gate. He's supposed to watch it at night."

"I'll look him up." Sheriff Walters motioned to

Deputy Graham, who leaned against the screen door. "You find out about him. If he's guardin', let him be. Cliff, you'd better go upstairs in the hall. Set in front of Miss Evans' room and don't let her come out."

Cliff picked up a pillow from one of the couches in front of the fireplace and started up the stairs. "Nobody's going to come out tonight," he announced from the top.

"I'll roam around a little as soon as things get set," Sheriff Walters said when the doctors and the deputies had departed. He stared disapprovingly at Crane and Mr. Penny, both of whom were sitting in front of the fire. "Don't you two intend to go to bed?"

"Sure," said Crane. "But we aren't sleepy. We thought we might help you a little."

"I don't need any of your help. I got trouble enough, now."

"Look here," said Crane. "You might as well use your head about this before anybody else is killed."

Sheriff Walters bristled. "What do you mean?"

Crane leaned forward in his chair. "Do you remember what I said about deduction? Well, there's something just as useful in detective work as that."

"Yeah?"

"It's called elimination. You've heard of elimination?"

Sheriff Walters nodded angrily.

"Elimination is even more accurate than deduction," said Crane. "Your wife has brown eyes, hasn't she?" The sheriff started. "I was lucky there," said Crane. "That was a deduction with the help of a gentleman named Mendel, who made up a law that blue- and brown-eyed parents have three brown-eyed children to one blue-eyed. Of course, I could have been wrong. That's where elimination is so valuable. You're never wrong with elimination."

The sheriff listened silently.

"Now let's take a try at some of this elimination." Crane spoke softly. "If the murders have all been done by the same person, I think we will get somewhere." He stood up and walked close to the fireplace. He leaned an elbow on the mantel and looked into the coals. "Who couldn't have killed Pittsfield is what we must first determine."

"I don't know," said Sheriff Walters. "I guess he couldn't have killed himself." He stared suspiciously at Crane. "But even if you tell me who couldn't have killed him, I don't know why I should believe you."

"You don't have to," Crane said. "Mr. Penny will back up what I say, and if you don't believe him, you can ask the others."

The sheriff's head nodded savagely in sudden decision. "All right, go ahead." He drew out a notebook and a cracked yellow pencil and sat down on a straight chair.

"The way I figure it out there are just five persons who couldn't have killed Pittsfield." Crane was still intent upon the soft coals which glowed in the velvet darkness of the fireplace. "They are Miss Van Kamp, who held hands with Nellie during the colorama, Mrs. Heyworth and Richardson, who also held hands, I guess, because each was sure that the other had not left; and the driver and Miss Twilliger. She was with the driver in the garage. I don't think a woman could have done it, anyway."

Sheriff Walters stuck the pencil under his sandy mustache, wet it, and then wrote down the names. "I wish Cliff was here," he said plaintively.

Lively points of light danced from unconsumed pieces of wood in the rear of the fireplace, but toward the front, in the beige and gray ashes, eyes of crimson and violet peered unwinkingly into the room. Away from the fire the air was cool and fresh.

"The second murder was that of Nellie Paxton," Crane continued. "There are so many who could not have done it that we'd better look for those who had the chance to stick that knife in her." He pushed a fresh piece of wood over the coal. "We won't consider the five we eliminated in the first murder at all. That leaves Blackwood, Mr. L'Adam, Miss Evans, the guy with the bandaged face, myself, Miss Queen, Dr. Livermore, Dr. Eastman, and that old fellow who watches at night."

Sheriff Walters wrote these names down. Crane continued:

"I'm not considering either of the two colored women because I am positive they are racially incapable of such purposeful crime. Charles is out because he was seen by Miss Evans going into the servants' bathroom for a bath, and Dr. Buelow and the patients are out, too, because they were all eating dinner together."

Sheriff Walters stuck the pencil into the corner of his mouth. "That sounds all right," he mumbled. "But how about yourself and Miss Queen? Didn't you have dinner with them?"

"I went up to get a drin—handkerchief," said Crane. "And Miss Queen got sore at me and left the table too. We both had a chance to do it."

"All right, all right," said the sheriff. "What next?"

Crane leaned both elbows on the mantel. "Now for the last murder. Who can we eliminate from those eight?" He looked at the sheriff and raised his eyebrows.

"I suppose you could count Blackwood and Miss Queen." Sheriff Walters was rubbing his neck. "We know they were both upstairs when Miss Clayton was killed."

"Then you can eliminate me," Crane said. "The deputy will vouch that I didn't leave my room." He smiled at the sheriff. "And if Miss Evans was the one who threw the chair at you, she could hardly have killed Miss Clayton."

Sheriff Walters balled his right hand and struck his left palm. "You're right. She couldn't be two places at once." He was quite pleased. "She's too nice-looking a lady to be mixed up in a murder." He reflected for a moment, his eyes closed. "Still, she might have thrown that chair anyway."

William Crane returned to the subject. "Now you've got only five different suspects left. Dr. Eastman, Dr. Livermore, Joe, Mr. L'Adam, and the old guard."

"I can't arrest all of them."

"No, but you have something to go on now." Crane caught Mr. Penny's attention and then glanced at the stairs. Mr. Penny blinked his eyes sleepily and nodded. "Of course, all the alibis may not be watertight. Particularly if the people are working together and one alibis the other. You better check over their stories and positions tomorrow."

Crane and Mr. Penny were nearly halfway up the stairs when Sheriff Walters coughed.

"Say, Crane, you seem pretty smart," he said. "What are you in for?"

"It was all a terrible mistake," said William Crane. He continued on to his room.

Chapter XV

CRANE FELT very strongly that he should, as a detective, keep a careful watch all night, but he was sleepy. The bed was inviting, the room was cool for sitting, and so he undressed in the bathroom. Against his skin the pajamas were smooth, but in tying them he found a new sore spot on his right hip. He examined the discolored welt, but he was unable to remember how he got it. He wondered if it was one of the early ones or if it had come from a kick in the second beating. His face in the mirror was still quite colorful, and he admired it critically. The blow Dr. Eastman had given him at dinner had left a red mark above two livid bruises, like something out of the Cubist school. He washed his face tenderly, and as a concession to being a detective he propped the door open a fraction of an inch with a piece of wrapping paper so that he would be awakened by any events outside, if they were loud enough. Then he shoved the windows all the way open and climbed in bed.

But when he finally achieved a really comfortable position with his knees pressed up against the wall, he found he was unable to sleep. There was a hollow feeling in his stomach, and his heart beat more rapidly than usual, causing blood to pound in his ears at each stroke. He felt a slight nausea, and he knew that either he had had too much moonshine or he was frightened. He hoped it was the liquor.

The room was quiet, but there was a soft wind outside which intermittently brushed a tree branch against the stucco side of the guest house with a furtive scratching noise. It sounded as though someone were crawling up the wall with finger nails and toes. He caught himself watching the open windows apprehensively, half expecting to see outlined a black figure. Once the curtain blew in a sudden gust, and involuntarily he sat up in bed. "What the hell!" he said to himself. "What the hell!" He rolled into a tight ball, pressed his face into the pillow, and closed his eyes firmly.

This seemed about to get him to sleep until, at a great distance, he heard the roar of running water. At times it was loud; at other times it was faint; as though somebody were touring the gardens in a portable bathtub with both faucets open. William Crane climbed wearily out of bed, put on his bathrobe, and stuck his head out into the hall. The noise of the water was clearer. At the other end of the hall, by the broken window, stood Cliff. His face was purposeful. He threw back his head and uttered an appalling scream. It started in a soprano's high C, dropped into a baritone bray, and ended in a giggly falsetto. Crane ran down the hall toward him, but he was only halfway when the door to the ladies' bath opened and Sheriff Walters emerged, red-faced and angry, amid a cloud of steam.

"Who the hell told you to scream like that?" he shouted at his son, who waited quietly, his face reposed as an opera singer's after a successful aria. Sheriff Walters put his hands on his hips. "What's the big idea?"

"Why, you told me to." Cliff stood his ground. "You said . . ."

"I said for you to call me, not scream your damn head off."

Cliff carefully rubbed his nose on his sleeve. "You found out what you wanted, didn't you?" he asked. "You could hear me holler even though the water was running." He grinned triumphantly.

Red in the sheriff's cheeks slowly became pink. "I'll say I did," he said. "I'll bet Ma heard you clear out the other side of town." Reflective wrinkles creased his forehead. "That gal musta heard that scream if she was really in there. There's something funny about her story. I'm glad we got her where we can watch her."

The sheriff went back to turn off the water, and Crane started for his room. Only one other door in the entire hall was open. In it stood Richardson, wearing a wool robe and brown pajamas. He was looking at Mrs. Heyworth's door.

"What happened?" he asked.

"More detective work." Crane passed him without stopping and went into his room. He left the paper in the door to keep it open a crack, threw his bathrobe across the foot of his bed, and slid between the sheets. They were still warm.

It was about 3 A. M. when Crane awoke. He did not move, but he was quite awake, and the muscles in his stomach and legs were as tight as bowstrings. It was deathly quiet. The wind had passed away, and with it the clouds, and the moon stared coldly down through the left-hand window and made luminous a rectangle of floor a few feet from the foot of the bed. The silence had a quality of listening, as though something had stealthily disturbed it without actually having driven it away. Crane listened too.

Over by the door there was a faint creak and the soft grind of hinges. Through the woolly darkness woven over that part of the room he could see nothing. He knew, of course, that it was the murderer. He felt a kind of horrible paralysis grip him. It was a strange feeling of weakness such as he had sometimes encountered in a dream when he was sliding toward a cliff or speeding down a hill in a runaway automobile, but he knew he was not dreaming. The noise softly and slowly approached, direct and relentless. He held his breath, and in a subconscious flash his brain told him it must be Dr. Livermore. He wondered whether the doctor would use a knife or try to strangle him; but he did not dare move or shout for fear that the doctor had a pistol.

Now the noise was close to the bed, and in front of the regular patch of moonlight was another glimmer of light. Suddenly this became a figure bending over him, and Crane sat up in bed and siezed it and pulled it over upon him, his fingers feeling for a throat hold. At the same time he rolled over on top, one leg hooked around the intruder's body.

It was a woman he had hold of, and she was naked. She seized his face between her hands and kissed him. It was Mrs. Heyworth, and her eyes were insane in the moonlight. Crane pulled himself free of her, and for a moment his mind stopped working. He heard himself scream twice, and then he climbed through the open window and jumped. Bushes broke his fall and scratched his face and shoulders, but he was immediately able to run. He raced through the garden and over to the high wall that stood between him and the auto trailer on the hill to the north. Glass and barbed wire along the top of the wall tore his fingers, and he finally dropped back into the garden.

He panted for a minute and found that his bare feet were very cold. With this discovery came a return of his senses and a feeling of shame of his cowardice. He wondered if anyone else had had a madwoman climb in bed with him, and if so, what he had done. He reassured himself by deciding that he had probably got the hell out of there, just as he himself had.

Then he wondered how he was going to get back to his room. In the garden even the soil was cold, and while there was no wind, the air was raw. Everything smelt of frost. In the distance he could see the guest house, ablaze with lights and alive with excited voices. Evidently his screams had been heard and search parties were being organized. He thought he could hear the voice of the sheriff giving hoarse orders. To get back to the house undetected, if possible, he moved to the other side of the garden, away from the wall. He walked tenderly, but small stones cut his feet, and once he whacked his toe against a heavy metal object. He reached down in the grass and lifted it. Beams from the moon showed him it was a shovel, and to his left, slightly out of his path, was another circular hole such as he'd seen the old guard dig. Crane was looking at this when his eye caught a movement in the shrubbery between him and the guest house. It was a man, and he was kneeling behind a bush watching the flashlights assembled by the guest house. Sliding his bare feet over the damp grass, Crane edged nearer the man and saw, to his surprise, that it was Dr. Livermore.

Now, fanwise, the searching party had spread out and

was slowly beating through the shrubbery in the garden. In the distance the lights were faint, lost in the torrent of clear moonlight which poured upon the trees and bushes and flowers. With a grunt of fear, Dr. Livermore stood up, and Crane ducked behind a bed of geraniums. He wished he had on socks, at least. Dr. Livermore hurried to where he had dropped the shovel, frantically felt for it in the grass, and shambled off toward a wing of the search party. He flung the shovel behind a clump of bushes as he passed them.

It seemed impossible to dodge the searchers, so Crane pulled himself out of the geranium bed, rubbed his hands on the seat of his pajamas, and sat down on a near-by bench. He lolled back comfortably and gazed up at a sky white with moonlight.

He was still admiring the sky when Deputy Powers and the driver came upon him. They halted at a safe distance. Deputy Powers, the reluctant authority of the law upon him, advanced a pace beyond his companion. "Hi!" he said. "Hi, there!" When Crane did not answer, he turned to the driver. "Maybe he's dead, too," he suggested hopefully.

Crane stood up. "No such luck," he said. "I'm just cold." He stepped gingerly across the gravel path to them. "Let's go back. I believe I have the next quadrille with you, Mr. Powers?"

"You got what?"

The driver seized Crane's arm firmly and spoke behind his back to Deputy Powers. "Don't pay no attention."

While they were walking back to the guest house, Deputy Powers left them to warn the sheriff. In the moonlight the garden was a photographic negative, all blacks and grays and whites, without depth and without relation to each other, as if they had been pieces of dark paper pasted on a blackboard. A savage slash of chalk was the path, while the shadows of shrubs and flowers were substantial blocks of black, and the vegetation itself was gray and unreal. Overhead there was the cry of night birds, sometimes angry and sometimes alarmed.

Crane and the driver were on the front steps when the sheriff and the rest of the party caught up with them. The sheriff was utterly outraged.

"What in hell were you trying to do?" He shook his arms like a preacher calling upon God. "Run clear to the Hudson in them pajamas?"

"No." William Crane spoke softly. "I just wanted to get out of my room."

The sheriff shook himself convulsively. "You just wanted to get out of your room." He repeated this to the entire world. "He just wanted to get out of his room. He couldn't wait until morning." A gnarled fist shook under Crane's nose. "For God's sake, why did you want to get out of your room?"

The arm was dangerously close, and Crane stepped back. "I thought somebody was in the room with me."

"That's no reason for screaming and scaring everybody half to death."

"Maybe not," said Crane.

"That's no excuse for jumping out of a second-story window."

"Maybe not," said Crane.

Against the gray silk sky, the sheriff's shoulders shrugged blackly. "Do you feel safe to go to bed by yourself now?" he asked with heavy sarcasm. "Or will we send somebody to keep you company?"

"Miss Evans would do," Crane said. He opened the screen door and let it shut gently behind him.

Sheriff Walters shook his head. "Crazy as a loon," he stated to the little gathering. "Crazy as a loon."

"I don't know," said Deputy Graham. "I wouldn't mind sittin' up with Miss Evans myself."

"You close your mouth," said the sheriff.

For the third time the silence of the night was broken by a gentle persistent knocking at the door. William Crane regretted leaving his bed. Tufts of wool in his trousers tickled his legs, but he fastened the belt securely. He was taking no chances. He flicked on the lamp at the head of the bed, and a subdued radiance made the room visible and ugly.

The subtle knocking continued.

He pulled open the door and retreated two steps. Mr. Penny was in the hall. He had on a Japanese robe and leather sandals, and his finger was against his mouth. He looked like an Oriental toy. Crane let him in the room. With a gesture of his wrist Mr. Penny indicated that the door should be closed. Magically, he produced a small pad of white paper from a hidden pocket. He held out his right fist, opened it slowly. William Crane watched suspiciously. There was a stub of a pencil in the open hand. On the pad Mr. Penny wrote: "*I might be able to help you.*"

Crane sat on the bed, smoothing beside him a place for Mr. Penny. "I need some help." He spoke conversationally. "I'd like to be able to stop all this."

Mr. Penny blinked his licorice-drop eyes. His pencil scrawled on the pad: "*I might be able to give you some background.*"

"Fine," said William Crane. "But first I'd like to know what's the matter with Mrs. Heyworth. Why is she here?"

The pencil wrote: "*Husband and child killed in auto accident. She won't believe they're dead. She thinks you look like her husband.*"

"She thinks more than that," said Crane. He grinned. "Now about that background?"

The pencil wrote: "*This might help. Dr. E. and Dr. L. have had dreadful quarrels.*"

William Crane moved his chin vertically.

"*Dr. E. threatened to cane Dr. L., so Dr. L. got a bodyguard. That's Joe.*" Mr. Penny turned the piece of paper.

Crane sucked in his under lip. "What were they fighting about?"

On the white paper the pencil spelled: "*E-V-A-N-S.*"

"Why?"

As a gourmet would on smelling terrapin cooking in white wine, Mr. Penny closed his eyes. Then he opened them, glared fiercely at William Crane, and doubled a chubby fist. Who wouldn't, he implied, fight over a beautiful woman?

His eyes twinkling with the sly humor of a perfect mime, Mr. Penny then wrote:

"*They are mad about the box, too.*"

"How about this box?" Crane asked eagerly. "Is it really filled with scraps of paper, or is it full of bonds?"

Mr. Penny wrote: "*Bonds.*"

"How do you know?"

The pencil trembled indignantly: "*I saw them.*"

"Why didn't you tell the sheriff?"

Mr. Penny had used up the reverse side of the page. He crumpled it crisply and tossed it into the waste basket. On the new sheet he wrote: "*Who'd believe me?*"

William Crane felt a little doubtful himself, but he directed what he hoped was a look of confidence at the little man.

Mr. Penny smiled understandingly. He wrote: "*One of them has the box.*"

Crane nodded and said, "How do you know that?" He propped his pillow against the head of the bed and leaned against it.

The pencil scratched hurriedly and triumphantly on the paper: "*I saw Miss Evans with the box.*"

Behind Crane the pillow plumped to the floor. "When did you see her with it?" he asked.

"The day you arrived."

"The hell you say! What was she doing with it?"

As he wrote, Mr. Penny shook his head. "I don't know. I met her in the corridor outside of Dr. L.'s office. She turned back when she saw me."

Crane forced air between his teeth. He thought this might be important if true. "Are you sure it was Miss Van Kamp's box?"

"Absolutely."

"What do you think she was doing with it?"

The pencil moved more slowly: "*Taking it from one Dr. to the other*"—the lead hesitated, then appended— "*?*" Mr. Penny's face was wistful.

William Crane's reverie was broken by the movement of the pencil. On the pad was written: "*Whoever has the box must be doing the murders.*"

"Why?"

"*Don't you know about the two keys to the vault?*"

Crane nodded.

The pencil hurried on: "*Nobody would want the second key unless he had the first one. That's why Pittsfield was murdered. He caught someone looking for that key in Miss Van Kamp's room.*"

"I guess you're right," said Crane. He slid off the bed, stretched his arms, and yawned.

Another sheet crumpled under Mr. Penny's fingers. He wrote something on a new sheet, tore it off the pad, folded it neatly, and handed it to Crane. The gay silk in his dressing gown shone red and blue in the light as he glided to the door. He paused there for an instant, beamed, and was gone. In the hall his sandals slid raspingly and unevenly.

The folded page was in William Crane's hand, and he opened it. It read: "*Why did the fountain stop the first night you were here?*"

The paper floated to the waste basket in quick zig-zags, and Crane returned to bed.

Chapter XVI

NEXT MORNING the tattoo of the curtain against the wall awakened Crane. Both the windows framed freshly scrubbed blue sky and fat clouds, and gay tree tops dancing to the tune of a northwesterly half gale. In the room the air smelled like that under a Mercury-Arc sunlight lamp. He drew in two deep breaths and climbed out of his bed. When he walked over to the windows he found his feet still hurt from the gravel. There were some people in the garden, around the hole he had found during the night, and he recognized Sheriff Walters, Deputy Powers, Dr. Eastman, and an exceedingly thin man in black whom he judged to be the coroner. Halfway between them and the detention building the fountain arched a silver back in the morning sunlight.

He put on a lemon-yellow and green striped tie, a brown Harris tweed golf coat, flannel trousers; tucked the suit he had been wearing the night Miss Evans had kicked him over his arm, and went downstairs.

"I'm hungry," he told Maria. "I want plenty of victuals."

"Yes sir," said Maria with approval. "You always does."

While he was eating some oatmeal with plenty of butter and sugar on it, Miss Evans came into the dining room from the kitchen. She was in a neatly starched white and blue uniform, and there was about her an air of having somewhere to go. She walked past him.

"Wait a minute," he said. "Won't you have a bloater or some curry?"

Miss Evans paused by the door. "I'm very busy."

Crane said, "I just wanted to ask you something. Is there any way of having clothes cleaned around here? These are so dirty I can't wear them."

"I think Charles sometimes does cleaning. You might ask him." With a crackle of linen, she was gone.

"Thanks," said William Crane. He returned to his oatmeal with relish. He had finished most of it when Maria came out of the kitchen with a platter full of fried ham and eggs.

"Who's that man out there?" he asked, helping himself to four slices of ham and three eggs.

"He's the one who looks at the bodies." Maria rolled her eyes. "He's important. He's the coroner of this county."

"Whew!" Crane took a piece of toast from the tray. "I hope he doesn't have to look at me."

"You said somethin'." Maria became slate colored. "I don't want no white man messin' with this corpse." The kitchen door quivered behind her.

When he had finished breakfast, he picked up the suit and stepped out into a golden day. Under the warm sun, roses hopefully spread petals chilled by the frost of the night before. Bees, like tri-motored transport planes, kept regular schedules under the bright, envious eyes of sparrows. The air was shadowed with perfume.

Crane found Charles near the garage. He was collecting apples which had fallen in the coarse grass under the orchard of six trees that pressed against the far wall of the estate. He had no coat on, and his skin, under the open collar of his shirt, was tan and finely textured.

Crane held out the trousers and said, "Do you suppose you could touch these up a little for me? I fell in them." As Charles looked dubious, he hurriedly added, "I don't care about anything except the spots on the knees and elbows. If you could . . . ?" He produced a five-dollar bill.

Charles smiled and reached for the clothes. "I won't charge you anything," he said, looking at the bill.

William Crane said, "If you can get me another bottle of that poison, I'll give you two of these." Charles nodded and accepted the bill. "I'll bring the stuff with the suit."

"When?"

"In about an hour."

Crane toed an apple, stooped and picked it up. It was red, with a tiny cluster of yellow specks on one side. It was firm between his teeth, and spicy sweet.

Charles said, "The frost did 'em a lot of good."

Crane smacked his lips. "You bet." He took another bite. "What do you think about all this trouble here?" Sweet juice ran down his throat from the pressure of his teeth.

"I couldn't tell you," said Charles. He shifted the clothes to his left arm and gestured with his right. "I wish I was out of here. That sheriff couldn't catch the smallpox. Before he knows it, everybody'll be dead." He moved toward the servants' house. "The smart thing to do is to stay inside at night."

Crane said, "I guess you're right."

Charles paused. "Every time that L'Adam gets loose, it gives me the willies." He leaned slightly toward William Crane. "You know I think he has some way of getting out of there whenever he wants."

"Why don't you tell the sheriff?"

Charles was on his way again. "An' get canned?" he asked over his shoulder. He walked rapidly to the house, disappeared inside.

Crane's nose got juice on it when he took his next bite from the apple, and he rubbed it with his arm. He picked up two more apples and put them in his coat pockets. Over by the front gate there seemed to be something happening. By the heavy iron grille a group had gathered, and through the firm aromatic air there came the sounds of conversation. He strolled over to the gate, making a circuit so that he passed the fountain and the pool. The stream of water, which rose about eight feet before it scattered into spray, came from a pipe jutting out of a cairn of rocks in the center of the circular basin. Fish moved skittishly as his shadow darkened the water.

Just outside the partially opened gate stood a man whom he recognized as a manifestation of Mr. Williams, the electrician. His face was clean, this time, and bloodless with rage. His jaw was thrust out, his arms waved; he had just finished a short speech. He had on golf knickers, and a large black camera hung from a strap around his neck.

Facing him like an angry bull was Dr. Eastman. "Get out," he said. "I don't give a damn who you are. Get out and stay out."

A small man standing behind Mr. Williams spoke eagerly. "But, Doctor, don't you see how it will appear to the public?" He had a black mustache. He was Tom Burns, and he was the one Mr. Williams had mentioned as camping with him on the hill.

Dr. Eastman roared, "No! Get out!" He tried to close the gate, but Mr. Williams put a brown shoe against it.

"What's all this?" Sheriff Walters pushed past William Crane. With him was the angular coroner. "What's the matter?" the sheriff demanded. The coroner had a soft black hat and a hooked nose and gold teeth and a large Adam's apple.

Mr. Williams's dissolute face assumed an expression of innocence. He said, "We're from the *Mirror*. We'd like to get some pictures and find out what's going on here."

Sheriff Walters crossed his arms. "I have nothing for you now." He nodded deferentially to the tall coroner. "Coroner Benbow and I are investigating. I can promise you speedy developments."

"Nuts," said Mr. Williams. "We want some stuff now."

The sheriff lost some of his poise. "You can't have it," he said shortly.

Mr. Burns's short figure thrust its way past Dr. Eastman. "So," he said. "You're going to keep off the press?" He sounded as though he were reading Shakespeare. "How'll it look to have a front-page story saying, 'Sheriff Walters and Coroner Benbow baffled. Helpless in the face of supercriminal. Citizens urge they be recalled.'"

Sheriff Walters was about to retort when the coroner put a hand on his arm. "Maybe he's right," he said. "It won't hurt to tell them what we know. They'll find out anyway." He stared commandingly at Dr. Eastman. "Open that gate." It did not matter that the gate was already open.

Dr. Eastman's face twitched. His brows met above

his nose. "This is an outrage," he said to the sheriff. "Publicity will ruin our medical standing."

Mr. Williams was already fidgeting with the black box. "You'll get plenty of publicity anyway." He wound up a screw at the right-hand side of the camera and pulled down the front and slid out the bellows along the nickel rails. "If you gentlemen would mind standing a little closer . . . ?"

"Certainly not." The coroner adjusted his tie with agitated hands. "Not if you think——"

A large fly, puppy-like in the warm sun, blundered about the black camera. Mr. Williams aimed a terrific blow at it. "The public will be eager to see who has charge of . . ." He snorted violently. "Get the hell out of here!" The camera jerked against the strap, and Mr. Williams made indignant motions in the air. The fly ridiculously and fatly spiraled up to safety. Mr. Williams continued: ". . . such competent law-enforcing officials."

His brown teeth fixed in a smile, and his hat held against his chest, Coroner Benbow posed for his photograph. Beside him, a stern silent man of the law, stood the sheriff. Mr. Williams got off at a distance and peered at them through the glazed glass in the box.

"Don't you use one of them wooden stands?" asked Coroner Benbow. He spoke through his teeth without disturbing his smile. "I should think it would jiggle."

Mr. Burns laughed easily. "Not him," he said. "No tripod. For an ordinary photographer, yes. But not for him. He don't need any help." He twisted his neatly waxed mustache. "He's the best photographer the *News* ever had."

Suspicion flecked the sheriff's blue eyes. "I thought you said you was from the *Mirror?*" He started to turn but thought better of it.

"I did." Mr. Burns had a slight difficulty with his throat. "But Phil here used to be the ace photog for the *News* before he came over to us." Mr. Burns laughed easily. "He's been on some of the biggest stories—the Lindbergh kidnaping, the Starr Faithful . . ."

"What difference does it make whether they're from the *News* or from the *Mirror?*" Coroner Benbow asked testily. "Go ahead and shoot."

Mr. Williams took a last hasty look through the plate glass, closed the back of the camera, and pressed a small spring. There was a surprisingly loud click. Mr. Williams held out his left hand, palm forward, and said, "Gentlemen, one more, please. Hold your positions, please."

Again the camera clicked. Sheriff Walters stepped away stiffly, as though he had a leg asleep. Coroner Benbow relaxed his face and said, "C. H. Benbow. That's my name. I wish you'd put in that I'm also head of the Benbow Mortuary Service in Torytown." Surprisingly, his Adam's apple quivered, and he giggled. "Business is pretty dead, you know." He jackknifed, slapped his knee.

Tom Burns laughed heartily too. "I'd like to ask the pair of you a few questions," he said. The three moved together by the gate, and the driver and Deputy Powers drifted toward the office. Dr. Eastman held his ground.

Occupied in closing his camera, Mr. Williams didn't seem to have seen William Crane until he had come quite close to him. "Which way is town from here?" he asked suddenly. He spoke in a loud tone of voice.

Crane walked a few steps further from the gate. He pointed an arm in the general direction of Torytown. "I didn't know you could use a camera," he said softly.

"I can't," Mr. Williams said. He carefully kept his voice low. "I didn't have any films in it." He leered at William Crane. "A dame wrote that letter to you." He handed the camera to Crane. "Hold this. When I take it back, grab this bottle from my hand. The Colonel found perfume on the letter, checked the smell and bought a bottle like it for you. All you got to do is to find out who has the same kind here."

"The Colonel's too smart," William Crane said bitterly. "He ought to be here with these monkeys and get smashed around a couple of times; then he wouldn't know so much."

Mr. Williams looked anxiously around. "Boy, he should hear you . . ." His eyes were alarmed. "You shouldn't talk that way." He took the camera back to Crane and slipped a vial in his hand. "Here's the letter, too. No prints on it. Now about that other fellow, the one with his prints on the glass. He's a small timer, sent up for two years on a con rap. He gypped a dame out of three grand with some phony stock. Used to be a vaudeville actor before that, juggled balls, tossed knives, shot things with a pistol, and did a little sleight of hand. Had a reputation as a heart-breaker. That's all we could get on him."

"O. K."

"Look here, kid." Mr. Williams affectionately regarded Crane. "If you get in any jams, you know how to signal us. We'll be down in a couple of shakes." Mr. Williams affixed the camera to the strap. "The Colonel says to hurry up. He says you should have finished a couple of days ago."

"Nuts to the Colonel," said Crane. "It was his idea to have me come up here as a patient, and now he can wait until I get through."

Mr. Williams paled. "I don't want any part of you when you talk like that," he said vehemently. "The Colonel's a smart man."

"Sure," said Crane. "He's so smart he can get one of his employees killed every time he sends him on a job."

Mr. Williams eyed him dubiously. "If it's as bad as that, the Colonel can get somebody——"

"Never mind," Crane said hastily. "I can take it."

"I can see that." Mr. Williams leered good-naturedly at him. "Mostly on your face." He moved closer. "Any more of that panther spit around?"

"Not a drop. The panther died."

"Oh, yeah?" Mr. Williams winked without moving a muscle in the rest of his face. "Well, so long." Abruptly, he swung about.

"So long," said William Crane. He moved slowly toward the guest house. From the front steps just inside of the shade thrown by the roof, he watched his friends shake hands with the sheriff and the coroner, climb into a car, and drive up the dirt road. Dust from the wheels flurried upward in tiny explosions and drifted diagonally upon the garden, covering green leaves with a film that glowed in the sunlight.

On his way upstairs he nearly bumped into Richardson.

"Where's Mrs. Heyworth?" Richardson blocked his way. His face was pouty mad. "What did you do with her?"

Alarm unsettled Crane's stomach. He wondered if Richardson knew about the night episode. "What do you mean?" he demanded.

"She went out a few minutes ago, I think to meet

you." He bulked above Crane. "She hasn't come back."

"I haven't seen her." Crane sidestepped and moved up two stairs, so that he was even with Richardson. "I've been standing by the front gate."

"If anything happened . . ." Richardson trembled in fierce uncertainty. "If you hurt her . . . I'll beat you within an inch of your life."

"Let me know when you decide to start," Crane said. He went to his room, feeling things were very unpleasant and wishing Charles would come with the bottle.

Once inside, with the door locked behind him, he took out the vial of perfume and poured a few drops on a clean handkerchief. This he waved in the air twice before he held it to his nose. It did not surprise him to find that it smelled like Miss Evans. He felt it would not surprise him to learn that she had written the letter at the dictation of Dr. Eastman.

He went to the north window in his room. Vivid in the sun, the garden looked like a gaudy foreign post-card. Green was so fresh on grass and yellow and green on leaves that it seemed as though the paint was still damp. A line of gladiolus in a bed were an unreal pink-coated company of infantry. Below the window there were broken bushes and scattered twigs where he had fallen. It looked an appalling distance in the daylight.

Feet crunched on the gravel path, and he saw Richardson and Mrs. Heyworth, arms linked, coming toward the house. Richardson was saying something to which Mrs. Heyworth listened intently. Her face was tan and lovely, and there was in her eyes, even at a distance, a melting softness. She glanced upward, and William Crane ducked from the window and returned to the bed. There was a knock on his door.

Charles's skin showed palely in the dark hall. He had the suit over his arm. He came inside, closed the door. "Here you are," he said. He put a quart of liquor on the bed. William Crane took the suit from him. It smelled strongly of naphtha, but there was no dirt on the elbows or the knees, and it had been pressed. He hung it in the closet and gave Charles another five-dollar bill. "Want a drink?" he asked.

"Not now," said Charles. He was polite about it. "I've got to see Dr. Livermore. If he smells anything, he'll fire me."

"Would that be so bad?"

"Jobs are hard to get now."

Crane pulled the cork out of the bottle. "Did you tell me what you were sent up for?" he asked. The liquor smelled good.

Charles's face was composed. "I didn't, but I don't mind." He paused for a second, fingering the top button on his white coat. "It's a funny business. I was going around with a woman, and I liked her pretty well. She liked me too. I was broke, and she wanted to give me some money. I didn't want to take her money as a gift, but I needed it. I had some oil stock that I bought, so I said to her: 'This is probably no good, but I'll give it to you as security for the money. Then you can give it back when I pay you.'" Charles was speaking tonelessly. "That was all right with her until we had a quarrel. Then she had me arrested for operating a confidence game, and they gave me two years for it."

The bottle was still in Crane's hand. "That's tough," he said. "It ought to teach you never to get mixed up with women."

"I haven't since I got out of jail," Charles said. He looked appealingly at William Crane. "You won't tell the sheriff about this? He's liable to arrest me on suspicion, and I'd lose my job."

"He's too dumb to arrest anybody," Crane said, "but you don't need to worry."

"Thanks." Charles opened the door. "If you want any more of that—cleaning fluid, just let me know."

As the door closed, Crane secured a glass from the dresser. He had a drink. He refilled the glass and sat down on the bed to think about the murders. He finished the glass and placed it on the floor, and lay down so as to be able to think better. Presently he fell asleep.

Chapter XVII

5:45 P. M.

When Crane awoke a serene dusk filled the room. It was late afternoon; only a line of flushed clouds showed that there was still a sun. The chill of night was arriving leisurely but unmistakably. Swinging out of the bed, Crane kicked over the empty glass on the floor. It did not break, and he put it on the white strip of linen running across the dresser top. He took off his shirt, doused his head in the wash basin, looked at the bruises on his face unfavorably, and dried himself. Then he put on a clean white shirt and his tweed coat and opened his door. He went back and had a drink and then hid the bottle of applejack in the closet.

Dishes and silverware were clinking in the dining room when he came downstairs. It was Maria. She was setting the table. She displayed an incredible number of gold teeth. "Mistah Crane," she said, "you is a sleepingest man I ever seen."

William Crane tried a green olive. "Dinner about ready?" The olive was good. It made him think of a Martini.

"It won't take more than fifteen minutes, Mistah Crane."

"Where is everybody?"

Maria pulled open a drawer in the walnut highboy and brought out a handful of napkins. "I think they is out in the garden." She placed one of the napkins at Dr. Livermore's place. "The coroner's gone to Torytown. I reckon he'll be back tomorrow."

The celery was crisp and fresh. He shook some salt on the part of the stalk he hadn't eaten. "Maria," he said, "who cleans Miss Evans' room?"

A brown hand held a napkin suspended over Miss Van Kamp's place at the table. "Why, I does. Has there been any complaints?"

"You always clean it?"

"Yes sir! I'm the only one that has ever cleaned it since she come here."

"Nobody else go in there?"

"No sir! She's mighty particular. I's the only one."

The ripe olives were a trifle soft, but he ate three, anyway. "Good," he said. "You can tell me if you've ever seen anything funny in the room."

"Funny?" Maria's dark face was puzzled.

"Has she got a typewriter? Somebody wrote me a note, and I think it might have been her."

"No, she hasn't got a writin' machine. Both the doctors have, though. I mean Dr. Livermore and Dr. Eastman."

"Hmm." William Crane nodded his head impressively. "Ever see anything unusual in her room?"

"No sir. Nothing unusual."

"Where does she keep her victrola?"

"Oh, she keeps that in her closet. On the top shelf. She don't hardly ever use it."

"Why not?"

"I don't know, unless'n it's cause she's got a radio."

"What kind of a radio?"

"One of those portable kind. Just a little one. But it sure plays swell."

"You don't play it while you're cleaning up, do you?" He waved his celery sternly. "You don't play it?"

Maria rolled her eyes wildly. "Just once in a while, Mr. Crane. Just a little, so as not to hurt anything."

Crane abruptly stuck the celery in his mouth.

"You won't tell on me, will you, Mistah Crane?" said Maria. "She'd be awful mad."

As soon as he was able to speak, Crane said, "Your secret is as safe with me, Maria, as if it were buried deep in the unfathomable tombs of the lost kingdom of Atlantis."

Maria opened her mouth, said, "Yes sir." She backed toward the kitchen. She had forgotten to put a napkin at Miss Queen's place.

Crane went outside. There was still enough light to see, but everything appeared soft and hazy and smoky.

The air, too, smelt of smoke, and he drew in long breaths as he walked to the garage.

Halting in front of the sliding door, which was partially open, he listened intently. There was the sound of voices inside the ambulance. An empty bucket stood at the corner of the building, and this he kicked over against the wall. A tousled head appeared out of the back door of the ambulance and scowled at him. It was the driver. "What in hell do you want?" he demanded.

"Nothing," Crane said calmly.

"Then get the hell out of here."

"I like it here." Crane put his hands in his pockets and leaned against the door. "It's nice here."

"You get the hell out of here!"

"Oh no." Crane's voice was small. "You see, I like it here."

The driver shoved shoulders and chest through the door. "I'm coming down there and beat the ears off you."

Crane pulled his right hand out of his pocket and scratched his shoulder. "You going to do this in front of Miss Twilliger?" he asked mildly.

Anger suffused the driver's face, turning it purple in irregular splotches. "You leave her name out of this." Crane saw he was drunk.

A hand appeared from behind the driver, fastened tenderly onto his throat, and jerked him back into the ambulance. "Yes, you leave me out of this." Miss

Twilliger appeared in the opening. She blinked at Crane. Her hair and her clothes were extremely disarrayed.

"Aren't you losing something?" Crane asked.

Miss Twilliger hurriedly tucked her brassiere under her dress and fastened two buttons near her neck. "Get out of here," she said. "You're nothing but a moron."

"Why, Miss Twilliger!"

Miss Twilliger took such a deep breath that her small eyes protruded from their sockets. She opened her mouth. She said, "You're a zany." She withdrew abruptly.

Crane heard the sounds of violent movement within the ambulance. "I'll clout him with this crank here," said the voice of the driver. There was a banging of pieces of metal on wood. "This wrench is heavier," Miss Twilliger's voice suggested. Crane hurriedly made his way into the orchard, and from the obscurity of the last tree he stood and watched the garage.

Presently the two of them came out. The driver moved his feet highly, like a spirited horse. In one hand he had the crank and in the other he carried his shoes. They were quickly blacked out by the falling night.

Crane hurried to the garage and climbed into the ambulance. It smelled of powder and cheap perfume and whisky and cigar smoke. On the front floor board was a litter of tools, and from these he selected a pair of pliers, a monkey wrench, and a hammer. He distributed the tools about his person, slipping the hammer handle down under his belt.

On his way up the front steps of the guest house he met Dr. Livermore, who said, "Nice night." Crane, passing, agreed: "Lovely." He went to his room and shoved the tools under the bed and had a drink.

7:45 P. M.

After dinner Crane went back to his room and got the perfumed note. The sheriff had appeared with a clean shirt for dinner, and he was now questioning all three of the doctors in the living room. Crane slipped out of the guest house unnoticed and made his way to the hospital building. He saw a man watching the front gate, but he was too far away to be recognized. He walked into the hospital building and down the hall and into Dr. Eastman's room. There was a typewriter on the table. The black rubberized cover caught for a second and then jerked free of the space lever. William Crane opened the drawer, took out a sheet of white letter paper, and wrote:

" The quick brown fox jumped over the lazy dog."

He compared what he had written with the perfumed note, and he had found several letters quite similar when Miss Evans came into the room.

"Well," she said, "are you taking up housebreaking now?"

William Crane stood up abruptly, but she did not seem frightened. Her pallid skin made her lips scarlet. He thrust the note he had received at her and demanded, "Why did you write this?"

As she read the note, Miss Evans's breasts moved evenly with her breathing. She looked wonderingly at him. "I never saw it before. You don't think I would . . ."

"I'm liable to think *anything*. But this time I know. You wrote that."

"What makes you think you know?" Miss Evans tossed the note on the table with a graceful turn of her wrist. "You think you know everything."

"You didn't wear gloves when you wrote it, did you?"

Miss Evans's eyes narrowed in quick apprehension. She said, "Fingerprints! You didn't show it to the sheriff?"

He took the note, folded it. "Look here, we've played ball so far," he said: "why don't you come clean?"

"How'd you know there were prints on it?"

"All it takes is a little powder and a magnifying glass."

"But how did you get mine?"

He smiled triumphantly. "From your radio. It was covered with them."

"So you've been in my room, too." Miss Evans's voice sounded like a phonograph becoming unwound.

It got deeper and deeper. "But you didn't find anything there to interest you, did you?"

"Not a thing besides some silk whachamacallems." This was pretty safe, as everybody, even Miss Evans, Crane felt, occasionally wore something under a dress. "They were pretty nice, though."

"Sometime I'll walk over you in my bare feet," said Miss Evans. "It's more fun that way."

William Crane ignored this. He said, "Are you going to come clean, or am I going to have to show this to the sheriff?" He held out the note.

Miss Evans was a scornful Max Reinhardt saint. "It won't do any good to tell the sheriff, but I don't mind saying that I did write the letter. My fiancé, Dr. Eastman, dictated it to me on this typewriter. He thought you came here as a bodyguard of Dr. Livermore, just like that man Joe. He was afraid you would do him harm."

"So he tried to harm me first?"

Miss Evans did not bother to nod. She left the room, her hips provocative and fluid.

8:20 P. M.

In the moonlight William Crane climbed the front steps of the guest house. There was a froufrou of garments, and Miss Queen glided over to him and grasped his hand. Her dark hair hung over her shoulders.

"Oh, Mr. Crane!" she said. Her fingers had no warmth in them. "I'm so frightened! You must save me."

"Why, Miss Queen!" Crane removed her hands. "What's the matter?"

"It's this place. I feel death all around. It's hovering over everything. It's terrible—terrible!"

In the distance there was the mocking call of a night bird, detached and impersonal and brooding.

4:20 A. M.

William Crane wished he had a watch, but he judged it to be well past three o'clock. He had been lying down fully dressed, and he got up, made sure the door was locked, and then pulled the sheets off the bed. The sheriff had again posted Cliff in the hall for the night. He partially filled the bathtub, soaked the sheets, squeezed them out, and knotted them. Sliding the bed over to the north window, he hooked the knot under one leg, allowing the two ends of cloth to hang out.

From under the bed he got the tools he had taken from the ambulance. He put the wrench and the pliers in his pocket and again tucked the hammer in his belt. From the closet he took out the Roman candle, and from his dresser a packet of matches. He resisted an impulse to take a drink.

Drops of water oozed between his fingers as he carefully lowered himself on the sheets. The sky was misty now, and the moon shone as through hospital gauze. Between his teeth the Roman candle tasted of gunpowder. Reaching the end of the sheet, he dropped five feet to the soft earth. Still damp and stringy, the sheet was hardly visible against the stucco wall of the building.

The garden smelled nice and clean and faintly perfumed. He stepped cautiously across patterned beds until he came to the edge of the pool. Goldfish and carp shied frantically as he bent over the water. His face was reflected obscurely on the surface, and nearer the center, where the white spray of the fountain descended, the moon was mirrored in futuristic angles.

He put the Roman candle on the grass, removed his shoes and socks, rolled up his trousers, and stepped into the pool. The water was cool and came up to his knees. Ripples clung to his skin as he waded out toward the cairn of rock around the fountain. A piece of pipe jutted up from the rock, and out of this flowed the water. There was a bolt about a foot from the end, and on this were fresh metal scrapings. He tried to turn it with his pliers, but it was too large to grasp. He was fitting the wrench to the bolt when there was a sound of feet on the other side of the pool.

"Who's there?" a male voice called.

It sounded like one of the deputies, but Crane wasn't sure. Splashing protesting waves of water up to his waist, he galloped to where he had left the Roman

candle. A shot sent up a silver geyser of spray beside
him and the report echoed crazily among the buildings.
He crawled out of the pool, snatched up the candle, and
started for the guest house. He was running cleanly
when a figure rose out of the bushes five yards ahead
and pointed an arm at him.

He swerved to the right; desperately put on speed.

Five times the gun barked in scarlet laughter. In the
silence that followed, Crane's feet pounded on the
ground. He headed for the servants' house.

"There he goes, men." It was the sheriff's voice.
"Shoot the bastard."

Another pistol coughed hoarsely, and Crane heard
lead hiss over his head. He rounded the corner of the
servants' house and halted by the wall that ran behind
the apple orchard. He remembered the glass on the top
of the wall. The sheriff was gathering his men in the
garden.

Crane saw that they had lost sight of him, and he
took the Roman candle from between his teeth and
stuck it in the ground. He shielded a match with his
body and lit the fuse. There was an angry splutter of
powder. He ran toward the garage, jerked the heavy
sliding door across the front until only a small opening
was left, and then leaned against the friendly wood,
gasping for air. There was a smell of grease and gasoline.
Through the opening he could see the sheriff and his
men coming slowly through the garden.

A shower of golden sparks arose in the orchard, lighting clouds of blue smoke. The sheriff and his men halted and let go a nervous barrage of shots.

"It's a bomb," shouted the sheriff. "Quick, boys, we gotta get it."

He and Deputy Powers advanced courageously upon the spouting stick and bent over it. Their faces were illuminated in the flickering light. Suddenly the Roman candle spat like a cat, and a brilliant blue star struck the sheriff's neck and exploded with a terrific report. Part of the weird blue flame enveloped Deputy Powers's face. He screamed, fell over backwards. Dr. Livermore and Dr. Eastman ran to him, lifted him between them, and started back to the hospital. Deputy Powers was still screaming. Sheriff Walters tottered after them.

The two remaining members of the party had seen Crane outlined against the garage door, and from behind shrubs they potted at him. They shot more deliberately, and the bullets tapped on the sides of the garage and sliced splinters off the wooden door. The candle was still burning, and the sky was filled with noise and bursting stars and colored balls of light. There was also a strong smell of sulphur and gunpowder, and a pall of smoke curtained the garden. While Crane watched, two more blue stars emerged, and then the candle quivered, shook itself, and cast out a red ball of stupendous size. This soared high into the night and suddenly vanished in yellow flame. After several seconds the garage door rattled, and there was a tinkle of glass in the guest house. The sky was split by a thunderclap of an explosion. A woman shrieked thinly, and then there was no more noise.

In the mask silence put on the night, Crane climbed into the front seat of the ambulance. The timid light of a match showed him that the key was in place. He had switched on the ignition when a voice called:

"Bill? Are you all right?"

It was Williams. Crane turned off the ignition and walked out of the garage.

"I was afraid you weren't coming," he said.

Two men were with Williams. One was Tom Burns. He introduced the other. "This is Sergeant Wilson of the State Police. He was having a bite to eat with us when we heard your signal."

Crane asked, "What did you do with those smart boys with the pistols?"

"They'll be along with the sheriff in a minute," Sergeant Wilson said. "What the hell has been happening here?"

William Crane told him.

5 A.M.

"I don't care," said the sheriff stubbornly. "He may be a private detective, but I don't think he's got a clean bill of health." He looked belligerently at Crane. His neck was stiff with gauze. "He certainly stepped right into our trap. Everyone was supposed to be in their rooms, and naturally whoever went out was certainly the guilty party."

Williams raised himself on his toes and pounded the palm of his left hand with his fist. "I suppose he did all of this so he could turn himself in and get a reward?"

"I don't care," Sheriff Walters said. "I don't see why he won't tell us what he knows. He hasn't any right to raise hell like this. He might have killed somebody. If I can't lock him up, I'm going to send somebody up to watch his room."

"You're a wrinkled-faced fool," said Williams.

"See here," said the sheriff. "Nobody can talk to me like that."

"You'll be lucky if you don't have to go to jail yourself," Sergeant Wilson said. He was almost as short and broad as the sheriff, but he was younger. His face was fresh and red and a little heavy at the jowls. He wore a blue uniform with a black Sam Browne belt. His shirt was clean. "Don't you know enough to notify State Headquarters when there's a murder?"

"I was going to——"

"You wanted to see if you could figure this out yourself," said the sergeant. "That's what they all do." His voice was unfriendly. "I'll take a look around in the morning, and then I'll make a report."

"Listen," said Crane. "I'm tired. I'm going to bed. But I think I'll have something for you this afternoon when I get up. Could you have everybody in the living room about three o'clock?"

"Sure," said Sergeant Wilson. "We'll have 'em."

Crane went upstairs.

5:15 A.M.

William Crane had just put on his pajamas, when there was a knock at his door.

"Maybe you'd better leave it open a little," Deputy Graham said apologetically. "I'm supposed to watch you."

"O.K." Crane pulled the spread off the bed. "How's the fellow the Roman candle hit?"

"That was Tom Powers. He's just burned a little. They say he'll be all right in a couple of days. Them things are certainly handy to have around. They're better than a revolver any day."

"Have a drink?" Crane held up the bottle. The deputy shook his head. "Mind if I do?"

The deputy said, "Not a bit."

The liquor tasted strong but good.

Chapter XVIII

IT WAS LIKE the grand finale of a musical comedy, in the living room. Everybody, with the exception of Mr. L'Adam, was there when William Crane and the faithful Deputy Graham walked into the room. Crane slouched to the long table with the magazines and sat down on it, smothering a yawn with his left hand. It was past mid-afternoon, and because of an uncertain drizzle the day was already on the dark side.

Sheriff Walters eyed Crane from the chair. "You've got some explaining to do," he said. "If it wasn't for these friends of yours, I'd toss you in jail and let you do your talking in court." There was a crust of dirt on his bandaged neck.

The patients and the doctors were grouped in front of the brightly burning fireplace, while the guards and the two nurses stood by the door to the dining room.

"Look here," Crane said. "Can't you wait until tomorrow?" He rubbed his nose. "I'm not altogether straight on this thing yet. Maybe you have an idea?"

Sheriff Walters snorted. "You're my idea, and you can start talkin' right now. You won't be here to-morrow."

"All right." Crane spoke wearily. "I'll talk. He looked at Sergeant Wilson, who was standing by a window with Mr. Williams and Tom Burns. "You got any ideas?"

The sergeant's puffy red face was apologetic. "This is a little out of my line. I might——"

"Never mind," Crane said. He motioned vaguely to the door. "Mr. Williams, will you and Mr. Burns stand there?" While they were crossing the room, he turned to Sheriff Walters. "Have you a monkey wrench in your car?"

"I don't know. I guess so."

"Would you mind having someone get it?"

Cliff Walters, who had been standing beside his father, was sent for the wrench. Deputy Powers stepped in his place. His face was all bandages, with dark slits for eyes and mouth.

At the other end of the room Dr. Livermore stood up and asked: "Where's all this mummery going to get us?" He nervously rubbed his long hands together.

Windowpanes shook in a sudden wind, and a puff of smoke backed out of the fireplace. "Sit down," said William Crane, "and shut up." He noticed that Joe Kassuccio was beside Dr. Livermore. The man's nose was still bandaged, and his eyes were disagreeable.

"Where's Mr. L'Adam?" Crane asked.

Dr. Buelow said, "He was so strange that I decided it was best to leave him locked up. I can get him if——"

"Don't bother as long as—" William Crane caught Charles's eye; Charles shook his head—"you're sure he can't get out."

"I'm quite sure. He's in a new room, one with a double lock on the door."

The screen door slammed. "Here's your wrench," said Cliff. His voice was respectful. Crane did not take it from him. He said, "Will you and Sergeant Wilson go out and turn off the fountain and let the pool drain? Under the stones in the center you will find a box. It'll probably be wrapped in oilskins. Bring it in."

"O.K.," said Cliff.

Crane paused until they had gone. "Do you mind if we wait until the box comes?" he asked the sheriff.

The sheriff grunted.

Against the windowpanes the wind rattled as though somebody outside were trying to attract their attention. Rain sifted through the chimney and hissed on hot coals. It was much darker.

"I don't suppose anybody would like to say what's in that box?" Crane asked. "I know some of you have seen it." He glanced at Dr. Livermore. "Are you still sure it's full of old papers, old newspapers?"

A quick fit of coughing shook Dr. Livermore's beard. "I merely said that when Miss Van Kamp showed it to me it was full of old newspapers. Dr. Eastman will tell you——"

Dr. Eastman said, "I never saw the box in my life." His unshaven blue face scowled over Miss Evans's shoulder. "I was told that it was full of papers."

Speculatively, Sheriff Walters observed the two doctors. "That wasn't what you two said at dinner. Dr. Eastman, you said you had seen it too."

"You must have misunderstood me," Dr. Eastman said. "I only said——"

Crane interrupted him. "Never mind. Wait until they come back."

Miss Van Kamp was sitting on the couch with Miss Queen and Mrs. Brady. Her fingers moved quickly with her knitting. She was nearly through with the shawl. "It will be full of bonds," she said reflectively. "My nice bonds."

Bending down in front of the fire, Charles lifted a fresh log and threw it deep on the andirons. Red and écru flames raced up the chimney.

"How do you know that box will be in the pool?" asked Richardson. He was seated on the arm of Mrs. Heyworth's chair. She had not looked at Crane once since he had come in the room. "Did you put it there?"

Crane said, "I don't know it's there; I just think so." Mrs. Heyworth's luminous brown eyes were lovely in the firelight. "Mr. Penny and I both came to that conclusion."

"Why?" Richardson asked.

"The first night I was here somebody turned off the fountain. It was stopped for nearly half an hour." Crane grinned at Mr. Penny, who was seated beside Blackwood on a carved wooden bench which had been pulled out from the wall beside the fireplace. "Why would anybody shut off the fountain at night?"

Sheriff Walters was becoming interested. "I don't know," he said. "Why would they?"

"They'd shut it off to drain the pool," said Crane. "And the only reason they'd want to drain the pool is to hide something there. The only thing anybody'd want to hide around here is Miss Van Kamp's strong box."

"That sounds reasonable." Sheriff Walters reached under his coat and scratched his ribs. "Who hid it there?"

"I'd like to see the box before I'd say," Crane replied.

It was dark now, and colder. Charles and the driver snapped on some of the lights. At the north end of the living room, just within the sliding doors to the dining room, the two colored women, eyes and teeth white in the gloom, were perched on straight chairs. Miss Twilliger caught Crane's glance, snorted audibly and contemptuously.

Presently Cliff and the sergeant came out of the rain. Water ran in rivulets from their hats and down their coats. Cliff handed an object wrapped in yellow oilskin to William Crane, who passed it on to the sheriff. "Open it," he said.

While the sheriff's thick fingers clumsily unwound the parcel, the old guard pushed his way to the front. He exclaimed, "Why, that there is my slicker!" His wrinkled face was surprised and interested.

Crane demanded, "How'd it get there?"

"Verily, I don't know." The old man's hands were veined and trembling. "It was taken from me pretty nigh a week ago. I bin lookin' for it."

"We'll give it back to you in a few minutes," said William Crane. He saw that the sheriff had the box opened. "What's in it?"

"Gosh!" Sheriff Walters fingered the box reverently. "It's full of bonds." He held up a neatly wrapped package. "Must be a million dollars' worth. Here's a key, too."

Miss Van Kamp did not miss a stroke of her knitting. "They're mine," she said placidly. "They're all mine." Her wrists were busy, and the green ball of wool made convulsive jumps in the wicker basket on her lap. "I'm going to put them with my other bonds in New York."

"You'd better," said Crane.

Sheriff Walters closed the box and put it under his arm. "Who stole it?" he asked.

"You'll grant we have a motive in the box, won't you?" said Crane.

Sheriff Walters nodded vigorously. "I admit you are right there. A lot of people would like to have some of this dough."

Crane said, "That's just why Dr. Livermore took the box from Miss Van Kamp in the first place."

Nothing moved about Dr. Livermore except his nervous fingers. He began, "I didn't——"

William Crane cut him off with a wave. "You took the box to your room. You told Miss Evans about it. I know because she told me." Dr. Livermore turned a stricken face toward Miss Evans. "But I'm not the only one she told," Crane continued. "She told Dr. Eastman about it." Dr. Livermore's pale eyes were fixed upon Miss Evans. They were red along the rims.

Crane said, "So Dr. Eastman took the box from you."

"What makes you think I had the box?" Dr. Eastman stepped around Miss Evans. His hand lingered on her arm. "You'd better be careful."

"Miss Evans again," said William Crane.

"You can't prove that."

"I can prove through Miss Evans you wrote me this letter." Crane handed the note to the sheriff. "You dictated it to her on your typewriter. And the letter tells about the box."

Dr. Eastman glared at Miss Evans. "I couldn't help it," she said. Her face was composed. "My fingerprints were on it."

Having finished reading the letter, Sheriff Walters said, "Now we're gettin' somewhere." His eyes gauged Dr. Eastman's strength. "What did this guy do, hide it in the fountain?"

"No," William Crane said. "Somebody else stole it from him." He put the palms of his hands on the table and slid himself back so that his feet were clear of the floor. "It's pretty involved." He crossed his legs. "Am I right so far, Dr. Eastman?"

"You've made some damn good guesses." Dr. Eastman chewed his thick lower lip. "I did take the box from Dr. Livermore's room. It didn't belong to him, anyway. Then somebody got it from me."

"Miss Evans helped you get it, didn't she?" asked William Crane. Dr. Eastman nodded. "And then you repaid her by not telling her about the eight hundred thousand dollars' worth of cash and bonds in Miss Van Kamp's vault. Were you going to double-cross her?"

Dr. Eastman's mouth opened slightly. "Why, I told her everything." His eyes blinked wonderingly at Miss Evans.

"Oh!"

Sheriff Walters asked, "What's this got to do with the fountain and the murders?"

"Wait a minute." Crane spoke thoughtfully. "What were you digging for in the garden that night I was running around in my pajamas, Dr. Livermore?"

"Miss Evans had an idea that whoever had taken the box from me had buried it somewhere. I found some signs of recent digging in the garden, and I thought that might be the place."

"You suspected Dr. Eastman, didn't you?"

"I thought of him."

"You thought you could force him to give it back, didn't you? That's why you had that gangster come up from New York."

Dr. Livermore's beard moved sorrowfully up and down and he said, "I might have had some such idea in mind."

"You also wanted to scare Dr. Eastman away from Miss Evans, didn't you?"

Dr. Eastman squared his shoulders. "Leave her name out of this."

"Sure," said Crane. "It's like trying to write a history of Egypt without mentioning Cleopatra." He leaned one elbow upon the table and looked at the old guard. "Why were you digging?"

The old man's blue eyes were startled. He shook his white head. "I heard Dr. Livermore say it was buried in the garden." He mumbled his words. "I knew God would want me to find it."

"What do you mean—'it'?"

"The lost words of the Lord. I know they are around

here somewhere." He shook with excitement. "They're wrote on tablets of gold."

"Nuts," said the sheriff. "Let's get on with our business."

Crane uncrossed his legs, admired his brown shoes. "I'll tell you why the murders were committed. Somebody wanted the other key to the safety-deposit vault in New York. The key that would give its possessor eight hundred thousand extra dollars. Who wouldn't murder for that?"

"Ain't that the key in the box?" asked the sheriff.

"That's one key, but it takes two to open the New York vault. The second key hangs around Miss Van Kamp's neck." Miss Van Kamp's needles continued rhythmically. "She wears it there except when she's taking a bath."

The rain hurried down the glass windows and beaded on the screens. From the eaves water dripped noisily into pools. Branches swished wetly in the wind.

"The person who stole the box from Dr. Eastman and hid it in the fountain is the one who committed the murders," William Crane continued. "He had one key, and he was looking for the other. He was looking for it when Mr. Pittsfield saw him going into Miss Van Kamp's room while we were all supposed to be at the colorama show." So savagely did the wind shake the panes that Crane was forced to pause for a moment. "The murderer strangled Mr. Pittsfield when he came in to ask him what he was doing in the room. The murderer was looking through the bureau, the next to the bottom drawer, when Mr. Pittsfield surprised him. He didn't know the key was around Miss Van Kamp's neck."

Tiny scars of flame, like cat's tongues after cream, lapped at the charred logs in the fireplace.

"Then, to cover the first murder, he was forced to kill the other two," William Crane said. "In the second and third murder, you will remember, the knives were identical. That's right, isn't it, Dr. Livermore?"

"There was a certain similarity," Dr. Livermore admitted. It was quite cool in the room, but his forehead was shiny with sweat. "It seemed that the same hand must have wielded both daggers."

Sheriff Walters said, "Yes, but who in the hell's hand is it?"

"It's cold in here," said Crane. He slipped off the table. "Charles, suppose you put another log on the fire and then tell us what made you kill all these people."

Charles had started toward the wood basket. He stopped, his eyes wide with surprise. "What do you mean?" Everyone was looking at him in astonishment. He drew a gasping breath and cried, "Why, he's crazy

I don't know anything about these things. He's trying to get himself out of a jam by fastening it on me." The rain in the bushes sounded as though somebody were wrapping bundles in tissue paper. "I'm innocent, I tell you. I swear I'm innocent."

"Never mind, Buddy." Williams was beside him. "You'll get a chance to talk later."

"I'm God-damned if I——" Sheriff Walters's face was very red. "Where does he come in this picture?"

Charles was standing, his face bloodless, with Mr. Williams on one side and Tom Burns on the other. "He stole the box on the day I got here," said Crane. "Isn't that right, Dr. Eastman?"

"I noticed it was gone that night."

Crane lifted a log out of the basket, tossed it on the fire, and stepped back to dodge the shower of sparks. "After he had taken the box, Charles found out about Miss Van Kamp's other key. Naturally, he wanted to get it from her; eight hundred thousand dollars is a lot better than four hundred thousand. He decided the key would probably be in Miss Van Kamp's room, but he needed an excuse for being in the building if anyone should happen to see him. So he took Miss Paxton's bathrobe, which he had just finished cleaning. He could say he was just returning it, if anybody asked. He went in to search the room while the patients were at the colorama show, but Mr. Pittsfield surprised him, and he strangled him with the cord on the bathrobe to save himself. That was a great mistake." The crackling young blaze was pleasant and warm on William Crane's legs. "You see, Charles is the only person who does any cleaning in the place. Miss Evans told me that."

Richardson spoke from the arm of Mrs. Heyworth's chair. "But how do you know Charles had the robe at all?"

"After Charles killed Pittsfield he realized the robe, if left on the scene, would incriminate him. So he hung it in Miss Paxton's closet, but in his excitement, he forgot the cord. That had slipped under the bed with Mr. Pittsfield's body, and that's where we found it. Naturally, knowing the cord did the murder, I was interested in the robe. I examined it in Miss Paxton's room and found the only noteworthy thing about it was a strong odor of naphtha. You couldn't miss it." Crane scratched his hair. "Poor old Miss Paxton may have realized the same thing after she found her bathrobe cord had killed Mr. Pittsfield. Anyway, Charles did. He was present when she identified the cord, and he knew sooner or later she'd remember she had given the bathrobe to him to be cleaned. So that evening, at dinner time, he crept up to her room and stabbed her to death."

Sheriff Walters raised an objecting hand. He had a paper in it. "We figured out that Charles had an alibi in the second murder," he said, consulting the paper.

"He was taking a bath at the time. Miss Evans said she saw him."

Crane asked, "Miss Evans, did you go in the bathroom with him?" She shook her blond head. Her eyes were amused and contemptuous. "You!" Crane spoke to the driver. "Isn't there a window in that bathroom?"

The driver fingered his collar. "Sure." His neck was dirty. "A big one."

"People climb out of windows," said Crane.

"But I heard the water running," interposed Miss Evans.

"You could have the water running if you didn't put the stopper all the way in and you turned the faucet up just fast enough."

"That's reasonable," Sergeant Wilson remarked to the sheriff. "It would sound just about the same, particularly if it filled up a little way."

Crane went on: "Charles climbed out of the window and came over here. He hung around outside for about half an hour before he had a chance to get in. Then he crept upstairs while we were at dinner and killed the old lady."

"Wait a minute." Sheriff Walters drew his eyebrows down in a frown. "How do you know he hung around outside?"

"We all got there a few minutes after Miss Paxton was murdered." William Crane was patient. "I touched the knife. It was very cold. It was also cold outdoors. Therefore I came to the conclusion that the knife had been outdoors for some time."

Cliff Walters's brown eyes were intelligent. "Why couldn't any of the doctors have carried in the knife and killed her?" he asked.

"There'd be no reason for them lurking around outside. They'd have a right to be in here, or in Miss Paxton's room, for that matter. Any knife they'd carry would be warm."

Charles cried, "That's all a pack of lies. I didn't——"

Williams held a fist in front of his face. He said, "Shut up. How'd you like me to shove this down your throat?"

"For a time Miss Paxton's murder seemed to cover up everything." Crane said. "Then Miss Clayton, who was Miss Paxton's nurse, got wondering about the cord. She knew the robe had been given to Charles for cleaning. So she went and asked him about it." Crane had to speak above the rumble of the wind. "So he killed her. He used the same kind of a knife, and she mentioned 'cleaning' as she died."

Dr. Buelow said, "That's right, I heard her."

"You're both mad," Charles said. His boyish face was distorted. "You could build up as good a case against anybody."

"Shut up," Williams said.

"I noticed something about the knives, too; they are

all Mexican and balanced for throwing—the kind they throw on the stage." Crane was warm now, and he moved back to the table. "Charles used to be a vaudeville actor. He did tricks, and he threw knives! That's where he got those two just alike."

"How'd you know he'd been on the stage?" asked Sheriff Walters.

"We checked up on his fingerprints."

"How'd you do that?"

"Mr. Williams here posed as an electrician. He came to fix the lights after I had put them out of order. I gave him a glass with Charles' prints on it."

Williams laid a friendly hand on Charles's arm. "We also found out this mug had been in the pen for a spell on a confidence rap," he said. "He tried to trim an old lady."

"A jailbird!" Sheriff Walters eyed Charles with disfavor. "That looks bad."

Crane brushed a spot of soot off his sleeve. "That's all I know now," he said. "Except that you ought to be grateful to us for calling you into this at all."

Sheriff Walters asked, "What do you mean?"

"It was me that gave you the tip-off on the murders up here," said Williams. "Don't you remember my delicate voice?" He laughed hoarsely.

Sheriff Walters stared from him to Crane and then back to him. His blue eyes were cloudy; his lips twitched.

"Aren't you going to lock him up?" Crane spoke gently, as to an invalid. "It might be a good idea."

Sheriff Walters rubbed his chin with his fingers. "Cliff, you go and tell Clem to get a cell ready. Use the doc's telephone." He heaved his bulk to his feet. "I'll be God-damned!"

Deputy Graham and the heavily bandaged Powers took Charles into their custody. They did not bother to slip handcuffs on him.

"I didn't do it," Charles said. His boyish face was sad; his eyes misty. "Before God, I didn't." He looked appealingly at the red face of Sheriff Walters.

In a moment Cliff returned, out of breath. "We got to stay here all night," he announced. "The bridge south of town is washed out. They're working on it, but Clem says it won't be clear until tomorrow morning." A drop of water ran down his nose and dropped to his chin. "What'll we do?"

"Can't you take him by way of Watertown?" Sergeant Wilson asked.

"That's too far on a night like this," the sheriff said decisively. "We'll lock him up here and take him in tomorrow. Dr. Livermore, you got a room we can put him in?"

Dr. Livermore looked ten years younger. Tiny lines at the corners of his eyes were all that was left of his strain. "We'll put him in detention," he said.

William Crane asked, "Not in the old room Mr. L'Adam used to get out of?"

Dr. Livermore smiled, shook his beard. "Oh, no. We have the very room for him. He'll never get out of it."

With heads bent under the frigid impact of the rain they sloshed along the path to the detention building. Noises of the storm filled the garden; wet branches rattled an accompaniment to the splashing of water and the irregular music of the wind. Somewhere in the distance a loose board was banging.

They stamped on the cement porch, kicking off mud, and then entered the hallway. Dr. Livermore led them upstairs, his shadow bulky in yellow electric light. "We'll put him in here, right at the head of the stairs," he said. "This room has a Yale lock on the door."

It wasn't a large room, and there was only a small window high up at the other end. Through the lower pane could be seen the waving limbs of a young tree. Crane noticed that the bed, the chair, and the desk were bolted to the floor. The walls were padded with mattress-like material.

Charles was searched for weapons and then pushed into the room. "I want a lawyer," he whined.

The sheriff slammed the door shut and, stamping his feet, led the way down the stairs. He pointed to a bench in the lower hall. "You set there, Ty," he said. "If he makes a move, plug him."

William Crane saw that the door to Charles's room was visible from the bench. "Don't fall asleep," he warned Deputy Graham. Outside, in the rain, he touched the sheriff's arm. "How about that window? Do you think he could jump out?"

Sheriff Walters's wet face glistened in the light from the window. "Naw," he said, "he couldn't. The only way he could get through that window would be head first, and if he come tumbling out of there head first he'd break his neck." He squeezed water from his drooping mustache. "I'd just as soon he'd break his neck."

They started for the guest house. Crane said, "It's your funeral." He stepped over a puddle dotted with specks of foam. "I think it would be smart to look for his collection of knives."

"I'll have Cliff make a search." Sheriff Walters waded right through the puddles in deep concentration. "I wonder if dinner is ready?"

Chapter XIX

DESPITE THE STORM, which had moderated, dinner was a jolly affair. Even Miss Queen had gone to pieces and giggled when Williams politely refused his finger bowl, saying he'd had plenty to drink already.

"You're such a funny man," she said, peering over the top of her napkin with roguish eyes. "And you have such a kind face."

Williams sucked in his lips. His predatory eyes were bright. "Funny kind," he said. He exploded with laughter.

Under cover of the general conversation, Mr. Penny slipped a piece of paper in William Crane's hand. He opened it on his lap. It read: "*Congratulations. I may have something for you later.*"

Crane looked up. The little man winked mysteriously. Crane winked mysteriously, too.

Comfortable, with blue smoke curling from his cigar, Sheriff Walters lounged back in his chair. He signaled Ulah. "Who's gonna' feed the prisoner?"

Ulah replied, "Miss Evans has got a tray made up for him. She jest went out with it."

"I suppose even murderers have to eat," said the sheriff complacently. "I might even be one if the food was always this good." He slapped the table.

"Look here." Dr. Livermore spoke to Crane. "How'd you ever get in here? Your papers were in order from Bellevue."

Tearing the note from Mr. Penny into shreds, William Crane dropped it into a pewter ash tray and said: "It wasn't hard. I just tried to direct traffic on Fifth Avenue. They took me to Bellevue and Miss Van Kamp's brother had me sent here. He had a business associate, Mr. Sloan, make the arrangements. I believe I was sort of a nephew of his." He drained his demi-tasse. "I might as well tell you that the only reason that I came here was to serve Miss Van Kamp and her brother. She wanted her securities back, and I got them for her. The murders were only incidental."

"I'd hardly call three murders incidental," said Blackwood. He was his old blatant self.

"Maybe not," Crane agreed. He watched Mr. Penny leave the room. "I think I'll go upstairs for a while. I'd like to pack."

On the way out, with Burns and Mr. Williams, he passed in front of Mrs. Heyworth. Her soft brown eyes looked at him, but there was no recognition in them. She had never seen him before.

With an elaborate gesture Mr. Williams poured himself a stiff drink of moonshine. The bottle was nearly empty now. He winked at Tom Burns.

"We sure put this job over," he said reflectively. "We're the goods." He got off Crane's bed and looked out the west window at the detention building. "We always get our man." The window was open a crack, and he closed it. "I see that Charles still's got a light in his room."

"Don't worry about that guy," said Burns. "We gotta save our strength for our next case."

"Sure," Crane said. He held a partially filled glass in his hand. "It must have been tough camping on that hill while I was down here enjoying myself."

Burns looked interestedly at William Crane's face. "It was probably that Evans babe who socked you." He preferred his drinks neat, so he didn't bother with a glass. "She looks hotter than the kitchen stove." He reached for the bottle. Crane jerked it out of his reach.

"When do we leave?" he asked.

"As soon as it stops raining," Williams said. He drank, made a contortion of his lips. "Listen, what did that old dame give you for gettin' her dough back?"

"Nothing."

"Didn't she even thank you?"

"No. Not even that."

"Well, I'll be damned." Williams sipped a little of the

yellow liquor. "She's positively ungrateful." He sat down on a chair and tilted it against the wall. "Did you ever find out who beat you up?"

"Dr. Eastman and that Evans woman."

"See!" Burns put his thumbs in his vest. "I thought there was a woman behind those beatings."

"Sure," said Crane. "*Cherchez la femme.*"

"Huh?"

Crane explained, "That's French for 'Look for the woman.'"

"I don't have to look for my woman," said Burns. "She's always lookin' for me."

The door of the room opened, and Sheriff Walters and his son and Deputy Powers walked through. "William Crane," said the sheriff, "I arrest you for murder."

William Crane slid off the bed, drew back a step. "Why, what's the matter?" he asked.

"Look out your window," said Sheriff Walters.

Crane looked out his window, the one facing the detention building. In the shaft of light from the window the rain was fine and silvery, and it fell gently on a figure in the path below. The figure was on its back, and its face was wet and peaceful and quite dead. It was the face of Mr. Penny.

Chapter XX

UNDER THE ANGULAR FALL of water from the blackness above, Mr. Penny's clothes were already sodden. Around his head a pool was forming, and small ripples caused by raindrops moved his black hair. Another pool, tinted a brownish pink, began under his neck. He had been stabbed exactly as had the other two.

"You thought you could put it on that Charles because the stab marks were the same," said Sheriff Walters. He wiped off his sandy mustache with the back of his hand. "Well, here's another, and it's just the same. But he couldn't have done it."

One of Mr. Penny's legs, twisted unnaturally under his back, must have been broken. His coat collar in the back was jerked up toward his head as though somebody had tried to pull it off. One of the coat's front buttons had been torn off.

"I don't know why I'm lettin' you look around," said Sheriff Walters. He was keeping close beside Crane. "I know you done it. You killed him and dropped him out of your window." He had said this several times before.

Williams had his coat collar turned up against his

neck. He peered up at the lighted windows in the guest house. Then he looked at the crumpled body with the bone-handled knife protruding from the neck. "Looks as though somebody threw him down here," he admitted.

"Sure he was thrown down," said Sheriff Walters. "He didn't walk here with that knife in his neck."

"Maybe he was dragged here," said Williams. He turned a small flashlight around the path and the soaking grass.

"He couldn't have been," asserted the sheriff, flashing his large electric lamp around the body. "There'd be a trail of blood from that knife wound."

"Look here," said Crane. "You don't know I killed him, you just think I did." He spoke soothingly. "Let me take a look at the detention building."

"I don't know you killed him?" Sheriff Walters spoke passionately. "I don't, don't I? What were you doing outside when Miss Clayton was killed? Miss Evans just told me how she met you."

"Maybe she lied," suggested Tom Burns. He stood miserably in the rain. "Where is she now?"

"I got Cliff guarding her in the living room. I figure Crane might try to bump her off, too."

"Give the guy a look at the detention building," said Sergeant Wilson impatiently. "It won't cost you anything."

The sheriff shrugged his shoulders.

Underfoot, the grass was a screen for water an inch deep. Disheveled flowers whipped madly in wind that was more moisture than air. Rain made dark gray stains on the stucco front of the detention building. There was a light in Charles's window and another in Mr. L'Adam's room, toward the end of the building.

Deputy Graham was seated in a chair at the foot of the stairs at the back of the detention building's hall. He awoke with a start. His broad face was surprised. "Where's my dinner?" he asked.

"You'll get it later," said the sheriff. "Is that fellow still upstairs?"

"Certainly. I been watchin' him, ain't I?"

Crane asked, "Has anyone been up to see him?"

"Nobody but Miss Evans and that little dumb guy. He came right after she brought up that tray full of dinner."

"You let Mr. Penny go up to see Charles?" asked Crane.

"Sure. Why wouldn't I?"

"Was Miss Evans up there when he went up?"

"Yeah, they come down together."

"You're sure Mr. Penny came down?"

"You bet."

"How are you sure? Did you see him?"

"Not exactly. But I heard Miss Evans say good-

night to him just outside the door. I was sorta keepin'
my eyes closed to rest, and I didn't see 'em come down
the stairs together."

"You're sure you didn't dream this?"

"Oh, I heard her all right. She said, 'Good-night, Mr.
Penny; hurry so you don't get soaked.'"

Sheriff Walters seized his new prisoner's arm impatiently and said, "This stalling don't get you nowhere."

Crane shook off his hand. He walked to the front door,
opened it, and looked out. The wind-blown rain fell
like the spray from a shower bath. Trees were bent in
the gale, and under Charles's window the bushes were
wet and flat.

After a time he said, "Let's go up and see Charles."

They tramped up the stairs, and the sheriff unlocked
the door with a key handed him by Deputy Graham.
Charles was surprised to see them, and for a moment he
looked furtively violent. "What do you want?" he
asked. His arms moved in short muscular jerks. He was
seated on the bed. He had on black trousers and a white
shirt, and his feet were bare.

"Did you have any visitors this evening?" Crane
asked him.

"Miss Evans brought my dinner." Charles's manner
was defiant.

"Didn't anybody else come up?"

"Mr. Penny looked in for a minute just as Miss Evans

was leaving. He just winked at me, and then he went away with her."

"He didn't show you the knives he found in your room?"

Charles appeared hurt and surprised. "You know you had my room searched, and there weren't any knives there."

"That's right," said Sheriff Walters.

Crane turned to Williams. "Frisk the guy," he ordered.

Williams ran his hands over Charles. Crane looked up at the storm through the room's one small, high window. The rain beat against the pane at intervals, as though someone were throwing cupped handfuls of water. The roar of the wind was sullen and angry. There were two small smudges of moisture on the floor below the window. He could just reach his fingers over the window sill. He looked at his fingers. They were dry and clean. He reached up again and tried the window. It was locked. He ran his fingers along the point where the glass entered the bottom of the frame and then wiped the dry dust on the seat of his trousers.

"Nothin' on this guy," announced Williams.

Crane tried the desk and the chair, but they were firmly bolted to the floor. He felt Charles's black socks. They were faintly damp. "Can you move the bed?" he asked.

Williams couldn't.

"All right," said Crane. He felt the covers on Charles's bed and then looked under the mattress. There was nothing there. "Let's go see Miss Evans," he said.

Miss Evans had on a black silk dress with an artificial crimson flower pinned over her breast. The dress clung to her hips, and her ankles were slim in sheer brown silk. She wore a bright red coral bracelet over the black sleeve of her left arm. She was standing with Cliff by the fireplace, and her blond hair was translucent and nebulous. She faced William Crane and his captors with feline grace. "I see they caught up with you," she said in her husky-harsh voice.

"Miss Evans," said Crane. He freed himself from the sheriff's grasp and walked toward her. "The sheriff has said I could ask you a few questions."

Miss Evans waited. Her eyes were mocking.

"Did Mr. Penny come up to Charles' room while you were there?"

She nodded.

"What did he want?"

She shrugged her rounded shoulders. "He just looked in and smiled. Then I walked downstairs with him."

"Didn't he show Charles anything?"

Miss Evans made an almost imperceptible negative

movement of her head. The glow of the fire accentuated the soft curve of her jaw.

"How long were you up there with Charles?"

"About fifteen minutes."

"Did he have the window open while you were there?"

"Of course not."

"Was there a napkin over the tray when you carried it down?"

Miss Evans arched her eyebrows. "I don't think so. No, there wasn't. You can ask Maria."

"There was nothing on the tray?"

"I don't know what you mean." Her blue eyes darkened. "There was nothing on it but dishes."

"Where did you go from the detention building?"

"I came over here and met the sheriff as I was going into the kitchen. I talked with him in the living room, and then he left me here with his son when they found Mr. Penny's body."

"You didn't go to your room and change your clothes?"

"No, I didn't!" Miss Evans appealed to the sheriff. "Do I have to stand for all this . . . ?"

"I'm so sorry," said Crane. He stepped close to Miss Evans and put his right arm about her waist. "Get away," she screamed in sudden rage. She slapped his hand down and drove her knee into his groin. He grunted in exquisite pain. He took hold of Miss Evans's dress just above the artificial flower and ripped the garment off to her hips.

Her firm breasts were encased in a flesh-colored silk brassière and below them was a line of white skin. Around her waist was a thin belt from which hung six sheaths. Three of these were empty, and from the other three jutted bone-handled knives.

"You see?" remarked William Crane. "That's how Mr. Penny was killed."

Miss Twilliger returned alone from the detention house. A drop of water rolled down one cheek, and her eyes were large. She had searched Miss Evans before Cliff and the deputies had locked their prisoner in a room next to Charles's. She said, "I don't see how she kept her figure, carrying all those knives around."

"Maybe she swallows them and they come out in different places like needles," Williams suggested.

Miss Twilliger held out the belt and the three knives. "What will I do with these?"

"I'll take 'em," said the sheriff. "You better help Cliff guard her in case there's something she wants."

"I'll help watch that babe, too," volunteered Williams.

Crane crooked a finger at him. "You stay here."

Sergeant Wilson stood squarely in front of the living-room fire. He rubbed his chin with the back of his hand. "I don't see yet how they killed Mr. Penny," he said.

"It wasn't so tough to figure out," said Crane. "Let me tell you about it." He slid onto his favorite place on the long table. "In the first place, we know that Mr. Penny went into Charles' room. The deputy saw him."

"Yeah, and the deputy saw him come out," said the sergeant.

"That's where you're wrong. The deputy said he heard Miss Evans say good-night to Mr. Penny. That's a lot different than seeing him come down the stairs. She warned Penny about not getting wet, but Penny didn't hear her. He was already dead."

"You mean she carried his body down the stairs?" asked Mr. Williams.

"No, she'd be foolish to do that. The deputy might have seen her. What she did was to go outside to the body, which had been thrown out of Charles' window."

Sheriff Walters scratched his head. "But that window was locked," he objected. "And besides, it is too high for Charles to reach."

"I thought so too. That's why I didn't object when we first put him in there. I figured nobody could get up there, and we decided, you remember, that even if somebody did come through the window, they'd have to come through head first, and the fall would kill them." Crane shook his head. "I never thought about Miss Evans. It was easy enough for Charles to lift her up so she could open the window. Then, when they wanted it closed, he just lifted her up again. I noticed two damp spots on the floor beneath the window, so I decided it must have been open. Those spots were there when we went up to see Charles. I felt along the sill, but it was dry and clean. Then I felt the bottom frame, and it was dusty. What does that suggest?"

Nobody answered.

"It suggests that somebody wiped the sill dry. If they hadn't, there would have been dust on it, too. It occurred to me that Charles might have stood on something to open the window, but I found all the furniture was bolted down. That meant he must have had help. Incidentally, I'm sure he used his socks to wipe the sill, as they were damp."

Sergeant Wilson moved a little away from the fire. "The idea is that they killed the little guy in the room and threw his body out the window?"

"That's right. He came up there with the knives, which he had found in Miss Evans' room. He probably didn't believe Miss Evans was implicated, and he knew she'd be arrested if he turned them over to the sheriff. He thought, at least I think he did, that he could scare a confession out of Charles with the knives and thus exonerate Miss Evans. But when Charles saw the knives, he knew the jig was up. He knew they could be traced to him. So he killed Mr. Penny."

"That's all right," said the sheriff, "and it accounts for the fall Penny must have had, but I'm damned if I see how he got under your window. Did Miss Evans wipe up the blood under Charles' window and on the path?"

"She didn't have to wipe up any blood. There wasn't any." Crane grinned at his impressed audience. "Mr. Penny was strangled to death in Charles' room. Miss Evans dragged him across the flooded grass—you know how easily anything slips across wet grass and how it doesn't leave any marks—to my window. Miss Evans probably walked in her stocking feet so as not to leave prints, and she didn't have much trouble pulling Mr. Penny because he weighs only a hundred pounds or so. Then, after she dropped him, Miss Evans stuck the knife in his neck so as to throw suspicion on me. It was a pretty neat idea."

"I thought Miss Evans was chummy with Doc Eastman," said Mr. Williams. "How'd she get mixed up with Charles?"

"Charles is a pretty good-looking fellow." Crane settled farther back on the table. "He's known as a heart-breaker in vaudeville circles. It's no wonder Miss Evans fell for him. I wouldn't be surprised if they are married . . . at least they ought to be. He's spent a lot of nights in her room."

Williams made a "tsk" noise three times with his tongue and his teeth. "How do you figure that out?" he asked.

"You'd never guess. Of course, she was Charles' alibi for the murder of Miss Paxton—she said she saw him go into the bathroom. But that didn't prove anything against her. We later figured out he could have climbed out the window and fooled her by leaving the water running. Another thing was that she helped Dr. Eastman steal the box from Dr. Livermore, then helped Charles steal it from Dr. Eastman. She must have had a hand in that second theft, because she was the only person who knew Dr. Eastman had the money box. Then she almost had me believing that Dr. Eastman hadn't told her about the eight hundred thousand dollars in Miss Van Kamp's vault. But those things aren't what gave her away." Crane swung around to the sheriff. "Do you remember when Mrs. Brady was trying her nudist act?"

Sheriff Walters nodded. "That's something I'll never forget."

"Do you recall Dr. Buelow asked Miss Evans if she still had her phonograph? She replied, 'Certainly. Charles, will you get it?' I found out from Maria that Miss Evans kept her phonograph under some things on the top shelf of her closet because she used the radio most of the time." Crane rubbed the bruises on the back of his neck. They felt better. "I also found that Charles, in the ordinary course of his work, would never have an opportunity to go into Miss Evans' room, much less her closet. Maria told me she was very particular about her things. It seemed strange Charles should be familiar enough with her room to get the phonograph without being told where it was."

The sheriff strode toward the door in sudden determination. "I'm not going to take any more chances with that pair. They're too slick." He opened the door. A cool stream of air poured into the room. "I'm going to take them to the jail, rain or no rain." He started to go out, then paused. "Say, who was it that threw the chair at me?"

"Miss Evans," Crane lied.

"I knew it." For the first time the sheriff was indignant. "The two-faced bitch." He slammed the door.

"Are we going to bed, or are we going to leave?" asked Williams.

"Let's leave," said Crane. "I want to get home."

Sergeant Wilson said, "I should think you'd want to go to a sanitarium for a week's rest after all this."

William Crane paused at the door. "Christ, no!" he said. "That's the last place in the world I'd go for a rest."